Hurricane

[a novel]

of the 1900
Galveston Hurricane

Hurricane

janice a. thompson

RiverOak®

Good News in Fiction

COOK COMMUNICATIONS MINISTRIES
Colorado Springs, Colorado • Paris, Ontario
KINGSWAY COMMUNICATIONS LTD
Eastbourne, England

River Oak® is an imprint of
Cook Communications Ministries, Colorado Springs, Colorado 80918
Cook Communications, Paris, Ontario
Kingsway Communications Ltd, Eastbourne, England

HURRICANE
© 2004 by Janice A. Thompson

First printing, 2004
Printed in United States of America
2 3 4 5 6 Printing/Year 08 07 06 05 04

Cover Design: Koechel Peterson & Assoc.

Unless otherwise noted, Scripture quotations are taken from the Holy Bible: New International Version®. Copyright © 1973, 1978, 1984 by International Bible Society. Used by permission of Zondervan Publishing House. All rights reserved. Other Scriptures are from the Holy Bible, New Living Translation (NLT), copyright © 1996 by Tyndale Charitable Trust, all rights reserved.

This story is a work of fiction. All characters and events are the product of the author's imagination. Any resemblance to any person, living or dead, is coincidental.

Library of Congress Cataloging-in-Publication Data

Thompson, Janice.
  Hurricane : a historical novel / by Janice Thompson.
     p. cm.
  ISBN 1-58919-020-3 (pbk.)
  1. Galveston Island (Tex.)--Fiction. 2. Parent and adult child--Fiction.
3. Fathers and sons--Fiction. 4. Journalists--Fiction. 5. Hurricanes--
Fiction. I. Title.
  PS3620.H68H87 2004
  813'.6--dc22
                                            2004008139

This book is dedicated to the memory of those who gave their lives in this, the most catastrophic natural event of twentieth-century America. Their heroism motivates us. Their song, still sung by those who remember, brings us hope.

This story of bravery is also dedicated to the memory of my dear friend Alix Silguero, who managed to keep her head above water no matter how high the tide seemed to rise. You will forever be a hero in my eyes, Alix.

Finally, it is dedicated to the ladies of Seared Hearts, my precious critique group. You have weathered many storms individually and come through them all stronger women of God. How amazing it has been to climb into the boat with you for this season of refreshing. At times, the waves have climbed to dangerous heights around us, but Christ, our amazing anchor, has held us in place. Together, we will not only survive, but thrive.

"Do not be afraid, for I have ransomed you.
I have called you by name; you are mine.
When you go through deep waters
and great trouble, I will be with you.
When you go through rivers of difficulty,
you will not drown!"

—Isaiah 43:1–2 NLT

Preface

The Galveston Hurricane of 1900 still remains the most catastrophic natural disaster in American history. For Galvestonians, Saturday, September 8, 1900, may have started out as a day of rest, but it quickly catapulted into a battle for life against the rising waters of the Gulf of Mexico. Unfortunately, nearly one-sixth of the island's population lost their fight that day. In just a matter of hours, more than six thousand men, women, and children lost their lives, victims of the rising waters and rushing currents. Their rest became an eternal one. Thousands of others were injured; many were left to fend for themselves. Countless numbers were suddenly homeless, many of them wandering the streets for days in search of loved ones. One storm affected them all. This is their story.

When writing a fictional story within the framework of a very real historical event, it becomes quite easy for fact and fiction to overlap. Such is the case in this story. While most of the characters in this story are fictional, there are references to very real people and places.

Some of those places include:

St. Mary's Orphan Asylum (on the low-lying west end of the island); the Galveston *Tribune* (whose real editor was replaced with a fictional character in this story); the Galveston *Daily News* (now called the Galveston County *Daily News*, the only surviving newspaper on the island); the Ursuline Academy at Galveston (a Catholic girls' school that sheltered a thousand refugees during and after the storm); John Sealy Hospital (the primary teaching facility for the University of Texas Medical Branch, which opened in October 1891); The Tremont House (a prestigious hotel, which is said to have housed presidents and other dignitaries); the Grand Opera House (one of the finest in the United States); the American Red Cross (founded by Clara Barton); *The New York World* (Joseph Pulitzer, publisher); The Strand (an amazing stretch of stores and businesses); and Broadway (an avenue of fine Victorian homes).

As for the very real cast and crew:

Isaac Cline was the chief of the U.S. Weather Bureau's Galveston station. He was the island's first real "weatherman," and people looked to him for any indication of foul weather. He had concluded, much to his later chagrin, that the island had no need for a seawall. In fact, he believed that no storm could pose a serious threat to the island. His theory was put to the test on September 8, 1900. Unfortunately, he lost the bet. That wasn't the only thing he lost that horrible night. Cline's precious wife, who was expecting their fourth child, was among those killed in the raging floodwaters. Her body was not discovered for nearly a month. Cline's home, which had been built to withstand the fiercest storm, had crumbled like a house of cards. Thankfully, his children and brother were among those who were saved.

Clarence Ousley, editor of the *Daily News*, was a very real newspaperman. He believed Galveston to be "a city of splendid homes and broad clean streets; a city of oleanders and roses and palms; a city of the finest churches, school buildings, and benevolent institutions in the South." However, on Sunday, September 9, 1900, he called that same place "a city of wrecked homes and streets choked with debris and six thousand corpses. It was a city whose very cemeteries had been emptied of their dead as if to receive new tenants." He was one of the men who captured the heart of the people with the written word. The *Tribune* rivaled the *Daily News* for readers. Richard Spillane, editor of *The Tribune*, became quite famous in his own right. Together, he and Ousley carried the stories of the storm and its victims. For the sake of the story, I have created a third newspaper, *The Courier*, to capture the spirit of competition that existed amongst all newspapermen of the day. The characters who work at *The Courier* are as fictional as the paper itself. In reality, a paper as small as this would never have survived.

Clara Barton, the wonderful woman who founded the American Red Cross, came to Galveston after the Great Storm to help re-establish a place of safety for the island's children. She, of course, did not interact with the characters named in this book, but did the island a great service with all of her work. It is in honor of her work that she is mentioned in these pages.

Joseph Pulitzer, founder of *The New York World*, was also a vital player in the reconstruction of the island, along with many reporters, both local and national. He had been severely criticized for his exaggerated headlines and for his ongoing battle with fellow editor, William Randolph Hearst. According to his employees, he was a very tough man to work for. He was quick to praise, but just as quick to reprimand. However, when it came right down to it, Pulitzer's contribution to the rebuilding process on Galveston Island was immeasurable.

Bishop Nicholas Gallagher was the third Catholic bishop of Galveston. He served thirty-six years as administrator and bishop of Galveston, bringing to the island many religious congregations and organizations, including the Sisters of Charity of the Incarnate Word of San Antonio, which played a vital role in the storm of 1900. They, along with others, were responsible for founding several churches, schools, and hospitals.

Perhaps the greatest heroes of all in the real story of the Great Storm were the ten Roman Catholic Sisters of the Incarnate Word who cared for the ninety-three children of St. Mary's Orphanage, which stood on the beach just three miles west of the city. This facility was operated by tenderhearted angels of mercy who made it their calling to care for the island's orphaned children. In their greatest moment of crisis, these brave women fought with unparalleled bravery to save the lives of their young charges. Knowing very little about these women, I could only speculate concerning either their emotions or their reactions to what happened. One of them, Sister Elizabeth Ryan, gave her life trying to make it to town to purchase food for the children. Her dedication to the children is without question. But how does one begin to do justice to these women who gave their lives so selflessly? As I sat down to write this story, that question seemed to haunt me. After great deliberation, I chose to give all of the remaining sisters (outside of Elizabeth Ryan) fictional names and situations, hoping to capture the "spirit" of the group instead of giving actual biographical information. Their story is told from the point of view of one particular nun, Sister Henrietta Mullins, a completely fictional character. While she does not represent an actual person from history, it is my hope that she personifies some of the caring, diligence, and spunk of those women who fought so valiantly during this awful night to save the children they loved.

In closing, every year on September 8, the Sisters of Charity still gather on the seawall of Galveston Island to sing "Queen of the Waves" at the site where St. Mary's once stood. This ritual has been carried down from 1900 until today. As a fellow Texan, I cannot help but feel pride as their voices rise in song.

My heart carries the emotion of that song as I pen the words of this story.

The Nation's Deadliest Cataclysm

Within the last two or three years, people have begun to think that the islands and peninsulas along the Texas and Louisiana Coast are unsafe for human abiding places. And Galveston Island is but a waif of the ocean, liable at any moment of being engulfed and submerged by the self-same power that gave it form.

—*Braman's Information About Texas, 1858*

One

I am going home.

Home: a place I scarcely know, and yet know as well as my own name. A place of sweltering heat and gritty, salt-stung eyes. A garden of wispy oleanders and tall, green palms dancing in soft evening breezes. A sandy retreat for sundials and sand dollars, angel wings and starfish. A hallowed habitat for speckled trout and flounder, red snapper and bluefish. A sanctuary for pesky mosquitoes and wide-eyed immigrants, both an unwelcome source of irritation to the locals. A pavilion where sweethearts, young and old, dance at open-air concerts. A leisurely place where rickety wooden piers tiptoe out onto the reaches of the warm, murky waters of the Gulf of Mexico ... brown, rolling waters that stretch for miles against the backdrop of a soft, powder-blue sky.

I am going home—to Galveston, the island of my youth. It draws me back as the tide pulls the restless waves to the shoreline, and yet I resist just as they do when they have had enough and wish to be released to the sea once again. Galveston Island. Every corner of my mind is clouded with memories, though I push them away with a vengeance. I don't want to remember. My conscience is seared with the guilt of trying to forget.

Six years away have put the past behind me, and yet it lies ever before me. My years in New York have transformed me. I left a boy, a dreamer. I return a man, a realist. Perhaps there is more of my father in me than I am ready to admit.

"Hey, mister. Whatcha writin'?"

Brent Murphy looked up from his tablet into the sharp olive-green eyes of the little boy sitting across from him on the train.

"I, uh ..." Brent tried valiantly to collect his thoughts, leaving his scribbling behind him. "Not much, really." What was he writing, after all: his wishes, his fears? He couldn't possibly share those things with a child, a perfect stranger.

"You a writer, mister?" The little boy's eyes were playful, inquisitive. They danced in the direction of his tablet, as if wanting to snatch it up and read it. Brent pulled it a little closer to himself.

"Well, yes," he answered. "Sort of, anyway." After all these years, it was still a difficult question to answer.

"Gee-willikins. Do you write books?" The boy's sparkling green eyes widened with excitement. Brent discovered himself in those eyes—a young man enthralled with the world of a writer.

"No, not books. I'm a reporter, a journalist." As he laid the tablet down on his knees, Brent couldn't help but notice the wrinkles in his trousers. Days of travel had left him looking a little less like a reporter, and a little more like a vagabond.

"Man, oh man." The little boy sat up straight, looking him squarely in the eye.

"Lucas, son, sit still and don't bother the nice gentleman," the boy's mother, a woman with stern brown eyes, scolded.

"Oh, he's no bother," Brent said. "No bother at all."

"Do you live in Galveston?" Lucas asked, unable to hold himself still for more than a moment.

"Yes, well, I used to."

"I'm gonna visit my Grandpa Frankie."

"Joseph Franks," his mother explained. "He's a deputy sheriff on the island. Do you know him?"

"No, I'm sorry. I don't," Brent said. "But I've been away for awhile. Six years."

Six wonderful, terrible years.

Lucas turned his attention to something outside the window, and Brent returned to his pondering. The flatlands of Southeast Texas rolled by, stark and dry. A drought had left the tall grasses as brown as autumn. The warm air wafted through the open window. Brent pulled at his collar, deep in thought. The gentle clacking of the train against the tracks lulled Brent back into a hypnotic state. He began to jot words down, almost uncontrollably:

We pulled out of Houston half an hour ago, headed south on the GH&H line, a railroad I know well. During the Civil War, the Galveston, Houston, and Henderson crossed this very spot with Confederate troops and munitions, their goal: to reach the island to break a Union blockade. My mission pales in comparison.

Houston has grown to an almost unrecognizable level. She will surpass Galveston's greatness if islanders are not careful. Perched on the brink of indus-trial eminence, the city that brought General Sam Houston fame is now overwhelmed with the scent of oil, industry, and new money. Houses are springing up all around the place, wood framed with indoor plumbing and electric lights, all the modern conveniences. It is dif-ficult to believe that Texas won her freedom in this once-barren place. Sixty-plus years have brought a lifetime of change. Time changes everything—and nothing—all at the same time.

Within another hour we'll cross the trestle over Galveston Bay. From there I will be within moments of home.

Home.

Galveston, to my understanding, is much the same as when I left: bustling with streetcars and tourists, though surely not many remain this late into the season. What draws them back? The island, in its own mysterious way, seems to lull them, year after year. I will soon join them. When I get home …

Here Brent paused, looking up from his tablet to reflect. What should he write? How could he even begin to predict the future when he still had so much trouble dealing with the past?

TUESDAY, SEPTEMBER 4, 1900, 12:30 P.M.
THE MURPHY VILLA

"Douglas, dear, do you really have to go?" Gillian Murphy forced the saddest face she could muster. Years of experience had turned her into a better than average actress. She knew how to play a role when the script called for it.

"Gillian, we've already discussed this." Her husband's stern face left nothing to the imagination.

"But dear, we've got such a grand party coming up this weekend, and there's so much work to be done. I'm simply lost without you." She did depend on him, perhaps more than she wanted to admit.

"You've got Pearl," he mumbled, straightening his jacket. "And I've got to work."

"Work, work ... that's all you ever do," Gillian said with a pout. How could he argue the point? In their thirty years of marriage, the couple had rarely taken so much as a well-deserved vacation. Douglas was driven to succeed. His years at the GH&H railroad had proven that. Forty-six miles of track from Galveston to Houston was all that lay between Gillian Murphy and her husband.

"I don't see you complaining about the home we're living in, or those expensive clothes you're wearing," he said, pulling a gold watch from his pocket.

"Yes, but ..." It was hardly fair to bring that up.

"Just how do you think we're going to pay for this little shindig anyway?" Douglas asked, running a comb through his jet-black hair. He used his fingertips to straighten the sharp edges of his carefully manicured moustache, staring at his reflection in the hall mirror. "You're liable to bankrupt us with this party of yours."

Gillian's heart gave a quick flutter. Surely he jested. She gauged his expression for confirmation. A bit of a twinkle in his dark-gray eyes let her know that he was not completely serious.

"Pish-posh," she said with a snicker. "You know perfectly well we're not hurting for money. Now don't scare me by saying things like that. It's completely unfair of you, Douglas."

Her husband reached over and gave her a light peck

on the nose. "For a middle-aged woman, you certainly still act like a silly schoolgirl."

"I'm not middle-aged," Gillian said defiantly. "I'm barely forty-six."

"Forty-eight."

"Forty-seven," she said stubbornly. She glanced in the mirror at her reflection. Her soft brown hair was swept up off her neck with an ivory comb, a Christmas gift from Douglas. There were a few streaks of gray in her hair, she noticed, peering a little closer, but not enough to rank her as middle-aged. Her hazel eyes were more blue than green. There was still plenty of youthful vitality in them, though the finely tuned wrinkles that had crept up alongside them argued the point.

"Gillian, dear. You were twenty-two when our son arrived, were you not? He's twenty-six now. That would make you ..."

Gillian turned, feeling her heart begin to swell. Why did he have to bring up their son now, just when things were going so well?

"Twenty-six years of misery with the laziest good-for-nothing of a son a man ever had," Douglas said, his face turning red. "If only he had been born with half the work ethic I have, we might be singing a completely different song today. Of course, there's good reason why he isn't much like me, isn't there, dear?"

"Darling, let's don't do this—"

"I'm just saying that things might have been completely different if you hadn't—"

Gillian had to turn this around. She had to. "Alright, I'll admit it. I'm forty-eight years old," she said. "Now, can we change the subject?"

"Maybe," Douglas said with a hint of a smile, "if

you're ready to admit you still act like a giddy schoolgirl when it comes to hosting those ridiculous parties."

"Oh, but this is going to be the party of the century. Everyone will simply be mad with envy." She hoped so anyway.

"Well, we can't have that," Douglas said. "I suppose we'll have to cancel."

His thick eyebrows furrowed, and her heart fell. But only for a moment. Gillian looked into his eyes. "Oh, you're teasing. I knew you were."

"Teasing or not, there's work to be done, and I've never been one to slack off."

No, he hadn't. And now that rumors of oil ran up and down the coast, his zeal for the railroad played second fiddle to the possibility of making a strike in the near future. That meant she now came in third, in the grand scheme of things.

"I'll be back on Saturday afternoon," he said, turning toward the door.

Gillian pouted, half-angry, half-disappointed.

"Chin up," Douglas said, leaving. "I'll be back soon."

The door slammed behind him, echoing the hollow emptiness of the large home, fashioned in the new Victorian style. Gillian dropped into a chair, deep in thought. Her husband was a strong man, stronger in so many ways than she would ever be. It was a man's world, or so he told her all the time.

"That may very well be," she said, shaking her head, "but when it comes to throwing parties, it's a woman's world." She grinned, standing. There was much work to be done, and she would never let it be said that Gillian Murphy wasn't up to the task.

TUESDAY, SEPTEMBER 4, 1900, 2:35 P.M.
ST. MARY'S ORPHAN ASYLUM

Sister Henrietta Mullins reached up with the back of her hand to wipe the perspiration from her brow. Her habit, dark and cumbersome, clung to her petite frame like a second skin. Had she chosen this life? Could she really take the credit or the blame? Henrietta's commitment to the Sisters of Charity had taken her far from home, far from those she loved, and yet it was clear: She felt God's call on her life. She had known it from the time she was a young girl, weeping at the altar's edge.

At the tender age of twenty-one, Henrietta had taken her vows with no hesitation. And when her superiors had assigned her to work at the beloved St. Mary's Orphan Asylum in Galveston just one year later, she had gone willingly. What a difference a few months could make. Even with the breeze off the gulf, she still felt as though she might suffocate. "I'm only in Texas," she wrote home, "but I feel like I'm halfway to Hades already."

Henrietta longed for the cool autumns of Virginia, her home. There was nothing as beautiful as the turning of the leaves, their reds and golds melting together into dizzying shades of orange. The cool, crisp fall breezes whipped through the trees, teasing the leaves and eventually coaxing them down from unwilling limbs. All of her life she had romped and played in the woods of Virginia. Among those trees, she had first felt the tug that would eventually bring her to Galveston Island.

"It's not *so* bad," she said, looking about. The two dormitories of St. Mary's lay on the outskirts of town, well out of reach of the yellow fever epidemic that had swept the island a short time ago. The infirmary was nearby. Henrietta had made it her mission to keep the children in good health spiritually and physically. Many of them had lost parents in the epidemic. Others had been abandoned at birth by parents who did not have the necessary means to care for them.

She had no right to complain about her life. After all, she had made her own choices. Her biggest struggle, at least at the moment, was this bulky habit and its constricting white collar.

"Look on the bright side," she whispered to herself. "At least I don't have to wear a corset." A smile made its way up her cheeks. Small waistlines had become ridiculously painful over the past few years with those tightly laced, strictly constructed corsets in the picture. Though they posed countless health risks, any woman who considered herself fashionable wore one to embellish her female physique. A corset provided the coveted curves, naturally, but it also constricted the abdomen so that a woman could barely eat or sit down comfortably. How wonderful to be rid of that agony!

"I'll take the good with the bad." Henrietta said, suddenly determined. "Learning will come with time and much patience." Heat or no heat, she had to learn to endure. Her calling required it.

Had she known how difficult everything would turn out to be, she might have requested a different calling.

Two

Room for one, please." Brent dropped his bag on the floor of The Tremont House lobby, exhaustion setting it.

"Name, sir?" The clerk asked, looking down his nose at him a bit.

"Mr. Brent Murphy." He looked around with a smile at the beautiful lobby. Large overstuffed chairs in soft mint-cream linen lined the wall, and an elaborate chandelier hanging over the center of the room provided a soft glow of light.

"How long will you be staying, sir?"

"Hmmm." A good question. Brent looked into the eyes of the hotel clerk. An older man, he had a somewhat comical face that resembled a carnival caricature: a long, exaggerated chin and protruding brown eyes that seemed too large for the rest of him. Even in his tailored suit and high-button collar, the gentleman proved to be an amusing contrast to the elegant room.

"I, um … I'll probably be here only a day or two," Brent said, trying not to stare. "Certainly not much longer."

"That won't be a problem, Mr. Murphy. Have you ever stayed at The Tremont before?"

Stayed at The Tremont? The Tremont had been a proud part of the Murphy heritage. Why, if this fellow only knew. Brent's father had been in attendance back in 1861 when then Governor Sam Houston addressed a Galveston crowd from the second floor Tremont balcony. There, the great general had taken a strong stand against joining the Confederacy. Brent had heard the story most of his growing-up years. Of course, that was the old Tremont. The original building had burned to the ground in 1865. Still, this newer, fresher version of Galveston's finery seemed like an old friend. Brent had played at its doorstep as a child. Why, how dare this ridiculous-looking fellow imply that he had never been here!

"The Tremont has quite a history," the clerk said, looking at him proudly. "President Lincoln visited in 1860."

"Beg your pardon, but that was President Grant," Brent said, trying not to appear sarcastic, "and it was 1880."

"Oh, I, uh …"

Brent continued. "It's also rumored that Rutherford Hayes, Grover Cleveland, and Benjamin Harrison signed your registry at one time or another. Not to mention James Garfield, Buffalo Bill Cody, and Chief Spotted Horse." Brent couldn't help but grin as the clerk's face fell dramatically. "Don't let it get to you, my friend," Brent said with a laugh. "I grew up on the island. My parents are still here."

"Then why … ?"

Brent gave him his best "Don't even ask" look. He glanced down before reaching for his bags. "I'll be headed home soon," Brent said curtly. "In the meantime, where can I get a paper?"

"I'll have the *Daily News* sent up to your room, sir. First thing."

"I'll be wanting to look at the *Courier*," Brent said with a smirk.

"The *Courier*?" the old man asked with a laugh. "No one much reads that one anymore."

Brent gave him another quick glance. "I'm a journalist," he said proudly. "And I used to work for the *Courier*. So if you don't mind ..."

"I'll have it sent right up, sir. You'll be in room 203."

Minutes later, Brent settled into the posh room. He melted into the thick beige coverlet on the tall four-poster bed. Large conch shells, polished and glistening, sat perched atop the large pin wardrobe. Brent picked one up, placing it next to his ear. The pull of the sea gripped him at once. He had forgotten how strong it could be. He quickly placed the shell back on the wardrobe.

Brent carefully balanced a cup of coffee in his left hand, a pen in his right, and his journal on his knee.

Galveston Island ... home of fifteenth-century pirates and nineteenth-century businessmen and entrepreneurs. Not much difference to be noted between the two. However, after life in New York City, this place seems almost backward. Most of the islanders move along at a languid pace, one that seems far too sedate for my taste. And yet, in some respects, they are far more civilized than I.

I sit, near happy, in The Tremont House. Men of fame have probably slept in this very bed, tucked away in

25

comfort. And yet I fear I will not find much rest here. Not when my own home is only blocks away.

A knock at the door startled him. Brent stood, accidentally knocking over the cup and scalding his left knee. Hobbling, he made his way to answer it.

"What is it?" he asked abruptly as he yanked open the door.

A bellboy stood there, eyes wide, with paper in hand. "The *Courier*, sir. Just as you requested."

"Thank you," Brent said, his eyes automatically shifting downward. It wasn't this boy's fault he was in such a bitter mood. As a token of kindness, he dropped a coin in the young fellow's hand.

"Why, thank you, sir," the boy said, tipping his cap. "Have a pleasant day."

"Same to you," Brent muttered, closing the door. He turned back toward the bed, anxious to get some rest. Something in the glass caught his attention. "What in the ... ?" Were those eyes in the window? But he was on the second floor. It wasn't possible. Still ...

Brent tiptoed toward the window, slowly, cautiously. A reflection of the lamp. That's all he had seen. Not eyes at all. No one was watching him. Not here.

TUESDAY, SEPTEMBER 4, 1900, 5:40 P.M.
THE COURIER

Everett Maxwell, editor of the *Courier*, ran his eyes down the page as he read. "Not much of a story," he mumbled, jabbing his finger at an article on beach erosion. "We've got to do better than this." He wasn't speaking to anyone in particular. In fact, he was quite alone in the drab upstairs office.

As much as he hated to admit it, there had been little worth writing about in recent days. Fashion fads had come and gone, with skirts rising above the ankle and then falling again. Factory workers had their share of complaints, to be sure, but he had done enough stories on their plight to turn the hearts of all those who might consider turning. William Jennings Bryan had come to the island in the spring to campaign for the presidency, of course, but that was old news now. They had already stretched that story as far as it would go anyway. The stories that dominated headlines these days were focused on garden parties, Opera House events, and the like. Nothing terribly exciting.

He stood, glancing out the window as islanders rushed up and down The Strand—the Wall Street of the Southwest ... that's what folks called it. And it was a pretty impressive row of buildings and businesses with electricity and telephones—all of the modern conveniences.

Galveston ... "a city of splendid homes and broad clean streets; a city of oleanders and roses and palms; a city of the finest churches, school buildings, and benevolent institutions in the South ..." that, according to Clarence Ousley, editor of the *Daily News*. Well, let him use the niceties. Everett was tired of it. He was ready for some adventure, some action. Even The Strand didn't impress him much anymore.

"There's got to be more than this," he argued with himself.

There had been some great stories in the past, to be sure. In fact, his first big break as a young reporter had come in 1885 with the great fire that had swept across the island, destroying lives and properties. Though he hated to admit it, the excitement accompanying the story had been a writer's dream. Why was it that journalists were always so excited when bad things happened? Just because it made good news?

"What we need is a story," Everett muttered. "A *real* story ..."

TUESDAY, SEPTEMBER 4, 1900, 9:17 P.M.
THE SANDERS HOME

Emma Sanders flitted around the quaint bedroom, all atwitter. She spun in front of the vanity, where younger sister, Sadie, sat brushing her curly chestnut hair.

"Oh, Emma," Sadie spoke gleefully. "It's all so wonderful."

"Isn't it?" Emma echoed, feeling a rush of pride. She had waited for this day for years, and now, finally, it was upon her. She glanced at her reflection in the large round mirror above the vanity. Her cheeks were flushed, probably from the excitement. She snatched the hairbrush from Sadie's hand and ran it through her own brown curls. They cascaded down onto her shoulders.

"Do you mind?" she asked with a giggle.

"Do you mind?" Sadie asked, grabbing it back.

Emma put a dab of fragrant Jasmine oil behind each ear, turning to the right and then the left. "I'm so excited, honey. But tell me, do you like my dress?" She pranced about in her bright-white ankle-length frock and matching shoes, waiting for her sister's stamp of approval. Tomorrow she would wear it for real, for the very first time.

"Oh my, yes. You look, you look—"

"Well, go ahead and say it," Emma exclaimed.

"You look ... angelic."

"Hardly angelic," Emma said, brushing back a loose hair. "But tell me, do I look the part?"

"Do you ever," Sadie said, looking at her from every angle. "How does it feel?"

"Oh, in many ways just as I expected," Emma said, "although I imagine it's not going to turn out to be all that one might hope."

Sadie's face fell immediately. "Someday I may want to be in your shoes, but if it's no fun, then maybe I'll reconsider now and save myself the trouble."

"Save yourself the trouble? You silly goose." Emma laughed heartily. "Don't give up the ship before it's even set out to sea, little sister. You're only thirteen, after all. Someday, I promise you, someday you'll stand in this same dress and join the ranks of every other young woman who ever gave her life selflessly to another."

"You make it sound so wonderful," Sadie said with a sigh. "So *very* wonderful. In fact, I can hardly wait to become a nurse like you."

They threw themselves onto the bed and giggled until each was thoroughly exhausted.

"I want to be pretty like you, Emma," Sadie said, coming up for air.

"You little ninny. You are lovely." She took the pillow and hit her younger sister in the head with it.

"No I'm not," Sadie said, rolling over and gazing at her mournfully. "My eyes are hazel—plain and dull. Yours are cornflower blue. I'm so jealous."

"Cornflower blue? You're so dramatic, Sadie."

"I'm not. And if I were pretty, I'd be the envy of all the other girls on the island at my debut."

"Your debut?" Emma doubled over with laughter. "You know that only the rich girls have a coming-out party. Girls like us go to work at the sewing factory, or, if we're lucky, at the hospital. And the boys who attend social functions with the girls from Broadway wouldn't give us a second glance."

"Life is so unfair," Sadie said with a pout.

Emma stood, looking carefully at her reflection in the mirror. Her eyes were a lovely shade, and she had grown a little too prideful where they were concerned. Of course, right now she had far more important things on her mind. "No more time for this," she said, a yawn escaping her lips. "I've got to be up early in the morning, and I need my beauty sleep."

"Do you ever," Sadie said with a laugh.

"Now listen up, you, you ..." Emma took the pillow and hurled it at her sister. The pillow fight that developed was enough to awaken their parents in the bedroom below.

"Girls, get to sleep!" Their mother's voice rang out, startling them.

"Now see what you've gone and done?" Sadie gave her a playful grin.

"Who, me?"

"Yes, you. You're going to get me in trouble. You know they always think I'm the one to blame."

"Well, aren't you?" Emma couldn't help but laugh.

"You just wait and see, smarty-pants. Someday I'll show you who's the better sister."

"Well, if that doesn't beat all," Emma said, tossing her curls defiantly. She promptly whacked Sadie with the pillow again.

"You're going to hurt me."

"That's all right," Emma argued, hitting her again. "After all, I'm a nurse. I can always make it all better again."

TUESDAY, SEPTEMBER 4, 1900, 9:22 P.M.
ST. MARY'S ORPHAN ASYLUM

Sister Henrietta Mullins tucked the girls in for the night. Their dreary second-floor dormitory felt about as homey as a hospital ward with its stark metal beds and thin mattresses. Thankfully, most of the girls were already asleep. There was one who struggled with bedtime each night. Henrietta knelt at the youngster's bedside in quiet reflection as she prayed: "Now I lay me down to sleep ... What's the rest, Sister?"

"I pray the Lord my soul to keep," Henrietta added, opening her eyes just a bit to peek at the nine-year-old. Lilly Mae was new to St. Mary's, and she needed all of the encouragement she could get. Her parents, immigrants from Italy nearly ten years earlier, had lost their battle against yellow fever when the epidemic had struck the island.

Lilly Mae had coped in the only way she knew how—through her music. The olive-skinned youngster had been raised by kindhearted, giving parents who loved opera. They had always encouraged her to sing. Already, she possessed a voice that could easily parallel that of some of the older women on the island. But any hopes of pursuing her dream to sing had seemingly died with her parents on that shrimp boat.

"I pray the Lord my soul to keep," Lilly Mae continued in broken English. "If I should die ..." Here she paused dramatically. When she did speak, it was almost enough to knock Henrietta off her knees and directly onto the floor. "Can't we just leave out that part? I don't wanta die, Sister Henri."

"Well, I don't want you to die either, baby," the nun answered. "But we've always got to be ready, just in case."

"I'm not ready," Lilly Mae spoke defiantly, her dark-brown eyes flashing madly, "and I'm not going to pray that part. I'm not!" Crocodile tears sprang from those eyes, and she wiped at them madly. Henrietta understood the child's wish to appear strong. They were a lot alike, perhaps more so than the youngster would ever know.

Lilly Mae hopped up onto the bed, pulling the sheet over her head, muttering all the while. "You don't think God will be mad at me, do you?" she mumbled through layers of sheet and blanket. "'Cause I wouldn't pray it?"

Sister Henrietta stood silently, shaking her head. How could she correct one so young who had just lost so much? "I sincerely hope not," she answered finally. "Though, of course, I cannot answer for him."

How she wished she could.

Three

Brent pounded his clenched fist into the feather pillow, shaping it to his liking. "Just a few hours of sleep," he muttered. "That's all I'm asking." Exhaustion overwhelmed him, but his mind wouldn't allow him to rest. The rhythm of the train still held him suspended in time. Brent closed his eyes, but the clack, clack, clack refused to release him.

This wasn't the first night he had struggled to doze off. He hadn't managed a good night's sleep since the train pulled out of Grand Central Station in New York. "I should be home, in my own bed." But he couldn't go home. Not yet, anyway. "I'm such a coward." He drove his fist into the pillow once again.

Emma awoke to the cry of seagulls outside of her window. She fought to remember her dream. Like a vapor, it seemed to fade from her memory, dissipating into a haze of gray. Ah, yes. Things were a little clearer now. She saw herself in a ballroom, dancing blissfully with a handsome young man. She wasn't sure of his identity, but wrapped tightly in his arms Emma had felt a degree of comfort she had never before known. Now, with the pinks and grays of dawn's light, she could scarcely remember the curve of his face or the color of his hair. There had been a phonograph in her dream, a Victorian beauty that had played out a familiar melody. However, it was also disappearing from her memory. All that remained was the pounding of the waves at the shore just a few short yards away from her window. Yet it had all been so real, so very real.

The seagulls called out to Emma with their familiar shrill cry. From childhood she had loved that sound. Living this close to the shore was such a blessing. Moonlit strolls along the beach's edge had become commonplace, but nothing could compare to the ocean's misty breeze first thing in the morning. However, this particular morning, she had other things on her mind. The elusive dream just wouldn't leave her alone.

"You don't have time to be thinking about men anyway," she scolded herself. "There are far more important things to attend to." Emma shifted back and forth in her opinion. To marry and have a house full of rambunctious children would be wonderful, but her career beckoned.

Still reeling from the pride of having been chosen to attend Galveston's school for nurses, Emma tried to remain focused. Only six years old, the school had already graduated some of the finest nurses in the state. What an honor to be among them. But now that she had graduated—actually had the certificate in her hand—the moment she had waited for so long had finally arrived.

She would walk into John Sealy Hospital and take everyone there by storm.

WEDNESDAY, SEPTEMBER 5, 1900, 6:42 A.M.
ST. MARY'S ORPHAN ASYLUM

"Sister Henri. You've overslept again."

Henrietta looked up groggily at Sister Abigail's stern face. "Oh no, not again."

The older woman glared down at her with narrowed gray eyes and thin, pursed lips. "Yes, again," Abigail said with a smirk. "And this is completely unacceptable. We are not running a hotel here, Sister. In case you've forgotten, St. Mary's is an orphanage and an infirmary. There are children to be cared for, and patients to be tended."

As if she could have forgotten.

"I'm so sorry," she said, rubbing her eyes. "It's just that I've had such a hard time falling asleep these past few nights." The tiny cubicle of a room they had given her had proved to be a far cry drearier than her bedroom at home. She had done her best to adjust, but it was still a drab place.

"A life of hard work will remedy your lack of sleep." Abigail turned abruptly toward the door. "And the sooner you get yourself out of that bed, the sooner I can light a fire under you."

"Yes, Sister," Henrietta said, standing quickly. "I'll be right out." She pulled the sheet up over her nightgown, remembering her modesty.

The door shut firmly—a little too firmly. Abigail had made her point.

Henrietta groaned loudly. "Lord," she prayed through her tears. "Help me, please. I'll never make it here without you."

WEDNESDAY, SEPTEMBER 5, 1900, 8:42 A.M.
THE MURPHY VILLA

Gillian Murphy ran her fingers through the warm dirt in the flower garden outside her back door, packing soil around the base of an exquisite rosebush.

"Lovely. Just lovely." She reached to pluck a loose brown petal from one of the yellow flowers. "Shame on you," she scolded. "I need you healthy and strong. Take a few lessons from the candytuft." She smiled at the robust lilac flowers to her right. Low and bushy, they had survived the summer months triumphantly. "See. They're behaving quite nicely."

Gillian reached up with the back of her gloved hand to wipe the perspiration from her brow. Surveying her rather large garden, she couldn't help but smile. To think that only two years ago, it had been a rather ordinary backyard. And now ... now this place of beauty seemed more like a sanctuary.

Oleanders beckoned with their wispy aroma. Rising to her feet, she drank in the heady scent. Though it had taken months of work to get them to this lovely state, Saturday night's gala would make all of her work worthwhile. Saturday night, other upper-class islanders would converge on this backyard for the garden party of the century. With tables and lanterns in place, the whole garden would spring to life.

Mealy blue sage lined the beds to her left. They were hardy and abundant, an exquisite shade of violet blue. But her favorite, she had to admit, remained the Purple Horse mint. Like Gillian, it was a native to the Southwest. Its deep purple flowers, arranged in whorls, stair-stepped up a single stem. They gave off an exotic citrus aroma that always seemed to captivate her. It would captivate her guests as well.

"I'm a shoo-in," she bragged, looking about. A shoo-in for president of the Grand Opera Society, she meant, a position she had craved for nearly two years, ever since Millicent Reeves had filled the position.

Gillian watered the rosebush carefully, humming a piece from a recent production at the Grand Opera House as she surveyed the colorful garden. "Millicent will cry with envy."

A delicious thought. Not that she necessarily enjoyed provoking jealousies. But someone with a house like hers deserved a reputation to match. A slate-blue Victorian home on Broadway in the very shadow of the island's elite, who could have asked for more? Gillian lived the good life.

Why shouldn't she obtain the coveted position? Her father had helped finance the island's first opera house back in 1870. As a child, Gillian had wandered through the beautiful building, examining its intricate features, loving every nook, every cranny. It had captivated her with its beauty, its mystery.

Of course, there was much to captivate the imagination on the island. Galveston boasted many "firsts." The first orphan asylum in Texas stood on the western beach in what had once been the estate of Captain Farnifalia Green. Gillian's connection with the asylum ran far deeper than most knew, but that remained her little secret. The island also erected the first medical college in the state in 1886, which her father had also had a hand in building. Yes, Galveston proudly hailed itself as the Jewel of the Southwest.

Her husband, Douglas, although not quite the man of

money her father had been, certainly didn't lack drive or ambition. His years at the GH&H railroad had supplied him with adequate wealth. Now, with all this scuttlebutt about oil, who knew how much money could be theirs for the taking? Oil lay deep, ready to be struck. Everyone knew it. Time would surely prove them right. Douglas was going to be there when it happened. Even now, he had his hand in the pot. So what if it kept him away from home for days at a time? Money had long since replaced intimacy in their marriage—not that they had ever been terribly passionate.

Gillian lovingly fingered the pearl necklace that hung around her neck, relishing the feel of the cold, hard beads. They always brought her such satisfaction. *Yes,* she thought to herself, *business will soon be booming.* She could feel it. Gillian lived the good life—and things were only going to get better.

A twinge of guilt stopped her joyful thoughts.

Better? No. Until her son arrived home, nothing would ever truly be better.

Four

What will it be, sir?"

Brent stared at the menu for a few moments, attempting to make a decision. "Um ... vanilla phosphate, please."

"Yes, sir." The waiter reached for the menu, and Brent settled back to watch the crowd make its way along the busy street. Through the large plate-glass window of the confectionery, he could easily see those running to and fro along The Strand. People in abundance.

Horses pulled decorative carriages with style and ease. From what Brent had been told, only two automobiles existed on the island, and the drivers of both of them seemed to be content to circle the boulevard, drawing attention from curious onlookers—when the trolley wasn't fighting them for street space. No. No shortage of busyness here.

The Strand. How I have missed it. It embodies the spirit of the island. People shuffle to and fro, back and forth, as if they have no limits. And yet they are limited on every side—by the warm waters of Galveston Bay on one side and the cooler waters of the Gulf of Mexico on the other. They are held captive and don't even realize it. They remain victims of their own choosing.

Are there stories here? I see stories in their faces. I choose not to ask for details, and yet details confront me at every turn. They are a busy lot, these Galvestonians. Men with thick handlebar moustaches strut back and forth in their tailored, three-piece suits and proper straw hats. Shoppers march about with packages under their arms. Mothers scold precocious youngsters who lick ice cream cones and nibble at taffies. Bathing beauties, still damp from the gulf waters, are content to ride up and down in trolley cars.

They are all such a happy lot. Simplistically happy. Women in their cumbersome bicycling costumes roll by on two-wheelers. With their ridiculous puffed sleeves and accommodating skirts, they draw the eye of any young man who might choose to give them a glance. Those same silly women scurry in and out of the millinery, where they purchase large, impractical hats with ribbons and feathers, or bonnets with huge satin bows. Long-nosed women with their waists pinched by rigid corsets saunter by with dainty parasols in their hands to keep out the sun. Dressed in the latest fashion, their backsides are blown completely out of proportion by layers of ruffled petticoats. Flowing skirts brush the tops of prim black boots or high-button shoes, which adorn their tiny, delicate feet.

Islanders. Are they really worth writing about? Is any life without catastrophe worth writing about? Have I made a mistake, coming back here?

"Well, if it ain't old Boomer Murphy." The familiar

voice startled him. Brent looked into the eyes of an old school chum, Kevin Porter.

"Kevin." Discovery. The moment of truth.

"Do your parents know you're back?" Kevin pulled up a chair, making himself at home.

"No. Not yet."

"You sly dog, you, hiding out. What have you been up to?"

Brent spoke carefully, almost afraid that once he started speaking, the whole story would tumble out in one mouthful. "I, um ... I spent some time at the *World*. Did a little sprinting for Joe Pulitzer." More than a little, truth be told. He had run himself ragged, searching for stories.

"Well, I guess we all knew that," Kevin said with a grin. "Your mother's done nothing but brag since the day you left."

"Really?" Those words suddenly gave Brent a surge of confidence. "To be honest, I—"

"You mean you don't know?" Kevin asked, obviously astonished. "She's all but blamed the Spanish-American War on you. In a proud sort of way, of course."

"What do you mean?"

"Oh, come on, man," Kevin said with a laugh. "Don't you read the papers? Those sensational headlines provoked a war."

"They weren't my headlines," Brent reassured him, though he had to agree that sensationalism had probably played a role in starting the war. *"If it isn't a story, make it into one!"* That had been the going motto. Not his. Brent never moved in that direction. Everything in him argued against it. He fought tradition all the way to the top, which had proven to be his undoing. Pulitzer wasn't partial to individuals with strong opinions, and Brent wasn't fond of being told what to do. Together, they made an impossible team.

WEDNESDAY, SEPTEMBER 5, 1900, 12:08 P.M.
ALONG THE STRAND

Henrietta strolled the alphabetized streets of downtown Galveston, sweat rolling down her back under the heavy fabric of the dark habit. She pulled at the large white collar, trying to loosen its grip on her throat. She nodded at those passing by. A few friendly shoppers spoke a cheery "hello," but most were barely cordial. A nod of the head seemed all they could offer. Who could blame them? Approaching a nun on a busy city street must be extremely embarrassing, she imagined.

Henri refused to complain, at least aloud. A trip into town had been a welcome change. Here, she would make a few necessary purchases for the orphanage on her very first venture into the island's heart since her arrival. The first two and a half miles had been by buggy. She and Sister Elizabeth had parted ways at the livery, arranging to meet again in an hour. Just one short hour. She longed for so much more.

Henrietta fought the temptation to stare at those walking by. How lovely the women looked, with their tightly cinched waists and romantic, flowing skirts. Lovely hats framed their creamy china doll complexions, still snowy white, in spite of the ever-present sun.

"How do you do?" a curvaceous woman walking a large poodle spoke politely. Her nose tilted a bit too high. Henri nodded a silent response, and scurried along in silence.

An elderly man stood at the corner of The Strand playing an accordion, an odd sight, she had to admit.

Henri took it all in, part of her envious, the other part curious. She had heard all about The Strand from Sister Abigail. "It is a wicked, sinful place," the older woman had warned, shaking her head firmly. "Nearly as dreadful as the bathhouses along the shore."

Wicked? Sinful? Henrietta looked about nervously. Regardless, she must reach the emporium. She must cross the Jordan in order to reach the Promised Land. Stepping out into the street, Henrietta found herself nearly run down by an automobile.

"Careful, miss!" A young man reached out to grab her arm, pulling her back. He tipped his hat at her. Henri felt the heat rise in her cheeks.

"Thank you," she mumbled, looking into his eyes. They were kind, but a little distant. "I think you probably saved my life."

"Happy to be of service," he said, turning to walk in the other direction.

The motorist, decked out with cap and goggles and linen duster, recovered his senses and moved on. Henri made her way across the street without further complication, pausing in front of the large confectionery where folks sat inside eating and chatting. Chocolates and taffies, in full view through the large plate-glass window, caused her mouth to water. Fine foods at a nearby restaurant also awakened her taste buds. Chicken salad. Roast beef. Sweet ham. She could practically taste it all. How she longed for an afternoon out with friends—and a meal, a real meal. What a welcome change it would be from the daily allotments of bland, unimaginative food she dished out at the asylum.

The Strand drew her in, tugging at her senses. How could she resist such temptation? And yet she must. She simply must. Henri took one last look at the tempting delicacies then forced herself to look the other way. She quickly made her way to the large emporium, stepping inside. An odd mixture of aromas greeted her: pipe tobacco, freshly ground coffee beans, and vanilla concentrate. Henrietta immediately felt at home. Fans whirred overhead, providing some relief from the heat. She took her time inside the spacious store, looking at the colorful fabrics and the ladies' pattern book, her usual routine in the emporium back at home. But home did not exist anymore.

Henri's eyes traveled to the candy counter, shifting madly from licorice sticks to jelly beans to chocolate-covered almonds. Finally she found what she had been looking for. "I'll have one of those." She pointed to a peppermint stick. What a rare delicacy. She would have to hide it from both Sister Abigail and the children, but she didn't mind one little bit.

"Certainly, miss—oh, I mean *Sister*." The clerk couldn't even seem to maintain eye contact as he spoke. Obviously uncomfortable with her presence, he wrapped the peppermint in paper with his eyes shifted downward. "That will be a penny, please."

"Thank you," she said curtly, handing him a bright copper penny of her own, which she had brought for just such an opportunity. "But I do need to make a few other purchases." She had been sent to fetch sugar, flour, and two new mops.

"Yes, Sister. Of course." His trim moustache twitched nervously.

She handed the clerk her list, and he quickly bundled the necessary items together. "Would you like to have these delivered?" he asked.

"No thank you," Henri said firmly. "I believe I can manage."

She would look quite a sight marching up the street like this, mops in one hand, bulky bundle in the other.

Henrietta stepped outside, sighing deeply as the heat overwhelmed her. She glanced up at the sky—as clear and as blue as any sky back in Virginia. The sky could not be blamed. Frustrated, she tugged at her collar. It choked the very life out of her.

WEDNESDAY, SEPTEMBER 5, 1900, 8:01 P.M.
THE COURIER

"You might want to hear this, sir."

Everett Maxwell looked up from his work at the young reporter who stood in his doorway. "What is it, Nathan?"

"You know that storm? The one off the coast of Africa?"

"Yeah?" Everett mumbled, distracted. Truthfully, he had given the storm little thought, though the look on Nathan's face now convinced him there might be a story brewing.

"I just heard Florida took a pretty hard hit. Maybe we'll be next."

"You think?" Now he had Everett's attention. "It's crossed over into the gulf? Are you sure?"

"Looks like it. And you know what happens when they hit the gulf. They pick up speed, and strength too."

He knew, all right. The warm waters of the Gulf of Mexico usually managed to strengthen storms, which allowed them time to build gradually before they finally slammed into land. Of course, where they would land was always a puzzle. But the waves themselves gave a few

45

clues. The time between them lengthened whenever a storm approached.

Everett thought about the possibilities and felt the gravity of the situation. He quickly pushed all fears aside. The island had suffered storms in the past. She could brave another one. "Thanks for the news, Nathan. Good job."

"From what I hear, it's a big one." The younger man inhaled deeply.

"Really?" Everett's heart began to pound with the usual zest at an incoming story. "A big one, eh?"

"They, uh ... they've already reported it in the *Daily*."

"Great. I should have guessed." The Galveston *Daily News* always seemed to beat them to the punch. What they missed, the *Tribune* picked up. The *Courier*—well, the *Courier* rarely topped the two big guys. *Never* would be more like it. "Where are they predicting landfall?"

"Don't rightly know."

"Well, let's see if we can't nail this one," Everett said. "People on the island take these storms far too lightly. Poor attitude equals more fatalities, that's my thinking."

"You know how these islanders are, sir," Nathan said with a shrug.

"Yes, I know. Complacent," Everett agreed. "But I've said for years that Galveston is completely unprepared for the big one."

"Let's not get ourselves all riled up, Mr. Maxwell," Nathan said. "It's just a storm. We've been hit by some mighty hard ones before. Remember the big one back in eighty-six?"

"Yes, well ..." Everett said. "Let's just hope this isn't like that one." He shook his head as he allowed himself to remember the horrible, vivid details. The storm of eight-six had been catastrophic. One hundred and fifty lives had been lost, in all. The island hadn't taken a direct hit, but Indianola, a near neighbor, had been destroyed.

No, Texans weren't interested in another storm like that, story or no story.

Everett left the office abruptly, walking out into the bright sunshine of The Strand. Everett made his way to Market Street, toward one of his favorite spots: Frankie Dolan's Barbershop. There, he could sit and swap stories with the guys about everything from sports to medicine to weather. The *Courier's* "lifeline," that's what he called it. And maybe, just maybe, today would be his lucky day. Today, maybe Mickey would be there.

Mickey O'Brien never claimed to be a professional meteorologist, not by any stretch. He worked as a shrimper in Galveston Bay. But he sure liked to try his hand at forecasting the weather. If anyone would know about this storm, Mickey would.

Everett made his way along Market Street, nodding impatiently at those passing by. A storm brewed in his mind. He needed a story, one that would save the *Courier*. He entered the barbershop breathlessly. "Hey, Frankie, how's it going?"

Frankie looked up with the usual grin. "Good, Everett. But it looks like you're getting a little shaggy around the ears. If you had as much hair on top of your head as you do on the sides, I could make you look like a real gentleman."

"Very funny," Everett responded. "But I could use a shave."

"Whatever you say. You're the boss."

"Try telling that to my wife," Everett joked, settling

back into the chair, ready to enjoy the moments of peace that lathering up brought with it.

"Guess you heard about the big one," Frankie said.

"Big one?" he spoke through the lather.

"Mickey says we've got a big one brewing out there."

"Yeah, well, he's said that before," Everett said.

"Hold still, or I'll cut your lips off," Frankie said, reaching for the razor. The sharp blade began to move across Everett's face, creating a smooth rhythm: back and forth, back and forth. Frankie continued to talk as he worked, relaying all of the news available.

"Surf's up today, did you know?"

Everett didn't answer, for fear of losing a lip.

"Well, it is," Frankie continued. "Sure sign of a storm. Mickey's right about this one. I can feel it."

Everett nodded numbly.

"You know how he is. He drew up a chart of sorts to track the storm out there. Says it's gonna strike to the east of the island."

"Where, exactly?" Everett said, sitting up.

"Well, now you've gone and done it."

Everett tasted the salty dribble of blood run across his teeth, mixed with the minty lather.

"Just lay back now. It's not a deep one, but it will need some tending to." Frankie wiped the rest of the lather off and placed a towel across Everett's lip, making it impossible for him to speak.

But he had to speak. One question still remained fresh on his mind. Through the towel, he mumbled the words, "What does Cline say?" Isaac Cline, the island's chief meteorologist, was skilled in weather prediction. The locals took his word seriously.

"Ah, you know how it is," Frankie said. "When Cline

walks out of doors with an umbrella on his arm, the whole island perches for rain. When he comes out without it, merchants lay their wares out for sale in the streets."

"No one is right all the time."

"Nope," Frankie said. "I reckon you're right. If I had to place any bets, I'd put my money on Mickey"

Five

A brisk morning breeze blew across the bay, attracting tourists and locals, anyone who wished to trade the mediocrity of the day for a trip to the Pagoda Bathhouse. Its octagonal pavilions were full of frolicking children, too young for school, with scolding parents at their sides.

Seagulls, white with gray wings, swooped and rose, diving into the water for any bit of food they might find. Ripples in the water lulled dreamers to dream their dreams, encouraged lovers to clasp hands and enjoy the moment in quiet solitude. Nothing could disturb the sea. Not the rattle of a mother's voice raised in consternation. Not a brisk, unexpected wind, nor a ship setting out on its course.

"What is it about this place?" Brent asked himself. "I thought it was out of my blood, gone forever. How does it pull me back when I've struggled so hard to keep it away?"

A cotton steamer made its way off in the distance,

leaving a trail of white water lingering in its wake, a gentle reminder that not all is destined to remain ashore.

A line from the epic poem *The Rime of the Ancient Mariner* suddenly ran through Brent's head: "Water, water every where, nor any drop to drink." How inviting, and how completely void of life.

Brent scribbled nervously:

I sit at the ocean's side, more observer than friend. There is a certain picturesque serenity here that captivates the imagination. The clamorous waves, a choir against the composition of the bustling city, still roll in and out, as always. They lap the shoreline with an eagerness that energizes even the most casual spectator.

I have never quite forgiven the waves for nearly taking my life as a young boy. They were restless then, and restless they remain.

The whole island is abuzz these days: electric lights humming, telephone wires tapping, horns blasting from the boats offshore. I catch the scent of fish, a familiar odor. Shrimpers pull in their catch, providing a meager income. They seem poor, compared to the well-to-do folks along Broadway. However, I have learned that, in many ways, they have a richness about them: a knowledge of the gulf, of the currents, and of the sadness of lives lost in an instant. I find no standoffishness in them. There isn't the time or the energy for it. Any glassy stares are usually directed at them, not from them.

A seagull, perhaps a bit too friendly, dove down to Brent's side in search of food. Startled, he turned his attention to the tiny creature. It remained quietly as he continued to write, a noiseless observer.

Some things are sure and certain: The tide continues to pull in and out at will. The sun rises and sets according to its own clock. The seasons roll by unhindered. My father is much the same. He is a constant in my life. He is, and always will be, my foe. His fingerprints press into my back until I ache with the pain of it.

I am his biggest disappointment.

Brent laid down his pen, taking a moment to contemplate the wonder and majesty of the ocean waves. Their white-capped peaks rose above the rocky shore, then fell back again in utter defeat. He remained just as defeated.

THURSDAY, SEPTEMBER 6, 1900, 11:35 A.M.
ALONG THE STRAND

"Good morning. Can I help you?"

Gillian looked into the eyes of the young man at the confectionery counter. "Thank you, yes," she said, pointing a gloved finger at a display of sugary delights. "I'll be needing some chocolates delivered for our gala Saturday night. And some taffies, too, I suppose."

"Would you like a soda while you're here?" he asked, wiping his hands on a crisp, white apron.

"Don't mind if I do," she said, seating herself at the tall marble counter. "I'll have a cherry phosphate."

"Cherry phosphate it is," he said, turning to prepare her drink.

Gillian looked around the large confectionery. Even as a child, she had loved this place with its taffy machine and flavorful smells. She watched, transfixed, as the sticky white mound of sugar pulled back and forth, back and forth, stretched to unreasonable limits. She wasn't so different, really. Life had pulled at her over the years, but she had come through it all triumphantly.

"Ma'am, your drink." The young man placed the large glass down in front of her. Gillian took a sip, the bubbles teasing her nose a bit. She sighed deeply. "You wouldn't believe what I've been through this very morning. Those ridiculous immigrants are swallowing up the island. Why, I saw two of them haggling over the price of avocados out on the street. I tell you, it's absolutely disgraceful."

The young man cleared his throat, a frown crossing his lips. Only then did Gillian notice his olive skin and deep black eyes. How very embarrassing.

"Of course, I didn't mean ... It's not as if all of you, I mean all of them ..." Better stop before she made things any worse. "You know, I saw the most amusing thing," she said, attempting to change the direction of the conversation.

"Ma'am?"

"Just now, out on the street. I saw a man with a monkey. Can you imagine that? He played an accordion. The man, I mean. Not the monkey."

"Oh, that's Mr. Miracel," the young man explained. "He's only just arrived from Greece. The monkey's name is Kita."

"Kita. How very interesting."

The young man turned to wait on another customer. Gillian was certainly glad to be rid of him, at least for the moment. Her mind shifted to the upcoming party.

She would be the belle of the ball, no doubt about that. Just this morning, her gown had arrived. An ivory princess cut with Valenciennes lace overlay, it was exquisitely embroidered. The square neckline, covered in delicate trim, was just a daring bit risqué, and the full sleeves employed yards of fabric. Appliqués adorned the cinched waist, which she often bragged to be a mere nineteen inches about. Her cream-colored petticoat, a rich taffeta, created a swishing sound as she moved in it. She could hardly wait to wear it.

"Saturday night." She giggled, just thinking about Millicent's eyes popping right out of her head. Far more conservative, Millicent was sure to turn up in a linen piece with high neckline and smaller sleeves.

"Mrs. Murphy?"

Gillian turned abruptly, finding herself face to face with Kevin Porter, one of Brent's old chums from high school.

"Why, hello Kevin. I never expected to see you here."

"I'm here most every day," he said, grinning. "Becky Ann and I are engaged." He pointed to a young woman cleaning tables.

"Oh, is that so," Gillian said. She would never have guessed it. The Porters were such a nice family, and from such a lovely home. Why in the world would Kevin want to marry a girl like that? She was so, so ... common.

"So how is Brent this fine day?"

What a ridiculous question. Surely everyone knew that Brent was away. "Posh," she said, sipping her drink, "he's all the way up in New York City. Remember? He's a big-time reporter for the *World*. In fact, he dines with Pulitzer regularly. Why, I received a letter from him just this very morning." She hadn't spoken the truth, but bragging about her son had become more than just a passing fancy. Over the last few years, she had turned it into an art.

"But Mrs. Murphy. Brent was ..."

"Brent was what?"

"Um ... never mind," he said, turning suddenly to walk away.

What an odd young man, she thought. *And to think, he used to be quite nice.*

THURSDAY, SEPTEMBER 6, 1900, 11:56 A.M.
ST. MARY'S ORPHAN ASYLUM

Henrietta read the letter slowly, savoring each word:

My dear Henrietta, we miss you terribly, though we pray that this letter finds you content in our Blessed Savior's arms. We are so proud of our little girl, for the courage you've shown in so many areas of your life. We pray for you daily and send all our love. Remember the words from the book of Psalms as you carry forth his message, "I sought the LORD, and he answered me; he delivered me from all my fears. Those who look to him are radiant; their faces are never covered with shame." Papa sends his love, as does little Katie. She asks about you daily. Love and kisses, Mama.

Henri clutched the letter tightly in her hand, tears of shame washing down her cheeks. To be honest, she hadn't been seeking the Lord. She had been angry with him, angry because he had sent her here. How could she possibly reconcile those feelings with her mother's words? The call that had seemed so clear just months ago was now nothing but a blur.

She couldn't escape the inevitable conflict. A war raged inside her. Would she ever find peace in the midst of this storm?

THURSDAY, SEPTEMBER 6, 1900, 3:56 P.M.
THE MURPHY VILLA

Gillian climbed the front steps to the house, wiping the perspiration from her brow. The ample front porch, which she lovingly called her gallery, beckoned to her with its cool breeze, but there was no time to stop and enjoy it now. Packages loaded down the carriage, and she desperately needed assistance.

"Pearl! Pearl, come here!" she called out loudly.

The large black woman who had become more family than servant entered the front hallway. She was covered in flour from head to toe.

"Pearl, you look a sight," Gillian said with a huff. "Now get cleaned up quickly so that you can help me."

"I thought I was helping you," Pearl muttered, wiping her hands on her apron. "I've been downstairs workin' in that kitchen from sunup till sundown, mixing and baking, getting things ready for this shindig. But don't you fret now, Miss Gillian. You and me's gonna get this get-together up and runnin'. If there was ever two women who could do it, it'd be us, 'cause we're the best party-givers on this here island."

"Pearl, you talk entirely too much," Gillian said, exasperated. "Just help me, please."

"Yes'm. I'm just sayin' that you got nothin' to worry 'bout, Miss Gillian. That's all."

"Why don't you let me be the judge of that?" she asked, turning to face the older woman. How could Pearl possibly understand? It was Gillian's reputation that was at stake. Pearl knew nothing of such things.

Pearl scurried in and out with her arms full, griping about the heat, the weight of the packages, and anything else she could find to complain about.

"I declare, Pearl," Gillian said finally, "you're about to wear me out with that whining."

"Oh, I don't whine, Miss Gillian," Pearl said with a grin. "I just trust the Lord. He gives me the strength to get through, day by day. That's all."

Gillian shook her head, more frustrated now than ever. "This is no time for a sermon, if you don't mind. We have work to do." She handed the last of the packages to the older woman, then dropped down onto the settee in the front parlor for a much-needed rest.

"When you're done with those packages," she said, "please bring me a glass of tea. And hurry, Pearl. It's been quite a day."

THURSDAY, SEPTEMBER 6, 1900, 7:30 P.M.
THE COURIER

"Nothing exciting ever seems to happen on this island," Everett said, looking out the window. "Day after day, it's the same old thing. The tide rolls in and rolls back out again. Predictable. Completely predictable."

"But that's a good thing, isn't it?" his wife, Maggie, asked, wrapping her arms around his neck. "No news is good news."

"Not in my business," he mumbled, turning to face her.

"Poor Everett," Maggie said with a grin. "Only happy when others are suffering."

He shrugged. It was a hard statement, but true. "It's not that I enjoy seeing people suffer," he said with a sigh. "It's just that it—"

"Sells papers." She finished the sentence for him. They had discussed this subject many times, so apparently she knew his thoughts before he even voiced them. He gave her a tight hug, choosing to ignore the hint of sarcasm in her voice. It wasn't her fault. She had been awfully good about everything.

Perhaps a little too good.

THURSDAY, SEPTEMBER 6, 1900, 11:42 P.M.
JOHN SEALY HOSPITAL

Emma left John Sealy Hospital at the corner of Eighth and Market at 11:42 P.M.. She had struggled through the second in a succession of unbearably long days at the hospital. Her shift was supposed to end much earlier, but she was always so far behind.

Darkness blanketed the island, making the walk home difficult. Her family was probably asleep by now. She turned for one last look at the hospital, its impressive white structure standing out against the shadows of the night. All of her hopes, her visions of what nursing would be like, had vanished. Within hours of entering John Sealy Hospital just two days ago, everything had changed.

Two days. It seemed more like two years.

Six

Brent rolled over in the bed, fighting a torment-
ing nightmare. The dream refused to release its hold on
him. In it, he stood face to face with his father, their eyes
locked in a showdown. Who would break the ice first?
Who would speak the first word? What would they say?
His father's eyes were cold, hard. Brent began to tremble, a sweat breaking out on his forehead. "Just say it!"
he cried out.

His father's mouth opened, but nothing came out. No
sound escaped his lips. Brent turned his face away, feeling the painful lump in his throat.

I'm your son. You can talk to me.

No response. Brent twisted and turned in the sheets,
finally waking in a pool of sweat. "I can't do this," he
whispered to himself. "I can't face him."

He stumbled his way along the bed toward the window. He could not see the ocean from here, though he
longed for it now with every fiber of his being. Why, he
could not be sure. Truth be told, the gulf waters had

terrified him since childhood. He picked up his journal, writing rapidly.

The waves pound the shoreline. The glistening sand, like packed asphalt, takes the beating all too willingly. I have never been such an eager candidate. My father's cruel words have lashed out at me again and again, each time leaving their salty sting. Somewhere along the way, my emotions started to erode, washing away any feeling at all for the man.

Except fear. Fear lingers.

Brent turned back toward the bed, pausing to look at his reflection in the mirror. His sandy hair stuck up all over his head. He worked it with his fingers, trying to force it into position. Everything had to be perfect. He leaned in for a closer look at his eyes. They were deep brown, tinted with flecks of yellow and gold. Nothing like his father's deep gray ones. Nothing. But, then again, they wouldn't be, would they?

"You are nothing like me!" How often I have heard those words. They strike me as odd, all things considered. I wouldn't be like him. I couldn't be like him.

Gazing once again into the mirror, Brent couldn't help but notice how young he looked tonight. Too young ever to face a formidable foe like his father.

FRIDAY, SEPTEMBER 7, 1900, 5:32 A.M.
ST. MARY'S ORPHAN ASYLUM

Henrietta tossed and turned in the bed. She should have risen more than half an hour ago. Wonder of wonders, Sister Abigail hadn't come and pulled her from her blissful sleep. But all seemed still this morning, a blessing in disguise.

Henri slipped down to her bedside, onto her knees, for private morning prayer. She made the sign of the cross more out of habit than devotion. Today she would tell them ...

She was going home.

FRIDAY, SEPTEMBER 7, 1900, 12:11 P.M.
THE COURIER

Everett paced his office, looking out of the window, searching for ... Funny, he wasn't quite sure what to search for. Some sign of impending doom, perhaps? Dark skies, violent, rushing winds? A few clouds would have brought him some glimmer of hope. Instead, a bright noonday sun glistened overhead. It seemed to laugh at him. Any approaching storm—any approaching story—seemed miles away.

Not too many miles, he reminded himself. And a storm of great proportions would mean evacuation for islanders. Should he go ahead and suggest that now, even without knowing? Would they leave at his bidding?

With the sun shining overhead, it was unlikely. Galvestonians had grown accustomed to weathering the storms. They didn't take such things with any gravity. They would board up their houses and businesses, perhaps, but they would not go. They were tough. They had made it through others. So had he, in fact.

Everett decided to wait until he heard from Isaac Cline at the weather station before offering any advice to the public. At that point, things would be out of his hands.

FRIDAY, SEPTEMBER 7, 1900, 1:14 P.M.
THE TREMONT HOUSE

"You're not scared to go home, are you?"

Brent Murphy pondered the desk clerk's words. They were laced with wisdom, but he would never acknowledge such a thing. This fellow was far too nosy.

"I'm not afraid," he mumbled halfheartedly, trying not to look him in the eye. "I'm just ..." The rest of the words refused to come.

"Well then, what's keeping you?" the older man continued, his unusually large chin jutting forward mockingly. "You've been put up here two days now. Thought you said you were going home." His protruding brown eyes stared into Brent's, making him uncomfortable.

That's none of your business, old man.

Brent couldn't deny the fact that he had spent the last two and a half days shuffling back and forth between his room and the dining room downstairs. Anxious hours had been spent staring out his second-floor window, worrying and wondering.

"'Course, if you're *scared* to go home, well then, that's another story," the desk clerk continued, an undeniable smirk on his face.

I've had just about enough of you. Any minute now I'm going to put you in your place.

"I told you. I'm not scared. I'm just ..." Brent stumbled over his own words.

"Just what?" The man leaned on the counter, looking down his nose at Brent.

Just avoiding the inevitable? Just rehearsing the speech over and over in my mind? Just trying to imagine how the parents I left behind six long years ago will respond to my unexpected arrival back on the island? Trying to envision their response when I tell them of my escapades in New York's newspaper frenzy? No, not when they were so opposed to my leaving.

"I don't know," he mumbled.

"For a newspaper fellow, you sure don't use a lot of words."

Brent shrugged. "So I'm quiet. So what?"

"Thought you said you were a big-time reporter," the older man said with a laugh.

Big time? Big talker was more like it. Brent's days in New York had more than proven he wasn't ready for big-time anything.

The clerk chuckled. "Bet you've never even seen the likes of New York City."

"Of course I have. I just don't feel much like talking, that's all."

"Well, if I were you, I'd be headed home. We've got a storm brewing over the gulf. Won't be long now."

"We've weathered some big ones before," Brent said, stretching. "I suppose we'll get through this one just the same."

"Too close to shore here. I'm headed up to my sister's place if the waters start rising."

Brent yawned. The last few sleepless nights had left him in a foul mood. "I'll read about it in the papers, old man," he mumbled, turning toward the door.

"You will at that," the desk clerk said smugly, eyes boring down on him. "You mark my words."

FRIDAY, SEPTEMBER 7, 1900, 1:23 P.M.
THE MURPHY VILLA

"So much to be done, and so little time." Gillian looked across the spacious dining room with its stenciled walls. A large oak table, with all five leaves in place, took the place of honor in the center of the room. Adorned with a hand-tatted ivory tablecloth, this piece of furniture was her pride and joy. Douglas had paid a hefty price for it. A silver candelabrum stood in the middle of the table, surrounded on every side by fresh flowers. Bright silver forks, knives, and spoons, recently polished, glistened at each place setting, carefully placed on delicate lace napkins. Gillian beamed, taking it all in.

"What should I do next, Miss Gillian?" Pearl asked, wiping her hands on an already dingy apron.

"Pull out the fine china, Pearl," Gillian said. "And then wax the floors. I gave you a list."

"I'm just tired, that's all," the older woman said. "We been working nigh on three weeks now getting ready for this here party of yours, and I'm just plum tuckered out."

Gillian scrutinized her carefully, trying to analyze her words. "You need some vitamins, Pearl," she said matter-of-factly. "I've been saying it for quite some time now. I'll pick some up next time I'm at the emporium. Vitamins can make a world of difference. Strong blood is necessary for strong work. That's what I always say. Now, in the meantime, you get on in there and get that china laid out the way you know I like it." She nodded firmly, to emphasize her words.

"Yes'm," Pearl muttered.

Gillian watched her walk away, shaking her head in disbelief. "It is so hard to get good help these days." She turned her attention back to the house. The handmade oak floor panels, laid in a complex herringbone pattern, shone brightly. Imported carpets showed virtually no sign of wear. She looked up to the electric lights along the wall, reaching up to wipe dust off two of the votive cups. "Pearl, you've missed a spot," she called out in disbelief.

A smile crossed her lips as she caught a glimpse of her own reflection in the large pier mirror. Despite the heat, her hair remained in a clean upsweep. No proper woman on the island would dare be seen in a state of disarray, despite the weather. Better hot than cold, like so many of her relatives up north.

Yes, Gillian had grown accustomed to the heat over the years, though she regretted the fact that her beautiful home had no wallpaper due to the island's battle with extreme humidity. "Oh well," she said, primping in the mirror. "It's just as well." The plaster walls were carefully stenciled in the most contemporary style. Perhaps one day she and Douglas would be able to afford gilded cornices in the parlor. They were the latest fashion along Broadway.

"No time to worry about that now," she mumbled, trying to stay focused. There were far more important details to attend to. The butler's pantry must be carefully arranged, with all of the china and crystal in place. Downstairs, in the large kitchen off of the servant's quarters, the menu must be meticulously carried out.

Hosting the party of the century was no small matter.

FRIDAY, SEPTEMBER 7, 1900, 1:52 P.M.
THE COURIER

Everett flipped through the messy stack of papers on his desk, looking for the necessary quote to go with his article. "Ah, here it is," he said, pulling it out to have a closer look.

"Isaac Cline, employee of the newly founded U.S. Weather Bureau, has stated that the potential of a hurricane posing a serious danger to Galveston Island is 'an absurd delusion,'" Everett typed. "His expert opinion weighed heavily into the city's decision not to erect a seawall, though many felt, and still feel, that such a wall may be necessary to save lives, homes, and businesses." Should such a storm hit, Cline had concluded, it would do little damage. This opinion he based on the shallow slope of the gulf coastline, which would allow the incoming surf to be broken up, causing it to become less dangerous.

Everett shook his head, questioning the weatherman's confident stand on the matter. He knew many depended on this man for their very survival. Isaac Cline remained one of the most skilled weather reporters of their day, a man who knew his business. If he felt the island was safe from hurricanes, surely there was little to worry about. Not that Cline would have called them hurricanes. Never one to romanticize, the ever-businesslike weatherman had taken to calling them tropical cyclones instead.

Everett paused, deep in thought. He knew Isaac Cline to be a good and loving man, a family man who wouldn't hurt a fly. Did he really have a right to question the authority of a man who had meant so much to the islanders?

Yes, Cline was a good, Christian man. Thinking twice about the matter, Everett took the piece of paper into his palm and wadded it up. He tossed it toward the wastebasket.

It missed.

FRIDAY, SEPTEMBER 7, 1900, 7:36 P.M.
JOHN SEALY HOSPITAL

"Emma, you're needed in the children's ward," Nurse Phillips shouted abruptly. "There are beds to be changed."

"I know, I know," Emma grumbled, reaching for an armful of sheets. She shoved them under her left arm, leaving her right hand free to reach for more. "I've just been so busy, I haven't had time yet." It seemed no matter how she slaved, she could never please the old girl. Emma marched across the meticulously clean hallway to the medicine closet, thankful for a moment alone. She worked the afternoon shift today, and early morning tomorrow. No rest for the weary.

"I'm never going to get to see my family," she muttered. "I might as well put a bed in here."

"What are you up to, pretty lady?" a familiar voice rang out, startling her back to reality.

Emma turned to see Rupert Weston, a new intern. Strikingly handsome, Rupert's deceptively deep blue eyes twinkled merrily. They seemed to tease her.

"I, uh, I'm about to give out meds."

"Here, let me assist you," he said, reaching to help her.

"Don't let Nurse Phillips catch you in here," Emma whispered, "or it will be the end of me."

Rupert touched his finger to his lips, as if hiding some great secret. "So, what's new with you?" he asked.

"Nothing much. Just work, work, and more work."

"And more to come," he said.

"What do you mean?"

"There's a storm headed our way. Didn't you hear?"

Emma couldn't help but notice nervous wrinkles creep across his forehead. "No," she answered, using the back of her hand to brush wisps of hair from her eyes. In the process, she nearly lost the sheets.

"Careful, there." Rupert reached out to clutch them before they hit the floor.

"To be honest, I've been so busy, a cyclone could have ripped the whole place to bits and I probably wouldn't have noticed," Emma said.

"Hope that's not a prediction." He laughed nervously. "But really, people everywhere are talking about it. It's supposed to be a big one. The whole island's bracing for it." His eyes suddenly reflected a genuine fear.

"No storms where you come from?" Emma asked.

"Not hurricanes anyway," he answered. "I hail from Oklahoma, remember? We get tornadoes, plenty of 'em, but no hurricanes."

"Don't get yourself all riled up." Emma yawned. "We've weathered some pretty big ones here before. This one won't be anything new."

"I hope you're right." He gave her a wink.

"Right as rain," she responded, walking away.

FRIDAY, SEPTEMBER 7, 1900, 8:42 P.M.
ST. MARY'S ORPHAN ASYLUM

Henrietta looked up into the sky, eyes resting on the moon. Full, and nearly as bright as the morning sun, it held her captivated for a few moments. Somewhere in Virginia, her family probably gazed at this very same moon, thinking of her. Sadly, even that thought couldn't lift her spirit tonight.

I'm such a coward.

Henrietta had to confess it. She hadn't told them. She couldn't do it. Fear kept her locked in its cage, a victim of her own choices.

"Sister Henri?" Lilly Mae's soft frightened voice startled her.

"Lilly Mae, you're supposed to be sleeping."

"I can't sleep, Sister," the youngster said, a tear fighting its way down her cheek. "I miss Mama."

"Oh, Lilly Mae," Henri said as she swept the youngster into her arms. "I'm here, baby. I'm here."

"Promise me you won't go anywhere," the little girl cried.

"That's not a promise I can make, dear. None of us can make that promise."

Tears tumbled out of the youngster's eyes as she

spoke. "But it scares me when people go away. Where do they go?"

"They go to heaven, of course," Henri said, trying to sound reassuring. She reached out to take the child's hand into her own.

"Not Papa," Lilly Mae said, beginning to sob. "I heard Mama say he was going to the devil. She didn't know I heard it, but I did."

"Oh, Lilly Mae." How could she respond to such a statement? But she must. "Sometimes people say things they don't really mean when they're upset or angry. I'm sure your mama didn't really mean it."

"But what if—"

"No 'what ifs,' dear. Let's not think that way."

"Oh, but Sister, it makes me so sad to think about Papa down there with the fire and the devil."

"I'll tell you what," Henri said. "Why don't you sleep with me tonight."

"Really?" Lilly Mae's voice was laced with a new energy.

"Yes, really. But we mustn't tell Sister Abigail. Promise?"

"I promise," the youngster said, eyes wide with excitement. Henri tucked Lilly Mae in, then crawled in next to her.

A direct violation of our rules!

She could practically hear Sister Abigail's stern voice now, but she didn't care. For once she had to follow her heart. This precious child needed her, needed the security of very real arms wrapped around her as she slept. She would give her that protection. Henrietta pulled the youngster close. They snuggled for a moment.

Henri felt the sting of tears in her own eyes as Lilly Mae wept openly. Somehow she couldn't help but think of her little sister, Martha, back at home. How many nights they had spent, holding each other until they fell asleep.

"Will you sing to me, Lilly Mae?" Henri asked.

"What shall I sing?" The youngster's voice sounded steadier than before.

"Let's see now. What was your mama's favorite song? What did she teach you to sing?"

After only a slight hesitation, Lilly Mae's voice broke forth into an Italian aria, gentle and yet as strong as that of any grown woman. For a brief moment, Henri worried that the music, which now seemed to dance against the night, might waken the others. Then, just as suddenly, she didn't care anymore. None of it mattered anymore. All that mattered now was this little girl—this gift from God.

Friday, September 7, 1900, 11:56 p.m.
The Maxwell Home

Everett looked out his bedroom window one last time before climbing into bed. A full, bright moon nearly blinded him. A cloudless sky seemed to taunt him. No rain. No storm. No story.

Irritated, he pulled the curtains closed on a long, miserable day.

Seven

Mr. Murphy! Mr. Murphy!"

A repetitive pounding on the hotel door awakened Brent from a deep sleep. He fought to focus, trying to make sense of it all. *Where am I? What is that?*

"Mr. Murphy, wake up!"

"What in the world ... ?" Whoever it was certainly sounded determined. Brent reached for his robe in the dark. He stuck his arm in the sleeve—the wrong sleeve. Reaching for his spectacles, he accidentally knocked a glass of water off the bedside table. The pounding continued relentlessly.

"Mr. Murphy!"

"I'm coming!" he hollered. He fought his way toward the door in the utter darkness, stubbing his toe on the bedpost in the process. "Ooow!" By the time he finally reached his destination, anger had replaced any fear or curiosity. He yanked the door open with a vengeance. "What? What's so all-fired important that you haul a man out of bed in the middle of the night?"

The pale face of the young bellboy greeted him. Something must be terribly wrong. The young man spoke hurriedly. "I'm so sorry to disturb you, Mr. Murphy, but we've been asked to inform all of our guests that we've got water up to the diner."

"What?" Brent looked frantically toward the window, imagining the worst. This made no sense at all. It wasn't even raining.

"It's the swell," the anxious young man explained nervously. "And it'll only get higher. That's for sure. Probably won't bother any of you up on the higher floors, but I thought it would be wise to let everyone know, just in case they wanted to find refuge elsewhere."

"Good grief. This must be a bad one." Brent headed over to look out of the window, amazed at the water in the street below.

"It's bad, alright," the young man said. "Do you have someplace to go, or will you be staying on with us?"

"I'm pretty sure I've got someplace to go," Brent said. "But could you hold the room for me, just in case?"

"Of course, sir. Anything you like. But the water's too high to send a carriage around. You'll have to go by foot."

"Sure, sure," Brent muttered, shutting the door. Like it or not, it looked like he was going home.

SATURDAY, SEPTEMBER 8, 1900, 7:45 A.M.
JOHN SEALY HOSPITAL

Emma arrived at the hospital, still reeling from her journey on foot to get there. Lightning had danced across the morning sky, casting an eerie green over the stark white exterior of John Sealy Hospital. "I hear they've already got water rising in the streets down off The Strand and Market." She reached for a chart on the wall.

"It's barely raining," Rupert responded. "Besides, I thought you islanders didn't get all riled up over storms, remember?"

"You've never been through this before," Emma said curtly. "I wouldn't expect you to understand."

"You're sure singing a different song this morning, that's all," he said with a shrug. "But it looks like we may have more to worry about than that."

"What do you mean?" she said anxiously.

"We've got an influenza epidemic on our hands. I admitted three more children just this morning."

"Oh, that's terrible."

"Don't you have work to do, Nurse Sanders?" The abrupt voice of Nurse Phillips snapped her back to reality.

"Oh, I … uh," she stammered.

The older woman glared at her, no hint of compassion in her eyes. "I thought I made it abundantly clear to you, Miss Sanders, that there was to be no—shall I say *fraternizing*—with other staff members here at John Sealy Hospital. Any attempt to do so will result in your immediate dismissal."

Emma felt her cheeks heat up immediately. She tried to answer, but the words couldn't seem to squeeze past the anger.

I'd like to tell you a thing or two, you old bitty.

"Your comment was entirely inappropriate, Nurse Phillips." Rupert said sternly. "And I take it as a personal insult. For your information, I was briefing Nurse Sanders on our new influenza cases."

Emma's gaze shot straight to the ground. "I'm headed to the children's ward now," she said, clutching the chart.

Her heartbeat echoed loudly in her ears as she turned. Imagine the nerve of that old bag, to insinuate such a thing. And what must Rupert be thinking? Did she look like an immature schoolgirl with a giddy crush? Nothing could be farther from the truth.

Rupert disappeared in the opposite direction as Emma headed to the bedside of Jimmy Peterson. Only six years old, he bore the marks of the flu ravaging his tiny body. Diagnosed with influenza just three days ago, pneumonia now appeared to be setting in. Emma reached inside the tent that surrounded the bed to take his temperature. "How are we doing today?" she asked.

He answered with a frown.

"Would you like me to read you a story a little later?" she asked, forcing a smile. She placed her hand on his forehead.

He's burning up!

The youngster nodded, squeezing her hand. "Thank you, miss," he whispered, then dissolved into a fit of coughing. Emma waited until it subsided, then placed the thermometer in his mouth. She gripped his delicate fingers tightly, fighting back the tears suddenly overwhelming her. Where they came from, she had no idea.

SATURDAY, SEPTEMBER 8, 1900, 7:45 A.M.
THE COURIER

Everett Maxwell paced nervously around his office, stopping to look out of the window every few moments. Less than a mile from the bay, this window gave him an undisturbed view. For the most part, the skies were completely overwhelmed with an ominous yellow-gray. He had seen that color before.

Everett felt the swell of the tide even from here. It filled the air with a tremor, an energy that couldn't be explained.

"What's the story on the Kodak?" he asked anxiously.

"I'm working on it, sir. The shutter's giving me fits," reporter Nathan Potter grumbled, tossing his unkempt red hair out of his eyes.

"We've got to get pictures," Everett mumbled nervously. "I hear Cline's getting restless. This is gonna be a big one. I can feel it. But what good will any of it be without pictures?" He twisted his hands nervously, turning back toward the window.

"Yes, Mr. Maxwell. I know. Have I ever missed a story?"

Might be best not to answer that.

"I'm just saying—"

"Cline's out in his buggy running up and down the coast telling people to get away from the beach," Nathan interrupted. "I'm gonna snap a photo of him if I can ever get this ridiculous thing fixed."

"Just do what you can," Everett said. "Is anyone talking evacuation?"

"Lots of people talking, but no one seems to be listening," Nathan replied. "We've got tourists gawking at the waves."

"Well, if that doesn't beat all ..." People sure acted crazy at a time like this. Everett paced across the room again, pausing to look out the window. Droplets of water fell steadily, and the wind picked up. Even so, things really didn't look too bad, at least not so far.

"Got it!" Nathan's words startled him.

"Well, what are you waiting for?" he said, turning to face the young would-be photographer. "Get out there and get to work."

Nathan answered with a salute. "Yes sir!"

"That's the trouble with young people," Everett mumbled to himself as the door slammed shut. "They've got no gumption."

SATURDAY, SEPTEMBER 8, 1900, 7:55 A.M.
THE MURPHY VILLA

Gillian stared anxiously out the kitchen window. Rain shot down from the skies. What had started as a light mist had escalated into an unimaginable deluge. What a terrible distraction. A wet yard would never do for a party. The flowers could use the moisture, naturally, but if the yard took in too much water, it would become completely saturated. The party couldn't be held out of doors if the rain continued.

"My poor flowers," she moaned, looking at the candytuft, her sturdiest plants. Their lilac petals drooped heavily toward the ground, weighted down with raindrops. "It's simply pitiful."

"Miss Gillian, you care far too much about them little flowers of yours," Pearl said sternly. "And I'm weary to the bone with hearing about them."

"Pearl!"

"I'm sorry, but I just don't know how, in your right mind, you could be so worried about flowers at a time like this." Pearl turned back to her work. Gillian did her best to ignore her. She turned her gaze to the front window, looking out onto the street. The shadow of someone passing by caught her attention.

"Do you see that, Pearl?" she asked, pointing.

"You'd have to be crazy to be out walking in this," the older woman muttered.

"Yes. I wonder who it is."

"Someone without a lick of sense is my opinion," Pearl muttered. "What sort of person stands outdoors in a rainstorm? Other than your party guests, I mean."

"Very funny." Pearl's attempt at humor struck a nerve. If only Douglas would come home. He would know just what to say to soothe her nerves. But his train wasn't due in from the mainland for three hours.

"We'd better get back to work on the hors d'oeuvres for tonight," Gillian said, feeling her face come to life again. "Nothing, not even a storm, is going to keep this party from taking place."

With a grunt, Pearl turned her attention back to the food preparation.

SATURDAY, SEPTEMBER 8, 1900, 8:02 A.M.
ST. MARY'S ORPHAN ASYLUM

"Sister Henri? Sister Henri?" Lilly Mae's voice irritated her almost as much as the constant tugging on Henrietta's hem.

"What, Lilly Mae? What is it now?" She looked sternly at the child.

"Where's Sister Elizabeth going?"

"She's taking the wagon to get food."

"But why? It's raining. She'll get wet."

Why, indeed? The very idea of sending anyone out in this rain made Henrietta nervous. But stubborn Elizabeth had her heart set on going, against everyone's better judgment. After all, with the pantry nearly empty and hungry children to be fed, someone had to purchase food.

"I want to go to market with her," Lilly Mae argued. "I always go with Mama to market."

"I'm afraid not, dear," Henri said, reaching down to pick up the youngster. "Not this time. It's far too dangerous."

"Then why is Sister going?"

She shook her head, watching anxiously as the horse pulled the wagon through ankle-deep water. Why, indeed? Once again, Henrietta found herself searching for answers to this precocious child's questions.

"Can we play in the water?" Lilly Mae tugged repetitively, almost pleading now.

"Play in the water? I should say not. You'll catch your death ..." She caught herself, and did not continue. At that, she turned on her heels and took Lilly Mae by the arm. Together, they made their way inside.

Eight

Just go in," Brent said, wringing his hands. "Just go in."

He stood across the street from his house in the pouring rain. The last hour and a half had been spent pacing up and down the street, trying to formulate the words. Now, the storm seemed to be taking control, soaking him to the bone. If he didn't go in soon, he would have to forget the whole thing.

The house, grander than ever, stood amid a host of other such homes on Broadway, the main thoroughfare through town. A towering beauty, the villa had always been his father's most cherished possession and his mother's pride and joy. A slate-blue, two-story master-piece, it remained one of the loveliest on the island.

Through the kitchen window on the lowest level, he could see the reflection of his mother's face. Though clouded vision limited his view, he did his best to overcome it as he observed her. She still appeared to carry a grace in her movement, her mannerisms.

Brent stood behind a lightpost, safely hidden from view. He toyed with the idea of going inside, longing for his mother's arms, but knowing it would surely be followed by a tongue-lashing from his father.

I told you! You just haven't got it in you, boy! You're never going to do anything with your life!

He had proven his father right—and hated himself for it. Brent stared at his mother's face once more, trying to etch the memory in his mind.

No. He could not go inside.

SATURDAY, SEPTEMBER 8, 1900, 8:17 A.M.
THE COURIER

"Now this is getting better," Everett said with a smile. He stared out of his office window in happy anticipation as raindrops plummeted toward the ground. "A little rain never hurt anyone." He stopped himself before continuing. He wouldn't wish anything bad on anyone. Not exactly, anyway. It's just that a whopper of a storm meant great headlines.

And great headlines meant great sales.

SATURDAY, SEPTEMBER 8, 1900, 8:34 A.M.
THE MURPHY VILLA

"What next, Miss Gillian?" Pearl asked, placing the tray of shrimp into the cooler.

"I suppose we should ..." Gillian looked around the kitchen carefully. "We should slice the vegetables and place them out on a tray. And then we'll start on the crab dip."

"Mm hmm," Pearl said, rubbing her extended belly. "That's my favorite part. I just love your special crab dip, Miss Gillian. Yes, ma'am."

"Thank you, Pearl. Perhaps there will be enough that you and I can have a little for our lunch," she said, reaching to rinse off a large bunch of carrots. "But if we don't get busy on these vegetables, there won't be any."

"The way it's looking outside, there ain't gonna be any party, anyhow," Pearl said with a laugh.

"Nonsense, Pearl," Gillian said, forcing herself not to look out of the window. "It's just a little sprinkle. Why, it will be gone in no time."

SATURDAY, SEPTEMBER 8, 1900, 9:09 A.M.
JOHN SEALY HOSPITAL

"How is Jimmy?" Emma whispered the words to Rupert, hoping the youngster couldn't hear her. He had drifted in and out of consciousness for more than an hour now. She had kept a vigil at his bedside, as time allowed. Nurse Phillips would skin her alive if she saw that the morning breakfast trays still hadn't been picked up, but there would be plenty of time for that later. Right now a little boy needed her.

Emma pulled a chair up to his bedside, and reached under the tent to take hold of his hand. Hot to the touch. Labored breathing had left his color very poor. She did the only thing that made sense at this point. She offered up a prayer for a very special little boy named Jimmy Peterson.

SATURDAY, SEPTEMBER 8, 1900, 9:45 A.M.
ST. MARY'S ORPHAN ASYLUM

"Sister Henri! Sister Henri!"

Henrietta turned to face the children, their squeals rising to an almost unbearable pitch. Water trickled in under the door, seeping slowly across the dining room floor.

"Merciful heavens. Up on the chairs, children."

The children, voices still rising, scrambled up onto the crude wooden chairs set before the large dining table. Dozens of children on dozens of chairs. Now what?

The water rose rapidly, surprising Henri. She peered out of the only window the modest dining room allowed, shocked to find how high the water outside stood.

"Sister Henri?" She turned to face another novice, her dearest friend, Grace.

"What should we do?"

"I'll do what I can to keep the children calm," Grace said softly. "You go and get Sister Abigail."

Henrietta ran to the tiny kitchen, trying to hide the fear from her voice as she spoke. "Sister Abigail ..."

"Yes?" The older woman, preoccupied with food preparation, didn't turn to face her. "Is Elizabeth back?"

"No, Sister. We've got a problem. Water is coming into the dining hall. Two inches, maybe three."

"For heaven's sake. Why are you just standing there? Where are the children?"

"I'm trying to decide what to do with them," she explained. "Should I take them over to the infirmary?"

"To the infirmary? Don't be ridiculous. Do you really want to risk illness?" Abigail asked.

"Of course not. It's just that—"

"Take the children up to the girls' dormitory," Abigail said, turning back to her work. "Get Grace to help you."

"Take the boys and the girls up?"

"Certainly. Now stop wasting time, Sister."

Why did Henrietta always feel so useless around Sister Abigail, so completely hopeless?

"Move quickly now," Abigail scolded.

Henri bounded back into the dining hall, hiking her skirts up to avoid soaking them in the dirty water that now covered the floor. The children stood safely upon the chairs, but the water below had risen to nearly five inches.

"Grace!"

Her fellow novice turned to face her, a look of calm on her face that instantly brought some sense of relief to Henrietta's soul. Gentle Grace always had that effect on her.

"Let's get the children upstairs!" Henri hollered, trying to be heard above the noise.

Grace nodded, grabbing two of the smallest ones and holding them around her waist.

"Children, come quickly," Henrietta called out, beckoning them. They swarmed to the two novices like flies to honey.

"I'm scared, Sister," little Dorothy whispered, grabbing her hand.

Henrietta understood her fear. How in the world could she comfort the children when she herself shook like a leaf?

"I don't like the thunder," Molly Aikens cried, pressing her face into Henri's skirt.

"Don't be a scaredy-cat," eleven-year-old Rex Simcox said, deliberately splashing her skirt and creating more squeals from the group. "Only dumb girls are scaredy-cats."

"Stop it, Rex," Grace's firm voice rang out.

Henrietta pulled the children to herself, feeling a knot grow in her throat. Whatever it took, she would protect these children. "It's going to be alright. God is with us. Now let's head upstairs where we'll be safe."

"Boys too?" Grace asked, eyes growing large. "In the girls' dormitory? Are you sure?"

Henri nodded quickly, and they began to climb. Grace led the way. Henrietta stood at the bottom of the stairs, making sure each child was accounted for.

"Sister Abigail, aren't you coming?" She spoke over the rhythm of the water, which had now risen to a good eight inches.

"I'll be up shortly," the older woman responded,

clutching at the hem of her wet habit. She began to stack chairs upon the wooden tabletop. "Now get those children up the stairs."

"Yes, Sister."

Henrietta scrambled up the steep steps, joining Grace and the children in the large dormitory above.

"Gee willikins!" Rex shouted, running to the window. "Look at our dorm, fellas!" He pointed across the open field to the boy's dormitory. The sturdy two-story structure stood knee deep in water. Henrietta watched, mesmerized, as the water continued to rise. The infirmary stood nearby, also taking in water. In the distance, she could see the gulf, waters rising and falling at unbelievable heights.

"We're too close to shore," she whispered. For the first time the thought occurred to her. They were precariously close to the island's west beach, on the lower end of the island.

Abigail, wet to the hips, made her appearance, her temper still flaring. "Come away from that window!"

"I don't suppose this is the safest place," Henri said firmly. "Everyone needs to move away from the glass and come into this corner with me. We'll sing songs and play games until the storm passes."

She prayed it would pass quickly. She also muttered a prayer for the safety of her dear friend who had braved the storm to bring food. As if she could read her thoughts, Lilly Mae spoke up.

"I'm hungry, Sister Henri," she grumbled. "I bet Sister Elizabeth's having breakfast without us."

"I doubt it, dear," Henri said, grinning in spite of herself. Somehow, even in the middle of the storm, Lilly Mae had managed to give her something to smile about.

Nine

*B*rent shook the water from his jacket as he entered the office of the *Courier*. Though rain poured in a steady torrent, The Strand remained safe from flooding—at least so far. Some along the way had not been so lucky. A temperamental nun had caught his eye crossing Market. Even with her wagon full of supplies, she fought the current with a holy vengeance, her skittish horse dancing like a child's pony at a fair. He prayed for her safety.

Brent shook his head in disbelief. Everywhere he looked, children and even grown women frolicked in the warm, rising waters. Their faces were joyous, carefree. "If they know what's best for them, they'd stay inside their houses and prepare for the storm," he muttered.

Foolish, really, the amount of people out on the streets at a time like this. Of course, he had been one of them, so he really shouldn't comment. Running his fingers through his drenched hair, Brent did his best to make himself look presentable. "Hello?" No response. The building appeared empty. Most of the field reporters must be out covering the storm.

"Can I help you?" An older man in overalls greeted him. "Why, Brent Murphy."

Brent recognized the fellow at once. "Hello, Gordon." He extended his hand toward the older man. "Good to see you."

"And on a day like today. Why am I not surprised?" Gordon shook his head. "You newspaper fellas are a lot alike, aren't you?"

"I suppose," Brent said. "Looks like you've got most of the presses lifted."

"Yes. But if you're looking for Mr. Maxwell, he's gone back upstairs to work on a story."

"Thanks." Brent made his way up the stairs to the familiar inner office, tapping lightly on the door.

"Come in." The same gruff voice of the editor he had left behind six years ago called out to him. Brent carefully opened the door, sticking only his face inside.

"Well, I'll be horsewhipped," Everett Maxwell said, the cigar slipping out of his mouth and scattering ashes across a cluttered desk as it landed atop a heap of papers. "If it ain't Brent Murphy, returned from the dead. Come on in here." He gestured enthusiastically, knocking a stack of books from a nearby chair to make room for Brent.

"Hardly dead," Brent said, sticking out his hand. His old friend shook it with a broad smile.

"Never thought I'd live to see the day …" Everett muttered. "Thought you had the writing bug. Thought those big-city fellers would have snatched you up by now."

Brent dropped down into the chair with a sigh. "Didn't care much for the taste of big-city life."

"Big-city reporting, you mean?"

"Maybe." Brent shrugged.

"Not all you thought it would be?"

How could he answer without giving away his frustrations, his fears? "What's the latest on the storm? I had one doozy of a time getting here from my parents' place with the wind like it is."

"Ah ha. So that's what's up," Everett said with a sly grin. "You smell a story."

"Right now all I smell are storm clouds and the slightest hint of a hurricane. Am I right?" He felt the familiar pangs of excitement as he spoke. A big story always seemed to do this to him.

"As always."

"Where's it headed?" Brent tried not to appear too anxious.

"The worst of it is supposed to pass over the west of the city. Just received a telegraph. And with the west end being slightly lower than we are here on the east ..." Everett's voice trailed off.

"Not good."

"You're telling me." Everett nervously pressed his cigar into an ashtray. "Places the whole island in the right semicircle of the storm. Mighty glad I moved my family farther inland two years back."

"You did?"

"Yep. You missed a lot during the last six years. A mighty lot. Maggie's had another baby ... just four months ago."

"Boy or girl?" Brent asked. Everett's wife, Maggie, had always been kind to him, treating him more like a son than a fledgling reporter.

"Boy. Everett Eugene."

"Spitting image of the old man?"

"Hardly," Everett said with a laugh. "He's got hair."

"I wasn't going to mention it," Brent said, trying not to stare, "but what happened to yours?"

"I pulled it all out over the past six years while you were gone," the older man said with a laugh. "Missed you."

"Very funny."

"So what happened in New York? Too much to talk about?"

Too much? Far too much had occurred to mention now. "I, uh ... well, I got hired on pretty quick at the *World*—"

"You actually got to work for Pulitzer himself? That's quite an accomplishment for a young whippersnapper like you."

Brent shrugged, not wanting to say much more on the subject. "Hardly. Never actually saw him face to face. Let's just say life was different in New York and leave it at that."

"Quite a battle going on between Pulitzer and Hearst, eh?"

"Battle is a mild word," Brent mumbled.

"Yep. Heard firsthand that you practically started the Spanish-American War all by your lonesome."

"I wish everyone would stop saying that." What a gut-wrenching job it had been, working for the big names. Though Brent had stretched a headline or two to sell papers, he would never have gone so far as to create trouble.

"Tell me everything," Everett said, sitting on the edge of his desk. "You know I could never resist a good story."

Brent hesitated for a minute before speaking. Suddenly, a burst of wind from outside caught the window, shaking it, and creating a racket that startled them both out of their seats.

"Looks like you've got a much bigger story of your own out in the gulf," he said, trying to put on his most professional face. "Anything I can do to help?"

"Uh huh," Everett said. "Just as I suspected. Your nose is picking up the scent."

The scent of a major story filled the air. That, Brent concluded, seemed undeniable.

SATURDAY, SEPTEMBER 8, 1900, 10:51 A.M.
JOHN SEALY HOSPITAL

"Nurse! Nurse!"

Emma turned as the door swung open, the air pressure catching her off guard. A woman with olive skin and deep jet-black eyes entered, laboring with child. She was soaked from head to toe. "Gracious! Rupert ..." She called out to him, but he did not appear. Emma knew she must collect her thoughts and find a room for the woman. "What's your name, dear?" she asked.

"Chloe," the young woman said, panting in rhythm with the contractions. "My husband should be in shortly. He's looking for a place to tie up the team where they'll be safe."

"I'm glad you made it this far," Emma said. "I've heard the coastal areas are under water."

"Yes," Chloe said, "We had water knee deep when we left our place. I had planned to deliver at home, but ..."

"I understand. Just glad you made it safely."

Rupert appeared from around the corner, just as Chloe's husband entered, wet from head to toe.

"We'll have to find something dry for both of you," Emma said, reaching to take his jacket. With Rupert's help, she managed to get the couple settled into a safe spot, then offered them hospital gowns to change into.

Nurse Phillips caught her by the arm moments later. "What do you think you're doing?" The older woman spoke through clenched teeth.

"Wha ... what do you mean?" Emma instinctively began to tremble, suddenly unable to defend herself against the older woman's never-ending assaults.

"Those people. They're immigrants. You know good and well they don't have the money to deliver in this hospital."

"But—"

"There are no *buts.*" Nurse Phillips stood with her hands on her hips.

"Their house has taken in water," Emma argued. "They have no place else to go."

"This is not a charity hospital, Emma. And if they don't come up with the money to cover their expenses, then you will have to find a way to do it."

She couldn't think of any way to respond to such absurdity.

"No more," Nurse Phillips warned, shaking her finger in her face. "We don't want islanders looking at the hospital as a refuge. We certainly don't need that."

Heaven forbid.

SATURDAY, SEPTEMBER 8, 1900, 10:59 A.M.
ST. MARY'S ORPHAN ASYLUM

Henrietta stared out of the upstairs window, knuckles turning white as one hand clutched another. She didn't speak a word. Even if she had, no one would have heard her. The wind outside pulled at the building with unbelievable force. It tore through her skin and pulled at the very core of her being. And yet it never touched her. Safe inside the walls of the girls' dormitory, she remained a mere observer.

But what about Sister Elizabeth? Had she located shelter somewhere between the orphanage and the market? God forbid she should.... No, Henrietta wouldn't let herself think like that.

She stared at the boys' dormitory, just yards away.

"Sister!" The shrieking of the children pulled her back into the room, back into the present—the awful present. Her eyes searched out Grace's. She held a tight grip on the smallest of the girls, lips moving constantly in prayer.

"What should we do?" Henrietta merely mouthed the words, realizing she would never be heard above the shrieking of the wind and the wailing of the children combined. The noise coming from the water below built to an impending crescendo. She could feel it, like one felt the sting of a wasp just as the stinger entered the skin. The water had almost reached the second floor.

Then she saw it. Crumpled on the floor, in the farthest corner of the room. Clothesline, for whatever reason, had been tossed carelessly in the corner. What a miraculous idea! They could—they should—tie it around the waist of each child. Then they would rope themselves into groups: she, Grace, and Sister Abigail. That way, just in case.... She hated to think about it.

"Children, quickly," she called out. "Line up in three rows, smallest on the left, larger girls on the right."

She began to rope them together as quickly as her hands could move.

"Help me, Sister," she cried out, handing Abigail another piece. In total silence, the older nun began to work.

"Sister, Sister," Lilly Mae cried out.

"Yes?"

"Dorothy's rope came untied," the youngster cried. "Can you fix it, please?"

She reached for the rope, securing it around the youngster's waist. Dorothy's hand reached for hers, squeezing it tightly. She answered it with a squeeze. Anything she could do to keep them calm right now, she would do.

The roar of water below now accompanied the splintering sound of beams giving way. Every moment felt more critical than the last. Henrietta took the group of larger children and fastened herself to them with the remaining rope. Using only hand motions, she signaled for Abigail to do the same with the smaller girls.

A tremor shook the building, followed by a deafening roar. Then, from across the room, Henrietta saw it ... through the window ... just yards away ...

The boys' dormitory melted into nothingness.

SATURDAY, SEPTEMBER 8, 1900, 11:02 A.M.
THE MURPHY VILLA

Gillian Murphy turned away from the window, tears streaming down her face. A good two to three inches of water covered the yard now. All hopes of a garden party had been washed away. Now she found herself praying that her property, her very life, would be spared.

"It's not fair," she shouted to the sky. "It's just not fair."

Ten

*B*rent left the office of the *Courier* with a smile on his face. The Strand, not far from the harbor side, already had water in the street, ankle deep and rising quickly. Pulling his light jacket up around his ears, Brent fought the blinding rain with a rush of excitement. He had seen the gleam in Everett's eye. This hurricane could very well turn into the story of the century. Journalists always seemed to hope for the worst, knowing that a great story might come of it. Though he prided himself on being different from the others, the magnitude of this story simply couldn't be denied.

Brent looked up and down The Strand. The risk for offices along this stretch of road grew as the wind picked up. Escalating from a whistle to a steady roar, the sound nearly deafened him. Most shopkeepers braved the noise and the driving rain to board up their windows. He nodded to a few of them as he made his way south, fighting calf-deep water. He mustered up the courage to continue, determined to make it as close to the coast as possible.

That's where the stories would be. According to Everett, rumors of cottages toppling on the east end were already circulating. People, cold and wet, pressed past him, moving away from the shoreline and toward the center of the island, where they hoped to find refuge. Most had frantic expressions their faces, and they clutched their children and possessions tightly. They were traveling away from the storm.

His path led him directly into it.

SATURDAY, SEPTEMBER 8, 1900, 11:59 A.M.
ST. MARY'S ORPHAN ASYLUM

"Sing, children, sing!" Henrietta's voice rang out above the roar of water below. With the energy of a freight train, she began to sing one of their favorites, the French hymn, "Queen of the Waves." The song suddenly took on new meaning, new depth.

Queen of the Waves, look forth across the ocean
From north to south, from east to stormy west,
See how the waters with tumultuous motion
Rise up and foam without a pause or rest.

The children, water creeping up about their ankles, joined her—first in fear, then with a triumphant blast.

But fear we not, tho' storm clouds round us gather,
Thou art our Mother and thy little Child
Is the All Merciful, our loving Brother
God of the sea and of the tempest wild.

Lilly Mae's voice rang out above the others. As they sang, the water appeared to stop rising, at least for a time. Soon enough, it began again.

"Into the beds," Abigail instructed. They gathered as teams onto the highest of the beds, giving themselves additional time to collect their thoughts. Hand in hand, the Sisters worked together to secure the children once again. Hands clutched together, they whispered a prayer for safety.

"Dear Lord," the words were fresh on Henrietta's lips, "Be our ever-present help in time of trouble."

And then a song rose from the group, as magnificent as any ever raised at the Opera House just miles away in the heart of town. A song that rode the winds of the storm. A song of hope.

SATURDAY, SEPTEMBER 8, 1900, 12:07 P.M.
THE COURIER

Editor Everett Maxwell peered up anxiously at photographer Nathan Porter as he entered the office. "What's the story?"

"Too much to tell," Nathan said, gasping. "Too much." He shook his head frantically back and forth, eyes wide with excitement.

"Well, catch your breath and tell me what you can." Everett didn't have time to wait. A newspaper business couldn't be kept waiting.

"The bridge is under," Nathan said. "Probably washed out, but we won't know for sure until the water goes down."

"Pictures?"

"You bet." The young reporter raised the camera proudly. "And all three train trestles are under."

"This is a bad one," Everett said, half-excited, half-nervous. "Maggie managed to get through to me on the telephone about twenty minutes ago. She says we've got water up to the tabletops in our dining room. Wish I'd been able to build a little closer to the center of town."

"Me too," Nathan agreed. "I haven't been home for

hours. I don't have a clue how my parents are faring. But this is bad, really bad. Problem is," he explained, "the tide has forced itself into the harbor, causing the bay waters to rise to perilous levels. That's why we've already got so much water here on The Strand."

"Thank God for second-floor offices," Everett said with a grin.

"Yes, well, have you been downstairs?"

"Yep. We worked like the dickens to get the presses elevated."

"Well, I hope it's enough. With water coming in from the bay side and the gulf side, we're talking big trouble. Very big trouble."

Everett understood the gravity of Nathan's comment, and the reality of it suddenly hit him with a vengeance. Unless some sort of unforeseen miracle occurred, the whole island could eventually go under.

SATURDAY, SEPTEMBER 8, 1900, 2:03 P.M.
ST. MARY'S ORPHAN ASYLUM

Two hours and counting. Thankfully, the water in the upstairs dormitory stopped rising at ankle depth. From one of the top bunk beds, Henri felt an odd sense of security, though the roar of the winds outside did little to support the feeling.

Through the window a strange drama unfolded. An assortment of debris floated by on occasion, a reminder of how the raging waters really were in control. Henrietta watched helplessly as what appeared to be bodies also floated by. She could hear the cries from the infirmary across the way as the Sisters worked to pull people in through the second-story windows—a puzzling, almost unreal, sight.

"Oh Lord," Henrietta repeated over and over again,

"be my ever-present help in time of trouble." She had the comfort of one who knew ... knew that in spite of all odds, her faith would sustain her.

The room sat in total darkness. In spite of the trembling of the dorm, many of the children had used the darkness as a cue to drift off to sleep. "Now I lay me down to sleep...." She couldn't help but think of Lilly Mae's prayer now. How defiant the youngster had been. And now, in a sound sleep, how peaceful and safe she seemed.

"Grace?" Henri whispered the word, hoping not to wake her, if she happened to be dozing.

"Yes?" The voice, as strong and loving as ever, answered back.

"I just wanted to hear your voice. Is Sister Abigail asleep?"

"I believe so," came the response. "Are you frightened?"

Henrietta hated to answer, for fear one of the children might hear her. Though she felt some anxiety, an amazing peace transcended it. In the very middle of the storm, she had located an island of safety.

"Whatever happens," she whispered quietly. "Whatever happens, I know God will use it to his glory."

"Amen." A faint response, but it seemed to shake the room with its strength.

SATURDAY, SEPTEMBER 8, 1900, 4:00 P.M.
JOHN SEALY HOSPITAL

Violent winds shook John Sealy Hospital, threatening to knock it off of its foundation.

"This is never going to end," Emma mumbled the words as she moved along, doing what she could to tend to the injured as they came in. So many came in; the task soon became overwhelming, almost hopeless. The loss of electric power created a near panic, yet somehow she kept going amid it all.

She could hear the snapping of tiles as they freed themselves from the roof of the building. Bits of plaster fell from the ceilings, covering patients in debris. In the children's ward, Jimmy Peterson's condition had worsened. His fever had spiked, and delirium had set in. Chloe's labor progressed in the room across the hall. A child would be born before the night fell.

"Are you all right?" Rupert's hand gripped her arm, giving it a squeeze.

She nodded, trying to force back tears. No time for fear or sentiment here; too much work to be done.

"I ... I'm fine." The words were forced as she pushed fears about her family's well-being out of her mind.

The door of the hospital flew open time and time again, floods of people rushing in. They were of every color, every nationality. Many were bloody and frail. Others seemed to be in a state of shock. Frantically, they cried out for any kind of help.

Emma shook her head helplessly. What could she do when so many were in need?

I'm just one person!

SATURDAY, SEPTEMBER 8, 1900, 4:00 P.M.
THE MURPHY VILLA

"Miss Gillian, I'm scared. This whole house gonna go under and get washed out to sea."

"Pearl, stop talking like that."

"But ma'am—"

"We built this home on Broadway because it's the highest, safest place on the island," Gillian said with an undeniable air. "So stop fretting, Pearl. You'll just wear yourself out, and I need you now, perhaps more than I've ever needed you."

"But this here kitchen is already ankle deep, and it's just a matter of time before the water rises to the main floor."

Gillian refused to respond. As long as the water remained in the servant's quarters, everything should be just fine. She headed up the stairs, water lapping at her heels. For hours, she and Pearl had worked at stacking kitchen furniture up as high as possible. They had managed to elevate most everything of value. The food for the party, along with everything necessary to serve it, had been transported upstairs before the water had entered the house. Right now, Gillian couldn't seem to think straight. What remained undone?

"Miss Gillian," Pearl called out from below. "What should I do with the tea service?"

"Put it on the top shelf in the butler's pantry," Gillian said anxiously. "Hurry up, now."

The older woman quickly placed the necessary items on a broad silver tray and ascended the stairs to the parlor, where the mistress of the house stood, impatiently waiting. Pearl's damp, heavy skirts caused her to trip at the top step, and a silver teapot flew across the polished oak floor.

"Do be careful," Gillian scolded, reaching down to pick it up. "You know that tea service belonged to Douglas's mother. He would just die if anything happened to it."

"Yes'm," Pearl mumbled quietly. She went about her business, carefully placing the plates on the appropriate shelf.

"Now, don't bother yourself with anything else down

in the kitchen," Gillian said. "I'm going to need your help up here for the next little while."

"Yes'm," Pearl said, making her way toward the butler's pantry. "Land sakes alive, I sure am gonna hate to clean up that kitchen after this water goes down, I am."

"Let's not worry about that now," Gillian said. "Right now we have to make sure we can save everything of value."

No sooner were the words spoken than she realized how futile they were. The two things most valuable in the world weren't even there to be saved.

Douglas. Brent. Where are you? I need you more than ever.

Eleven

Brent turned and headed back toward town. The level of water, now well above his waist, made it impossible to go on. He joined the hundreds of others who fought their way toward the center of the island, shivering against the cold as the sting of water slapped him across the back in riveting pellets. The wind, stronger than any he had ever imagined, would drive him under if he didn't make it to higher ground soon.

"No story in the world is worth this."

Sheets of rain whipped across his face, blinding him. His glasses ripped off abruptly, leaving him without any sense of direction. He groped for them in the water, but couldn't locate them.

No, not that.

Suddenly it didn't matter anymore. A current of water tore at him, pulling him under. He fought to regain control, spewing the dirty saltwater from his mouth. Just as his feet hit the ground, pieces of broken timbers began to move toward him, striking him on every side. Brent groaned in pain as each new object struck. "Stop!" His cries were lifeless against the crescendo of water. Despite his pleas, debris raced swiftly along—a sure sign that homes and businesses were going down. Telephone poles, broken glass, wagon wheels, bits of furniture—all traveled inland at high speed, the water guiding their every move.

"Help me!" A man to his right clutched at a moving plank of wood. He disappeared as the current pulled them in opposite directions.

The lack of glasses threw everything into a blurry whirl, and Brent could not seem to respond with clear thinking. "I ... I'm trying," he called to the man in distress.

He suddenly felt the power of a large piece of timber hitting his flesh. It struck him in the right side. For a moment everything went black. Forcing himself to stay focused, he latched onto the piece of wood for safety. Large, dark: a telephone pole.

"Dear God, please ..."

If he could just get back to the center of the island, if he could only make it home, he would go inside and face his father.

SATURDAY, SEPTEMBER 8, 1900, 5:14 P.M.
THE MURPHY VILLA

"Miss Gillian!" Pearl's voice shattered the darkness just as the round stained-glass window above the front door split into a thousand pieces. "Come quick."

"I'm right here, Pearl," Gillian said, looking down from the safety of the balcony above. "But it's too dangerous. We need to get to the center of the house. Where is the safest place, do you think? The bathroom? The bedroom?"

"I'm not sure, Miss," Pearl said nervously. "There's a

big window in your bedroom, and one to match in Brent's room. What about a closet?"

"A closet?" Gillian said breathlessly. "Pearl, you're a genius. Douglas's closet is large, and it's far from any windows. I daresay it's the safest place in the house."

Once they were settled in the closet, Pearl asked, "Are you alright, Miss Gillian?"

All right? How in the world could she answer Pearl's ridiculous question? Of course she wasn't all right. There would be no party now. Her home might not survive the impending waters, her husband remained lost somewhere out in the storm, her son ...

At the very thought of Brent, tears began to slip down Gillian's cheeks. If her life ended this night, she would never get to see her son again, never get to tell him how much she loved him, how much he meant to her. She had to let him know. He would always be more important than her fancy home, her dinner parties, her favored guests. He had been given to her by God and would always remain her most beloved possession, her most precious jewel.

"Miss Gillian?" Pearl spoke again anxiously.

"I'm fine. Just fine." She clung tightly to the door-knob of the upstairs closet, where she and Pearl had taken refuge just moments before. Water had entered the prized mansion in shallow inches. Gillian saw no point in taking any chances. All around her, roofs and telephone poles tumbled to the ground. Pieces of masonry from nearby homes and businesses raced through the torrents of water that now ran down Broadway. One last glance out the window had been all she could bear.

Safely tucked away in the closet, it all seemed a distant

dream. But no dream should end this way. Gillian, for whatever reason, remained here, without her son or husband. Would she really have to face death alone?

SATURDAY, SEPTEMBER 8, 1900, 6:09 P.M.
THE COURIER

The downstairs office of the *Courier* stood waist deep in water. Everett pulled his way through it, frantic to see if the printing presses were safe. Gratefully, they were elevated enough, at least for now. "Stay on top of this!" he hollered above the roar of water to a group of young men working at protecting the valuable equipment.

Making his way to the window, he had a good, long look outside. The noise of the wind and the sight of debris being pulled rapidly along The Strand startled him. *God, help anyone who is out in this.*

At last report, the wind blew at eighty-four miles per hour, with gusts topping one hundred. Never in his lifetime had Everett experienced such force, and yet he didn't feel it either. He remained here, safe, inside—but for how long?

Making his way back to the stairs, he turned to survey the room. If this went under, it could very well be the end of the paper. Just the thought of it sent a sudden, sharp pain through his chest. He trudged up the narrow stairs, anxious to get back into his office where everything was still high and dry.

Dropping into his familiar chair, Everett lit a cigar. It dangled from his lips as he sat, deep in thought. Reporters roamed the streets. He had sent them there. Everett couldn't help but think of Nathan, back out for more photographs. He had practically pushed him out the door with instructions to take "the best possible photographs." If anything happened to him, he could never forgive himself. But that's what this business was all about, right?

Not much of a praying man, Everett now found himself muttering a choppy plea for the safety of his wife and children. As far inland as they were, they probably hadn't taken much water yet, but the wind might be sufficient to blow their wood-framed house to bits. The phone lines had been down for hours now. Guessing had become the fashion of the day.

And as for Brent Murphy, the prodigal news reporter, he had headed out to brave the storm for a story. Not much had changed there. That kid had always had a nose for the news.

SATURDAY, SEPTEMBER 8, 1900, 6:11 P.M.
ST. MARY'S ORPHAN ASYLUM

"Sisters!" Abigail's shrill voice roused Henrietta from her dozing. The shattering of glass followed. The dormitory window gave way under the pressure of rising water, both inside and outside the room. Henri watched in horror as the current began to pull at them, dragging the beds toward the open window. Now waist deep in the cold, murky water, she prayed as she had never prayed before. Salty waves washed over her, chilling her to the core of her being. The scene was so dark and foreboding that she could barely make out the outline of the others in the room, but she could hear their voices. The children's screams were deafening.

"Henri, are you here?" Grace's voice seemed amazingly steady and strong.

"I'm here," she cried out.

"Hold the children as tightly as you can."

"Be my ever-present help in time of trouble ..." the words crept from Henri's lips repeatedly as she clutched the children. Her hands shook uncontrollably, making her task almost impossible. The cold water left her so numb she could scarcely think.

"Lord, help us!" Sister Abigail's voice rang out from the darkness then disappeared altogether.

The cries of the children rose to a fevered pitch. Many were screaming, pleading. All but Lilly Mae. In a language still unfamiliar to Henrietta, the youngster sang the familiar aria, in Italian.

The beams above cracked with a deafening roar, and the walls began to move in slow motion toward the center of the room, allowing tiny bits of light from the heavens above. The water suddenly enveloped them all, its sheer force almost sending Henri out of her own skin. She felt herself pulled off the bunk and well underneath it.

Mouthfuls of saltwater choked her. She fought to keep her head above water, clutching at anything and everything. The current pulled her under again to face the darkness. The salty water stung her eyes, blinding her. She squeezed them shut. Another thrust sent her topside, gasping for air, screaming at anyone who might be listening. "Help us! God, help us!"

The weight of the children roped to her pulled her in every conceivable direction. The speed of the thunderous current picked up, pulling her under once again. She gave herself over to it. She felt herself being pulled out, out, out ...

Out of the window and into the night.

Twelve

*B*rent fought the rushing current with slow, unsteady strides. His legs grew numb, his breathing labored and painful. The force of the water seemed nearly unbelievable at times. For every step he took toward town, he found himself pulled back that much further. He clung to anything that might keep him steady.

"Help me, please!"

Brent turned to find a young woman clutching a telephone pole for dear life. She couldn't be very old, maybe thirteen or fourteen, and appeared to be in bad shape. Her hair, wet and matted, appeared to be covered in blood.

"What's your name?" he hollered against the sound of the wind as he reached to free her from the pole.

Shaking uncontrollably, she couldn't seem to answer. She seemed disoriented, dazed. When she did finally speak, the word was difficult to understand. "S-S-S-ad-ie."

"Sadie?" He held her tightly, fighting the push of the

water. She nodded, eyes beginning to roll back. "Hang on, honey."

The young woman slipped into unconsciousness even as he spoke. Fighting the wind and water, Brent struggled up to the highest point he could reach. He had to get her to the hospital, but how? Several long blocks lay between him and John Sealy Hospital. Would the trip be futile?

Did Galveston Island even have a hospital anymore?

SATURDAY, SEPTEMBER 8, 1900, 6:15 P.M.
JOHN SEALY HOSPITAL

"Chloe, how are you doing?" Emma asked kindly. Despite all odds, she must remain focused. This young woman needed her. Right now, nothing seemed more important.

"I ... I ..." Chloe didn't answer right away, another contraction speaking for her.

"I'm sorry it has to be like this," Emma whispered in her ear. "But everything's going to be all right. I'm not going to leave you."

The wind outside shook the building. Pieces of timber hit the sides of the hospital with great force, and the glass at the windows rattled. They were bound to give way any minute. Emma fought to ignore it all, to remain clear-headed.

Chloe's face reflected her fear. "We're not going to make it," the young woman said with a gasp.

"Of course we are." Emma tried her best to be reassuring. At that very moment, one of the glass windows shattered, spraying tiny fragments all over the room. The wounded began to cry out in pain. The frantic young nurse raced from patient to patient, doing what she could to care for them. Fortunately, no one was badly hurt, but the wind, once held safely outside by the glass, now pulled at the room with an unbelievable force. Sheets of rain poured in from the gaping hole. Cold as ice, it stung with a hard bite.

"Help me move the beds to the center," Rupert called out, appearing from out of nowhere.

Emma turned, relieved to see him. Tears began to pour down her cheeks, unashamed. "I'm so glad you're here."

"Sorry it took me so long," he muttered, pulling frantically on Chloe's bed. "I couldn't leave the patients downstairs. I've got a dozen or more that aren't going to make it. And now, on top of everything, the wind has damaged a couple of the exterior walls on the west end, and we've started taking in water."

"How deep?"

"About a foot right now," he said, trying not to let Chloe hear. "On the southwest corner. But it doesn't look like it's stopping anytime soon."

Emma closed her eyes for just a moment, fighting the nausea that suddenly hit her. "If the water is this deep here," she whispered to herself. "How high is it at home?"

SATURDAY, SEPTEMBER 8, 1900, 6:29 P.M.
ST. MARY'S ORPHAN ASYLUM

Drifting in and out of consciousness, Henrietta had no choice but to release herself to the pull of the water. The current swept her well past the wreckage of the boys' dormitory and beyond.

Up. Down. Under. Over. The waves pulled her to and fro at will. Gasping for air, Henrietta choked on mouthfuls of grimy water. Salt and sand lodged in her throat, nearly strangling her. She coughed up as much as she could, shaking violently against the cold water. Would this nightmare ever end?

Alive. Dead. Alive.

Alive. And in tremendous pain. Henrietta's legs felt as if they had been ripped from underneath her. Her head hit against something hard, jarring her. She struggled to clear her thoughts.

Occasional flashes of lightning overhead lit the skies, giving her moments of clear vision. No sign of Abigail or Grace. Several of the children who had been roped to her had apparently slipped away, victims of the gulf. She could feel it, sense their release. There was still the weight of someone, something, but she couldn't quite place who it was. Did it even matter anymore?

Up. Down. Over. Under.

Her habit became entangled on a piece of debris and pulled off easily. Undergarments were all that were left to guard her dignity, had she been worried about her dignity. Her teeth chattered violently, the cold water having its way.

All around her, people were screaming, fighting for breath. Babies in their mothers' arms, fathers crying out for lost children, and wives reaching out for husbands who no longer existed, they all floated by in a dizzying array. Buildings smashed into nothing but sticks of wood, furniture, animals, they all drifted by as if they belonged there.

Henri reached out to grab what looked like a tree branch, only to discover the arm of a man who had become tangled in the debris. It hung limply as she tried to free him.

God, help!

The current caught her up once again, and she felt her fingers slip through the man's. He drifted below the water, crying out in pain as he disappeared in the murky depths. Henrietta found herself once again pulled under, then up ... under, then up. Gasping for air, she prayed this nightmare would end, regardless of the outcome.

If it's my time to go, Lord, I will gladly trade this moment for the bliss of eternity.

Her ears rang with the madness of it all, the screams, the howl of the wind, the rush of the water.

Then, from out of the night, she heard it ... the sound of a child crying.

SATURDAY, SEPTEMBER 8, 1900, 6:48 P.M.
THE COURIER

Everett paced frantically through the upstairs halls of the *Courier* building, shouting orders as he went. "Get those papers up as high as you can. Lift those chairs up on the desks. Stay away from the windows, do you hear me?"

Try as he may, he couldn't seem to keep his thoughts straight. Perhaps the sound of the wind whipping at the building kept him distracted. The fevered frenzy had already taken out two windows; others were sure to follow. Water had risen to an alarming level in the pressroom. Everett calculated it to be at least chest deep now.

Nothing could be done about that, but he could certainly do something about the rooms up here. All of the *Courier*'s back copies were up here, carefully categorized. He would do anything and everything in his power to keep them from being destroyed, no matter what it took.

Thirteen

Brent struggled to the front of the *Courier*, clutching the young woman tightly. Though clearly unconscious, she still appeared to be breathing. Water stood chest deep at the office door, far too deep to force it open. The winds had blown the front glass window out, leaving sharp fragments everywhere. He pulled himself through to the inside.

Brent accidentally bumped her head against the windowpane as they crossed through it. She cried out, unconscious no more. "Help me."

"I'm trying." He shook violently as he spoke, fighting both the chill and his nerves. She hung limp in his arms once again.

"Is anyone here?" Brent called out. The office sat in pitch darkness. Even so, he could see it: debris everywhere, desks overturned, newspapers in wet masses. A glimmer of light peeked from the back room where the presses sat, but his destination lay elsewhere. Brent needed to get upstairs to the safety of Everett's second-story office.

He climbed the stairs carefully, the darkness sending a shiver of fear through him. He blinked his eyes frantically, the sting of saltwater compounding his vision problem. Slowly climbing the stairs, he counted: one, two, three ... Fourteen in all. Now safely on the second floor, he squinted to make out anything familiar.

Working his way to the back, he saw it. At least he thought he did. Inside Everett's office, the older man sat perched atop his desk, pecking away at the type-writer, a lit cigar dangling from his lips.

Any other time, it might have seemed humorous.

SATURDAY, SEPTEMBER 8, 1900, 7:31 P.M.
JOHN SEALY HOSPITAL

"Nurse Phillips." Emma felt the catch in her throat as she cried out. Fear held her in its tight grip. "Nurse Phillips, we've got water inside."

"Get these people upstairs," came the older nurse's stern reply.

Emma turned to face the crowd of people, trying to imagine how she could possibly begin such a large task. All afternoon they had fought the wind and the onslaught of people flooding through the doors of John Sealy Hospital, but now, with water at their doors, she seemed to be losing her ability to think clearly. Emma's body ached with exhaustion. A long shift yesterday, very little sleep in the night, and now all of this ...

I can't take much more.

The anxiety over her parents and her younger sister had almost driven her to her knees in terror more than once today, but in light of everything that was happening right in front of her, she couldn't leave.

Jimmy Peterson's fever had broken less than an hour earlier. Chloe had progressed in her labor and should deliver before midnight. Rupert continued to make the rounds, caring for those who came in injured from the storm. And she ...

"I said, let's get these people upstairs." Nurse Phillips's stern voice jarred her back to reality.

"Yes ma'am," she muttered.

She began to usher people up the stairs to the ward above. It would have to be converted, and quickly. How could they possibly accommodate so many? And who knew how many more were to come?

SATURDAY, SEPTEMBER 8, 1900, 7:58 P.M.
GALVESTON ISLAND

For what seemed like hours, Henrietta drifted along at the water's discretion. Though it swept the others away, far beyond her grasp, still she held tightly to one. Lilly Mae. Fate bound them with its fragile cord. They remained fastened as one, and yet completely distant from each other. The youngster's tiny voice occasionally rose above the din in a chattering, but angelic song. The Italian aria became a source of strength for Henrietta, a reason to stay alive.

As a shock wave of lightning tore through the skies, she forced herself to focus. All around her, bodies drifted hopelessly, helplessly toward certain death. They would all be dragged into the sea with a back sweep. If only ...

If only she could find something, anything, to grab hold of. *Lord, help me!* Miraculously, Henrietta found herself lodged on a rooftop, wedged near a brick chimney. Somehow this home had gone untouched. But how?

Every bone, every muscle, in Henrietta's body felt bruised or broken. Little strength remained. Frantically, she pulled at the rope to see if Lilly Mae could be aroused. Groping through the darkness, she found the child still and cold, her hands as limp as wet rags, her breaths stark and shallow.

After hours of silence, Henrietta now found herself free to weep.

SATURDAY, SEPTEMBER 8, 1900, 8:00 P.M.
THE MURPHY VILLA

"Where do you suppose he is, Pearl?" Gillian asked the question carefully, thoughtfully. She could feel her own heartbeat against the flow of the words. "Where is my son?"

"Why, Miss Gillian." Pearl said. "I haven't heard you talk about Brent in years."

"He's been on my mind so much tonight," she said, feeling the tears begin to well up. "I can't stop thinking about him. If only ..." Her voice faltered.

"There are no 'if onlys' when you love someone, Miss Gillian," Pearl said softly.

"But Mr. Murphy—"

"Pooh on Mr. Murphy," Pearl said stubbornly. "You just never mind what he's got to say about all of this. That boy is your son, and you're hurting for him. It's no sin to admit that."

Gillian pulled her knees up to her chin and broke into huge, unstoppable sobs. She felt Pearl's strong arms reach across her shoulders and clutch her tightly.

"There, there now, Miss Gillian," she whispered. "You just let it all out now."

SATURDAY, SEPTEMBER 8, 1900, 8:03 P.M.
THE COURIER

"I'm going to try to make it now," Brent said.

"Are you sure?" Everett's words were not terribly reassuring.

"If I don't get her there soon, there's no point in going at all."

The young woman had lost a lot of blood. Even in the dark, he could tell the situation grew darker with each passing moment. He must get her to the hospital, but did he dare leave with events outside escalating?

"It's not safe," observed Everett.

"It's as safe as it's ever going to be," Brent said, now determined. "And I don't have any choice."

He picked up the young girl, cradling her like a small child, and headed for the door.

SATURDAY, SEPTEMBER 8, 1900, 8:10 P.M.
GALVESTON ISLAND

Henrietta clutched a sleeping Lilly Mae in her arms, still shaking violently from the cold. The youngster stirred slightly, the first glimmer of hope for a terrified Henrietta.

"Sister Henri?" The youngster spoke suddenly, with a clarity that shocked Henrietta.

"Yes, darling?"

"We're not alone, Sister."

"Yes, Lilly Mae. I know."

"We're not alone," the youngster repeated, her voice beginning to drift off again. "The angels are singing over us. They're coming close now."

Yes. There was a sound from the heavens above—a rush of wind, as if angels' wings held them in place. Henrietta heard it now.

But, no. It was just the roar of the water below.

SATURDAY, SEPTEMBER 8, 1900, 9:17 P.M.
THE COURIER

Everett sat at his typewriter, typing frantically. The wind shook the window with fervor, startling him, but not swaying him. He had a job to do. This story would be written; it had to be.

His fingers moved swiftly across the keys with only the glimmer of a candle to guide the way. It didn't matter. He could have typed in total darkness. His fingers knew the keys. They were his best friends, his closest allies.

"The Storm of the Century," he typed.

The truth of that statement hit him like a ton of bricks. The tiny office window suddenly shattered into bits, ribbons of glass flying across the room. Everett felt the pain as a large piece sheared into his left thigh.

Everything after that became very dim.

SATURDAY, SEPTEMBER 8, 1900, 9:47 P.M.
THE MURPHY VILLA

"Do you ever pray, Miss Gillian?" Pearl's voice spoke from out of the darkness of the closet.

"Of course I do, Pearl." What an absurd question, and what inappropriate timing. *I pray, Lord. I'm a God-fearing woman, and I attend church nearly every Sunday.*

"I pray all the time," Pearl continued, her voice steady against the wind that continued to pound the house from outside. "I do believe in the power of prayer."

"What are you getting at?" Gillian asked as she shivered against the cold.

"I was just wondering ..."

"Yes?"

"Well, Miss Gillian, I was just thinking that this might be a mighty good time."

Fourteen

*B*rent pressed against the torrent of rushing water, moving forward step by awful step. The hospital should be just another block north. For more than two hours he had fought the good fight against the wind, the rain, and the weight of the child in his arms. The trip up The Strand had been bad enough, but beyond there ... beyond there, the city lay in ruins.

Escaping the flying debris had proven to be half the battle. Brent's thighs took a continual beating as bits of lumber, glass, and other items forced themselves through the current and pressed into his flesh. Snakes appeared, as if by magic, floating on the water's surface, in search of potential victims. Brent's eyes darted to and fro continually, taking it all in. He inched his way along in the darkness, fighting to maintain some sense of sanity, of clarity.

The girl in his arms would stir upon occasion, seemingly aware of her surroundings, her situation. He would console her as best he could. Sadie. Thirteen. She had family, somewhere. Or at least she once had.

In the distance, the hospital loomed. Glimmers of lamp-light, or possibly candlelight, drew his attention from inside, along with the shadow of people moving about on the second floor. The building itself remained intact, with only roof tiles missing in places.

The last few feet toward the door of the hospital were the hardest Brent had taken all night. It had nothing to do with the depth of the water, which seemed considerably lower here. For the first time all night, the exhaustion and the sheer magnitude of what had happened finally caught up with him.

This was no story. This was the real thing.

SATURDAY, SEPTEMBER 8, 1900, 11:06 P.M.
JOHN SEALY HOSPITAL

Against the flicker of candlelight, against the backdrop of the storm of a lifetime, a child made its entrance into the world. Emma stood nearby, watching over the mother as a final push ushered the youngster out of the safety of the womb and into the madness of the storm.

Mother and newborn daughter had no privacy, no quiet moment to themselves. The ward had filled quickly with refugees, some sick or injured, others looking for shelter. But Chloe didn't seem to mind. With her baby, Dominique, now safely pressed to her breast, there was no storm. Nothing but peace lay wrapped in her arms.

Emma left them alone to share the moment. There were other, more overwhelming tasks. All around her, people shouted in fear and grief. "My wife needs help over here," an older man, obviously agitated, cried out. She made her way to the corner where his wife lay, huddled, hands clutched to her chest.

"Are you in pain?" Emma asked, kneeling beside them. The woman nodded, face frantic.

"Rupert." He came at Emma's beckoning and checked the woman's blood pressure.

"She's in shock," he whispered. "We've got to find a place for her to lie down." He looked about, frantic. No place. The corner would have to do. "This is absolutely ridiculous," Rupert said angrily. "We've got more coming in, and there's no sign of any of the night shift doctors."

"How many have we lost?" Emma whispered the words.

"Too many to count," he said, shaking his head. "And I'm afraid we're about to lose another. They just brought in a girl with a head wound. She's critical."

"Can anything be done?" Emma asked, peering anxiously at his face.

"She's lost a lot of blood. If we could get some blood into her, maybe ..."

"That's an idea!" Emma practically shouted. "We could round up the ones who aren't sick or injured and draw blood." She jumped up excitedly.

"Emma, that's not going to be possible. You can't be serious." He continued working on the older woman as he spoke.

"I am serious, Rupert. We can do this. I'll get some of the ones who aren't injured to help. When this is all over, we're going to need blood, lots of it."

"I'm busy here, Emma."

"I know that," she said, almost defiantly. "I'll take charge. I can do this."

"If you think so, be my guest."

"Where's the girl?" Emma said. "I want to do what we can to save her."

"Don't get your hopes up," Rupert said, shaking his head sadly. "She's a lost cause."

"Where is she?" She looked about, overwhelmed with the ocean of bodies in the room.

He nodded toward the hallway. "Out there, on a stretcher. There wasn't any room in the ward," he argued.

She sprinted toward the stretcher, her mission clear. She would take care of this girl first, and then she would form a brigade of sorts to collect blood for others who might yet need it.

"Hello." She nodded politely to the young man who stood at the foot of the stretcher. The young man, soaked to the bone, looked to be in his mid-twenties. He clung tightly to the hand of the young woman on the stretcher.

"Is this your sister?" Emma asked, handing him a blanket. She would do what she could to lift his spirits.

He shook his head, pulling the blanket around himself. "I don't know who she is, to be honest. I found her down on The Strand. She's in pretty bad shape. I got her here as quickly as I could."

"Well, let's see what we can do to help," Emma said. Glancing down at the young woman on the stretcher, she suddenly felt her knees give way.

No. It wasn't his sister. It was *her* sister.

SATURDAY, SEPTEMBER 8, 1900, 11:45 P.M.
THE COURIER

Everett wrapped a cloth around his thigh, pressing his hand against the largest wound. For two and a half hours he had been like this, alone and bleeding. He had managed to keep the blood loss to a minimum, but any hopes he had had of typing up the story were shot to pieces with the blast of that window. Now it was all he could do to hang on until help arrived.

SUNDAY, SEPTEMBER 9, 1900, 12:01 A.M.
THE MURPHY VILLA

"Where do you suppose Mr. Murphy is, Miss Gillian?" Pearl's voice pulled Gillian from a tremulous sleep.

"His train was due in so long ago," she responded. "I don't know if they ever made it to the island." Her heart lifted, just thinking about Douglas.

Please, Lord, let him be alive.

"Maybe they didn't leave Houston at all," Pearl said in a reassuring voice. "Maybe they had good enough sense to just stay put till the storm blew over."

Gillian suddenly felt a sense of relief, some assurance that her prayer would be answered. "Oh, I hope you're right, Pearl. I do hope you're right."

SUNDAY, SEPTEMBER 9, 1900, 12:05 A.M.
GALVESTON ISLAND

Henrietta stared in desperation at the dark skies. For hours they had been perched here, atop this miraculous house. She and Lilly Mae. They were as one.

"Now I lay me down to sleep ..." Henrietta whispered the words softly. "If I should die ..." The revelation of those words now left her speechless.

Occasionally, she did drift off to sleep, but oh, what miserable sleep. She would awaken, shaking with fright and cold.

Through the haze, a dizzying array of things floated by. She saw them only as flashes of lightning danced across the sky and gave her moments of clear vision: people on makeshift rafts, bits of masonry from houses, clothing, pots and pans. A horse, eyes wide in terror, jutted by. Their eyes met briefly before he was swept downstream. A frantic older man, arms wrapped around a piece of timber tried valiantly to reach for the roof. His cries for help nearly ripped her heart out, but she could not let go of the youngster long enough to offer any assistance. He miraculously caught hold of the roof's edge, but lost his grip almost immediately. Henri cried out as the current pulled him under and out of sight.

She shuddered, trying to still her mind, but it would not be stilled. Like the water, it raced forward. The orphanage, the sisters, the children, her family—they were all pieces in this soggy, horrifying puzzle.

She stared silently out into the night and tried to make sense of something, anything. Clearly, the water had begun to recede now. The rain slacked off. In her rather catatonic state of mind, it all seemed to make sense. It was all a part of the show.

"Now I lay me down to sleep ..."

The words continually tripped across her tongue. She shivered against the night.

"If I should die before I wake ..."

Henrietta gave herself over to the exhaustion.

Fifteen

Sir, are you all right?"

Brent looked up, through clouded vision, to face the young nurse. *Pretty. Really pretty.* Even with the salt in his eyes, he could tell that. Her soft brown hair shimmered against the lamplight, but he couldn't seem to make out the color of her eyes. Ah yes. Blue. As blue as the Galveston sky on any normal day. He nodded as he spoke, "Yes. I, uh ... I'm fine."

"That's good. Listen, I really need you to stay here awhile." Her voice, laced with concern, pierced through him.

"I shouldn't." He attempted to stand. "I need to get back out there and— "

"And what?" She reached to place her hands on his arm in an attempt to stop him.

"And help."

"Your help is needed here," she said, taking hold of his hand. "That's what I was trying to tell you. Do you know your blood type?"

"O-positive. Why?"

"You've just become our first donor." She spoke matter-of-factly.

"Oh no," he said, pulling his hand from hers. Brent had always hated needles, ever since childhood.

"You're not scared, are you?" she said, nearly mocking. "Not after all you've been through tonight."

"Scared isn't the right word," he said. "It's just that I—"

"I, nothing," she said, rolling up his shirtsleeve. "This is my sister lying here, and she needs your help."

"Sadie? She's your sister?"

"Yes." She prepared the needle, flicking it with the tip of her finger.

"I'll do whatever you say," he said, helping her pull the sleeve up as quickly as he could. "Just say the word."

SUNDAY, SEPTEMBER 9, 1900, 12:15 A.M.
JOHN SEALY HOSPITAL

Emma worked quickly to get the necessary blood flow started. Whoever this young man was, he had probably saved her sister's life. A hero. "Rupert," she cried out nervously.

The frustrated doctor rounded the corner, his face nearly expressionless. "Yeah?"

"Can you help me?"

"I told you, Emma. I've got work to do." He turned abruptly.

"Rupert." She turned on her heels, anger building. "This is my sister!" Anger swelled with each word. He was going to help her, come hell or high water.

"Your sister? Sadie?" His disposition softened immediately. "The one you're always talking about?"

"Yes," Emma said defiantly. "And you're going to help

me save her life. I don't care what else you thought you were going to do."

"Yes ma'am," He saluted her, coming to immediate attention. "Let's get busy."

SUNDAY, SEPTEMBER 9, 1900, 12:42 A.M.
GALVESTON ISLAND

Henrietta slept as she could, waking every few moments to fend off insects and free-flying debris. She shivered until her body felt it might give way under the pressure of the movement. Many times she thought they would slip from their precarious perch, but she and Lilly Mae held on for dear life.

Snakes slithered alongside her, terrifying her and preventing her from sleeping for long. When she did doze, her dreams swept her away.

Up. Down. Over. Under. No, not that! Not again!

SUNDAY, SEPTEMBER 9, 1900, 1:04 A.M.
THE COURIER

Everett awoke to a piercing pain in his belly. He jumped up instinctively, realizing his cigar must have dropped out of his mouth onto his shirt. Burning embers made their way into his cold flesh. He slapped them away with a vengeance until the red glow disappeared into the night.

Could have burned the whole place to the ground.

The pain in his leg caused him to double over, reminding him of the earlier injury. He tugged at the cloth wrap, trying to put pressure on the jagged cut to keep it from bleeding further.

If they don't get here quickly, I may very well bleed to death.

Who "they" were didn't seem terribly important right then.

SUNDAY, SEPTEMBER 9, 1900, 1:27 A.M.
THE MURPHY VILLA

Gillian awoke to near silence. "Pearl," she whispered. "Pearl, are you awake?"

"Yes'm," a groggy Pearl answered.

"It sounds like the worst has passed."

"Heaven be blessed!"

"Yes, well ... we should probably go out now," Gillian said. She didn't want to. Truth be told, Gillian was scared to leave the safety of the little closet. She worried about what had become of her lovely home. "Do you have the lantern?"

"Yes'm," Pearl answered, reaching for a match to light it. Strange, how her dark face appeared almost angelic against the soft glow of the lantern.

"Let there be light," Pearl said with a grin. Somehow it comforted Gillian that Pearl always managed to keep her sense of humor. The two inched their way out of the closet, carefully examining the room. The window glass lay shattered on the floor, and lamps were overturned. Otherwise, things looked remarkably good.

They made their way from room to room, surveying the damage. A couple of windows had been broken, and a tree branch had forced its way through the ceiling in the guest bedroom, but little more. Gillian breathed a huge sigh of relief.

"Let's go downstairs."

About halfway down, Gillian faced the inevitable. The first floor of her beautiful home stood in at least three feet of water. Her prized stained-glass window, a jewel in her social crown, had disappeared from the spot above the front door. A gaping hole with bits of tree limb hanging precariously from it now replaced it. Dark, hollow spaces remained where larger pane-glass windows once stood.

"Lord, help us," Pearl whispered. "Do you see that, Miss Gillian?"

"I see it," she whispered back. There was so much to see, so very much.

"No, Miss Gillian. Over there." Through the glow of the lamplight, Gillian's eyes followed Pearl's pointing finger. There, in the middle of her living room, perched atop her cherry dining table, sat a group of people, staring at them with wide eyes.

"Please, ma'am," one of the men spoke out. "Please don't be angry. We was just lookin' for a place to stay alive, that's all."

"Please, ma'am," a little boy's voice rang out, followed by anxious tears.

Gillian's heart began to race. Who did these people think they were, coming in her house at a time like this? Were they vagrants, with no place else to go? Or worse still, were they vandals, here to rob her of what little she had left?

"Pearl," she whispered gruffly. "Go upstairs to the bureau and get Mr. Murphy's gun."

"But Miss Gillian, they—"

"Pearl, do as I say."

As the older woman moved up the stairway, the light disappeared with her. Gillian stood clutching the stair railing, hoping against hope no one moved toward her. Just as Pearl approached with gun in hand, Gillian heard it: the sound of an infant crying.

SUNDAY, SEPTEMBER 9, 1900, 2:30 A.M.
JOHN SEALY HOSPITAL

Brent yawned and stretched, his body aching all over. He longed for sleep, but didn't dare. He looked into the eyes of the young nurse. She had worked diligently to save her younger sister's life. "You look like you could use some sleep," he said.

"I can't look any worse than you."

"Gee thanks."

Brent gazed at her closely. Even through the exhaustion, one thing was obvious. She was a beauty. That was clear enough, glasses or no glasses.

"So," Brent said carefully, "what's the story with that doctor friend of yours? His bedside manner leaves something to be desired."

"He's young. Besides, he's just an intern," she explained.

"Uh huh."

"And he's been on his feet for almost twenty-four hours straight," she added.

"So," Brent said, working up a little journalistic courage, "there's no story—"

"Story?" the nurse asked. "What story?"

"I mean …" he stammered. "Are you two …"

"What?" she looked stunned, almost insulted. "I should say not."

"Ah ha." That was all the answer he needed.

SUNDAY, SEPTEMBER 9, 1900, 2:35 A.M.
JOHN SEALY HOSPITAL

Emma, completely exhausted, pressed herself into bed next to her younger sister, Sadie. She had gone for far too long without sleep, but guilt hadn't allowed it until now. How could she sleep when so many others were suffering, when others needed her so desperately?

"Sadie, can you hear me?" she whispered.

"Mmmm."

"You're going to be all right, sweet girl," she continued. "I'm going to make sure of it."

She closed her eyes, and visions of her mother and father swam before her. Where were they? Had they survived the storm? Giant sobs began to overtake Emma. She cried in silence, forcing herself not to wake her younger sister or any of the others nearby. The exhaustion forced the tears away after only moments. She clutched the hand of her sister, drifting off to sleep. At least Sadie was safe. That, for now, would have to be enough. The angels had brought Sadie here. On a wing and a prayer, they had brought her.

That is, the angels and a very nice looking young man named Brent Murphy.

Sixteen

*B*rent awoke, stiff and sore, after sleeping only a couple of hours. The hospital sat in an eerie, dark silence. Only the occasional whimpering of a child stirred the night. He rose quietly, dreading the task ahead, yet knowing he must face the inevitable.

He must go home.

Brent made his way out of the hospital door, gazing at the heavens. Dawn promised to break soon; the distant sky shone pink with anticipation. The water had receded, a welcome piece of news. But nothing could have prepared him for the scene that contrasted with the warm glow of the sunrise.

Bodies. Bodies everywhere. A mangled, twisted mess.

"Dear God." Brent clutched his stomach, afraid for a moment he would lose its contents. In a state of shock, he turned toward Broadway and began to run.

SUNDAY, SEPTEMBER 9, 1900, 6:22 A.M.
THE COURIER

Everett Maxwell pulled the newspaper off of his face and yawned. He had slept only a handful of hours, but they were enough—probably too much, all things considered. The sun had risen over Galveston Island with an unparalleled brilliance, casting ribbons of pink and lavender over the twisted rooftops. Nice contrast to the preceding night

"Well, look at that," he said, stretching and moving toward the broken glass for a closer look. Beyond the dawn lay the most amazing blue sky Everett had ever seen. He stared up at it, forgetting the magnitude of the night, resting in the assurance that all was well.

Then he looked down.

Nothing could have prepared him for what lay below. All of his years in the newspaper business hadn't equipped him, though he had certainly seen his share of disasters. His heart ached with a sudden fierceness he had never before experienced. The Strand lay torn to shreds. Most of the water had drained off, leaving a trail of debris: everything from telephone poles to pieces of buildings to bodies.

Bodies everywhere.

SUNDAY, SEPTEMBER 9, 1900, 6:53 A.M.
GALVESTON ISLAND

Henrietta awoke to a groggy sky. For a moment, she forgot where she was ... where they were. Just as suddenly, she remembered. She trembled uncontrollably, trying to gain control of her senses, to think clearly.

She and Lilly Mae remained pinned against a chimney, atop a house. This brick haven had saved them from certain death, at least in the night. But now, with the rush of dawn, it all seemed a distant memory, a faded photograph of someone else's tragedy, not her own.

From her perch, Henrietta could almost make out the coast. She squinted to see more clearly. The morning had summoned a sleepy sea. But what lined the coast set her hair on edge. Along several miles of shore lay mounds of wreckage. Buggies, streetcar rails, bodies, lumber—these all formed a momentous semicircle around the business district. Buildings were down all over the place. Rubble replaced what had been a lovely, well-kept city. Milling through the rubble, there were people.

Henrietta fought to catch her breath as she turned to look in the opposite direction. People everywhere. Many of them stumbled about naked, or nearly so. They crawled in and through the water and debris, searching, calling out the names of loved ones. Even from this height she could hear the faint cries of those who had been buried alive beneath it all.

"Dear God," Henrietta cried, tears flowing in torrents down her cheeks. "Help them." She fought the temptation to leap from her perch to help them herself, but fear wouldn't allow it. She would stay in this spot forever. She wouldn't move. She couldn't.

But she must. Someone depended on her, someone who could not care for herself. Leaning down, Henri groped for the child. "Lilly Mae?"

No answer came.

SUNDAY, SEPTEMBER 9, 1900, 8:04 A.M.
THE MURPHY VILLA

Gillian Murphy threw open the front door of her Broadway home, determined to make the journey to the train station. *Douglas, you have to be there. I can't do this without you.* She quickly surveyed what had once been Broadway, realizing the futility of her mission. She slammed the door shut. "Pearl!"

"What, Miss Gillian?"

"Forget the wagon. We'll have to try it on foot."

"But what about all these people? Who's gonna take care of them? They need food and—"

"Pearl!" Gillian knew her voice sounded stern, but didn't care. "I don't care whether or not these people have a hot breakfast. I do care whether or not my husband is alive and well."

"But—"

"No buts. I don't care how improbable or how impractical it sounds. You and I are going to that train station, and these people can just make do without us. Now come with me before I lose my temper."

Pearl's face dropped, but she didn't speak a word in reproach. Instead, she reached for a shawl to wrap around her shoulders. Gillian softened, watching her, suddenly coming to the realization that everything she had once thought about herself had now been washed away in the salty waters of the Gulf of Mexico.

SUNDAY, SEPTEMBER 9, 1900, 9:34 A.M.
GALVESTON ISLAND

Brent stopped to catch his breath as he hit the familiar stretch along north Broadway. And yet, nothing about this street looked familiar today. While most of the houses remained intact, masonry, telephone poles, and wheels from coaches filled the streets. *Few bodies here. That's good news.*

He rounded the corner and began to run once again. There, in the distance, loomed the Victorian mansion he had avoided only hours before. Inside, he prayed he would find his mother and father—the parents he had left behind as he had set out to find himself as a stubborn, rebellious young man.

Now, standing so near the home he had left, Brent found himself at last.

SUNDAY, SEPTEMBER 9, 1900, 10:15 A.M.
JOHN SEALY HOSPITAL

"Have you heard anything yet?" Emma asked Rupert, clutching his arm.

"No, honey. I'll let you know the minute I do."

"Don't call me honey." His choice of words nauseated her, especially at a time like this.

Rupert shuffled off, obviously ignoring her comment. She shouldn't have asked him. But he had ventured out into the madness an hour or so earlier, hoping to get news of his own family. His visit to the outside world had been short-lived. He had returned with stories she, as of yet, refused to believe.

Surely his tales of destruction were exaggerated. Nothing could be as bad as all that. She made her way to a window, peering outside. A tree had fallen, blocking her view. She shifted to the right a little, straining to see what lay beyond the fallen branches. Just as quickly as she saw, she wished she hadn't, wished she could take it all back again.

Suddenly, the room began to spin. Everything faded to black as Emma's knees buckled.

"Miss, are you all right?" A child's voice rang out, reverberating around the hollow shell of a room.

"I, uh ..." She clutched at the wall, trying to hold herself upright. "I'm fine."

She took several deep breaths, until the dizziness stopped. *I won't go down. I won't.* Madness surrounded her on every side, and yet Emma fought to be strong. Someone had to be there to help the hurting, crying, grieving. She would be that someone.

SUNDAY, SEPTEMBER 9, 1900, 10:21 A.M.
THE GALVESTON COURIER

Everett Maxwell worked alongside the others at the *Courier* to clean out what had once been a perfectly respectable newspaper office. The early morning heat set in, making the task even more unbearable. But he couldn't seem to keep his mind on the work. His thoughts shifted continually to his family. If only he could have gone to check on them himself. But the pain in his leg wouldn't allow it. He could barely make it across the room, let alone across town.

Nathan Potter stormed into the room, soaked from head to toe. "It's hotter than blue blazes out there," he exclaimed. "As if we didn't have enough to worry about."

Everett turned to face him. "Well," he asked impatiently, "What's the word? Were you able to get to my family?"

"Found 'em, high and dry," Nathan said. "There's been some physical damage to the house: a few windows out and a hole in the roof over your kitchen."

"But Maggie and the kids? They're ... ?"

"They're fine," Nathan assured him. "A few minor bumps and bruises, that's all."

"Thank God," Everett whispered. "Thank God." They were alive. They were safe.

"You'll be happy to know that you now have a house full of guests," Nathan added.

"Guests? How many?" Everett thought about their modest home.

"I'd say forty or fifty, easily."

"Forty or fifty? Are you kidding me?" *How in the world could Maggie—*

"I'm not kidding. And there are plenty more out on the streets looking for a place to stay. I just came from the mayor's place. He says we're probably looking at seven thousand or more displaced."

Everett had to sit down. "How many do you think are ..."

"No way of knowing yet," Nathan said. "Probably pretty close to that number."

"We only had thirty-seven thousand on the island to begin with," Everett mumbled. "That's a third of the island dead or homeless. We're completely dependent on help from the mainland now."

"Mainland?" Nathan echoed. "Don't forget. We're shut down from the mainland completely."

"Shut down." Everett pondered the words. Being disconnected from the mainland meant several things—in particular, getting food and medical supplies to the people on Galveston Island would be a nightmare. There must be something he could do, but what?

SUNDAY, SEPTEMBER 9, 1900, 10:26 A.M.
GALVESTON ISLAND

Gillian trudged along Broadway, forcing herself not to look at the debris. *This is too horrifying, too awful.* People, half-dressed, lurked on every side, crying out, screaming, searching for loved ones.

"Horrible. Horrible." She pressed a handkerchief against her face, fighting a wave of nausea, trying to think clearly. Douglas hadn't been at the train station. Hopefully he had remained safely behind in Houston, but how could she know for sure? She had no peace. Her mind moved constantly, imagining every possible scenario. Was there nothing she could do in the meantime?

"It's about time you let the Lord use you, Miss Gillian." Pearl's voice resounded against the cacophony ringing in her ears.

"Use me? What do you mean?"

"To reach out to others," Pearl said firmly. "To be a blessing to someone."

"Be a blessing?" Those were strange and unfamiliar words. "I don't understand your meaning."

"We all have a responsibility," Pearl continued, "a responsibility to help our fellow man as much as we are able."

"I help my fellow man, Pearl," Gillian argued. "I'm very charitable. You, of all people, should know that. Didn't I take you in when your husband was killed? Haven't I always been good to you?"

"Oh, yes ma'am," the older woman continued. "Yes ma'am. It's just ..."

"What?"

"Well," Pearl stammered, "Those folks at the house. They ain't your garden party set, but they gonna need a place to stay for awhile."

"What are you getting at?"

"I just been thinking. It's such a big house, and the storm hardly touched it. You could put lots of those folks up for a few days."

"Douglas wouldn't hear of it," Gillian said, horrified. *Why, the very thought.*

"How do you know, ma'am?"

"Well, I ..." Truth be told, she didn't know.

Seventeen

*B*rent paced around the house, nearly frantic. The large home was bursting at the seams with people, none of them familiar. His parents were nowhere to be seen.

"What time did they leave?" he asked a young woman who had made herself at home in the kitchen.

"*Que?*"

"What time—? Ah, never mind."

Brent made his way through the house, looking for any clues. The dining room stood cluttered with trash, no doubt washed in through broken windows in the night. Everything from the waist down looked terrible. Everything from the waist up remained the same. How ironic to see his mother's beautiful china spread out across the dining room table, as if in preparation for some great event. The silverware seemed to be disappearing before his very eyes. *Is that little boy slipping forks into his pocket?*

"Let me have that," Brent said nervously. He emptied the boy's pockets, finding a sight more than just a few pieces of silverware.

"I want all of you out of here right now!" he shouted. "Do you hear me?"

"But sir," an older woman spoke with a strong Irish accent. "The lady, she said we could stay until the water went down."

What a ludicrous thought. His mother inviting strangers in off of the street? A total and complete impossibility.

"The water's down," Brent said. "And I'm saying it's time for you to go."

He pulled the door open, completely unprepared for what met him on the other side.

SUNDAY, SEPTEMBER 9, 1900, 10:35 A.M.
THE MURPHY VILLA

"Brent?" Gillian's heart leaped for joy. The boy who stood before her was her son. And yet she didn't appear to be looking at a boy. The face staring back at her belonged to a man.

Gillian's arms instinctively flew around his neck. "Brent. Oh, Brent."

His silence seemed to speak more than words ever could. They held each other for what seemed like an eternity.

"Praise be to the Lord!" Pearl spoke the words, reaching around the pair to grab Brent by the neck. "Oh, praise him!"

"I will, Pearl," Gillian said, "just as soon as you give me a chance."

SUNDAY, SEPTEMBER 9, 1900, 11:17 A.M.
GALVESTON ISLAND

Henrietta clutched the child in her arms, wading through the debris toward John Sealy Hospital.

According to all of her calculations, John Sealy would be a good bit closer than St. Mary's Infirmary—if it even existed anymore. Perhaps it had melted away with the dormitories.

She had to find medical care, and soon. Lilly Mae needed help, and as quickly as possible. The youngster hadn't stirred in hours. Her breaths were shallow and slow.

"Can I help you, Miss?" A black man spoke from her right. Henri turned, half embarrassed to be seen by a man in little more than her undergarments, and half relieved that someone was actually offering to help.

"I have to get to the hospital," she said. "This little girl is hurt badly."

"Could I carry her for ya?" the grey-haired man asked gently.

Henri looked into his eyes. They carried a bit of a sparkle, which she imagined must have been even brighter before the storm.

"You don't mind?" she asked.

"Of course not, Miss," he said, scooping Lilly Mae up into his arms.

Henri breathed a sigh of relief, and felt the tears start once again. "The hospital ... ?" she started to ask.

"It's still there, Miss ..."

"Henrietta. My name is Henrietta." It seemed pointless to share that she was a nun. What difference did it make, all things considered?

"Well now, Miss Henrietta, I got good news for ya. Mighty good news. The hospital's still standing tall."

"Thank the Lord," she whispered the words.

"Oh, I do," he said with a smile. "I been thankin' him for a mighty lot this morning, Miss Henrietta, that I have."

Henri trudged along behind this man, who shared at length his stories of the night. His name was John, though folks along the way called him "Big John." She couldn't help but notice the respect he commanded, and the inner strength that guided him as he moved them toward the hospital. She forced herself to remain focused, for had she chosen to absorb all that lay around her, it would have been her undoing.

"My wife, Vada, she's as strong as a mule and sly as a fox," John said. "She crawled up on the rooftop down to the church with all the young'uns in tow. They lasted through the night same as you—up in the air. They all alive and well, praise be to the Lord."

Henri wondered how it was possible that a man such as this, who had been through far more trials than she in the night, could have so easily forgotten his own misery when he saw her with Lilly Mae. His faith in God seemed evident, though her own had all but vanished.

"This little 'un," John said softly, looking down at Lilly Mae. "She's doin' mighty poorly, Miss Henrietta. I don't believe any hospital can help her now."

Henri did not respond. She couldn't. The lump in her throat wouldn't allow it.

SUNDAY, SEPTEMBER 9, 1900, 11:33 A.M.
JOHN SEALY HOSPITAL

"Can I help you?" Emma looked into the kind eyes of a large black man who was carrying a small olive-skinned girl. She didn't feel like helping them. She didn't feel like helping anyone. What she wanted, what she needed, was sleep, and the assurance that her mother and father were alive and well. And Sadie. Dear, darling Sadie. Even now, staring into the face of this child, she could not help but feel the familiar tug of love for her darling baby sister.

"I'm guessin' it's already too late for this little angel." The man spoke with tenderness.

Too late? Emma quickly checked her pulse. *Are we too late already?* They must try to save her. A young woman, about her own age, stood near the man. She looked frightened, and clearly in need of medical attention too.

"What's your name?" Emma asked.

"Henrietta."

"Henrietta. We'll have to find something to put on you. You're soaked to the bone. And who is this little one?" Emma glanced down at the child in the man's arms. It was clear she was barely breathing.

"Her name is Lilly Mae," the young woman said. "She's one of the orphans from St. Mary's."

Emma's heart twisted, as it had done so many times over the last several hours. Where would they put the little girl? The wards upstairs were full; the downstairs remained a muddy mess. But she had to find room for her, no question about that.

"Come upstairs with me," she said, stepping out ahead of them. She would find a way. She didn't know how. She didn't know where. But she would find a way.

SUNDAY, SEPTEMBER 9, 1900, 12:00 NOON.
THE COURIER

"Is there anything left standing on the island?" Everett asked the question almost sarcastically. His humor had waned as the day wore on, hot and sticky. The smell of death was everywhere, even permeating the walls of his second-floor office.

"The east wall of the Opera House has collapsed,"

Nathan said. "But a host of people are taking up refuge there anyway. Refugees are everywhere."

"Looting? It's inevitable, I suppose." In fact, the view from his window had convinced him the lowest forms of life were already doing their seedy work on the streets below.

"Of course. But the deputies are out in force, as many as can be, that is."

"I'll be out, myself, as soon as this place is back in some kind of working order."

"If you don't mind my saying so," Nathan said, "I don't think you need to be going anywhere with your leg in such bad shape."

"It's not so bad, really," Everett said. He knew he needed medical attention, but there were far more pressing matters at hand. Besides, his wife would give him enough coddling when he got home—if he ever got home. "I'll have it looked at when I'm able. What's the story on the train station?"

"People down there in droves, trying to get off the island. But it's impossible with the bridge down."

"Anything else I should know? Any good news at all?"

"A strange story, if you're looking to print something a little bizarre."

"Try me."

"There's a child out on the east end who's alive because her mother nailed her hand to the wall."

"I beg your pardon?"

"It's true. Seems it kept her from being washed away. Saved her life."

"Amazing. Anything else?"

Nathan looked down, biting his lip. "The orphanage is gone."

"St. Mary's Asylum? What's become of the children?"

"It's too soon to tell, Everett. I know that at least one or two of the boys have survived, but I've not got any news on the girls yet."

"And the infirmary?" Everett knew full well the ramifications of losing the infirmary. Other than John Sealy, it was the only hospital on the island.

"Still standing, but not functional," Nathan said breathlessly. "The patients have been moved upstairs, but there's no telling what kind of shape they're in. My guess is they'll need to be transported to John Sealy as soon as possible. Could be there are some orphans among them; I don't know."

"Well, get yourself down there and see if there's any sign of them anywhere. We can't sit on this story."

"But Everett, my own family is needing me. I have to get home."

"Get home? Kid, we're in the middle of the story of a lifetime. There's no time to go home now."

Eighteen

How long has father been gone?" Brent asked the question hesitantly, half-afraid of the answer his mother might give.

"Since Tuesday."

Tuesday—the same day he had come to the island. They could very well have passed right by each other at the train station and not even known it. The crowd that afternoon had been particularly thick.

Dear God, please let him be all right. Please let him ... Brent tried to turn his thoughts to his mother, who sat across from him, paler than he had noticed before.

"Mother, what are you going to do about all of these people?"

"Pearl is in there now cooking up a storm," Gillian said, looking nervously about. "But after that, I just don't know. She says that we should let them stay here."

"Stay here? That's crazy. Father would never allow it."

"I know," Gillian said, eyes constantly moving. "But

he's not here right now, and we are. We have to begin to make some decisions without him."

She sounded fiercely independent for a change. Brent wondered at such a thing. His father wouldn't like it, certainly. And yet ... He looked around, his eyes resting on a little boy no older than two or three, curled up in a weary mother's lap in the corner, sound asleep. There had been a time in his life when he had needed help. His mother had been there then. It made sense that she would now offer to help these people.

Yes. It suddenly made perfect sense.

SUNDAY, SEPTEMBER 9, 1900, 3:45 P.M.
JOHN SEALY HOSPITAL

"Miss?"

Henri felt the gentle hand of the nurse rousing her from sleep. She had been enjoying the most wonderful dream. She and Lilly Mae were swimming at a west-end beach. They had been playfully jumping the waves, enjoying the pull of the water together as Lilly sang gleefully.

But the dream ended abruptly. Henri shook herself awake. *Where am I? Why am I here?* She glanced down at her gown, a hospital gown. For the life of her, she couldn't seem to remember why she wore it. The garb seemed to swallow her up. Henrietta forced herself to look into the eyes of the young nurse, who attempted to speak to her.

"I'm so sorry, Miss. The little girl ... the one you brought in with you ..."

"Lilly Mae?"

"Yes, Lilly Mae ..."

Henrietta's heart began to pound wildly. *Don't say it!* her mind screamed. *Don't say it!*

"I'm so sorry to have to tell you this ..." The nurse spoke with compassion, tears streaming down her own cheeks. "But ..."

An intense pain, greater than anything she had ever experienced, suddenly gripped Henrietta's chest. "No!" The word shot out, instinctively. "No!"

"I'm so sorry," the young nurse said quietly. "We did everything we could."

The sobs that overtook Henrietta were as sudden and intense as the storm itself.

SUNDAY, SEPTEMBER 9, 1900, 3:56 P.M.
GALVESTON ISLAND

Emma raced from the hospital, tears streaming down her cheeks. She had been the bearer of bad news more times than she could count over the last day and a half. *Enough is enough. I just want to go home. Mother will be there, waiting. She has to be there. And Papa. He'll be sitting on the sofa, reading the morning paper, wondering why I haven't arrived home yet. Papa will fix everything.* Strong and steady, he would mend the broken pieces of their lives, putting them all back together again. That's what he did. That's what she counted on.

Help me, please! she prayed as she ran.

Not yet a block away, and Emma found herself lost in a maze of bodies and rubble. *This way is east, and that's west.* She stood, staring, hoping to read the sun for direction. *I'm headed toward the beach, at least I think so.*

"Which way is the beach?" she called out.

"To your right. But I wouldn't attempt it, Miss," a large man with tattoos on his bare chest called out. "There's not much left in that direction anyway."

"I have to get home," she shouted, pressing through the debris toward home. Toward safety.

On she ran, the tears nearly blinding her at times. Fighting them was easier than seeing clearly. She wouldn't see clearly. She couldn't. The smell alone overpowered her.

"Miss, you shouldn't be going that way, now," a young immigrant with a strong Italian accent called out. "Nothing but death and destruction down there."

But I have to. Emma fought her way past the young woman, past her words of defeat, *I'm getting closer now. I'm nearly home.*

A large pile of debris appeared before as she made the turn onto what had once been her street. Rubble. Rubble everywhere. A piano, completely intact, lay on its side in the street. Dead, swollen bodies of people lay scattered about like trash. Her home, what remained of it anyway, stood as a hollow shell, a reminder of yesterday. Of countless yesterdays.

SUNDAY, SEPTEMBER 9, 1900, 4:36 P.M.
THE MURPHY VILLA

Gillian scrubbed diligently at dishes alongside Pearl. The tears flowed down her face: tears of exhaustion, tears of relief for a son lost no more, tears of anguish for a husband whose presence remained a mystery.

"Could I be of some help to you, Missus?" Gillian turned to see a woman about her age in tattered clothes. She spoke with a thick Irish brogue.

"I ... I don't know." Gillian quickly brushed aside her tears, not knowing whether or not to trust her good dishes to this woman. Heaven only knew what she might do.

"We can always use two more hands," Pearl said, matter-of-factly. "Just you come on over here, missy."

Gillian turned her attention back to the sink as Pearl tied an apron around the woman's thin waist. She took a dishtowel in hand and began to dry each dish as it came her way. Gillian couldn't help but wonder about her. She seemed quite pleasant, but she was obviously ill-bred. Her intolerable language served as a source of irritation, and her clothes were ... well, they were nothing short of awful. Yet, there was something inviting about her, something Gillian couldn't quite put her finger on.

"How long have you lived on the island?" she asked, finally working up the courage.

"Ah, yes ... I came over in ninety-six with my husband and our son," the woman said.

"What's ya name, dearie?" Pearl asked.

"Brinna O'Shea. My husband, God rest his soul, was named Kieron. Our son is sleeping in there in your parlor. His name is Michael."

"How old is he?"

"Nine next month," Brinna said proudly. "And he's th' spittin' image of his father, that one."

"I'll bet you're mighty proud of him," Pearl said.

"You've a son, haven't you?" Brinna asked, looking at Gillian. "The young man who stopped by earlier?"

She nodded lamely.

"Well then, you know the love of a mother as well as I do."

"Yes." She knew that love.

A knock at the door interrupted their conversation.

"I'll get it, Miss Gillian," Pearl said, reaching to pull her apron off.

"No thank you, Pearl," she said, quickly drying her hands. She wanted to be the one to answer it. It might be Brent, or possibly even Douglas. Gillian made her way to the door, dodging children and mothers on every side. She pulled the door open anxiously. On the other side ...

"I don't believe it! I simply don't believe it!" The ever-familiar voice of Millicent Reeves shattered her illusions of reconciliation.

"Millicent."

"I just had to come by," the older woman said, "and see for myself."

"See what?" She knew, but needed to hear the words herself.

"Well, the rumor is all up and down Broadway that you've taken in refugees. I've told everyone that it's simply not possible, that the Gillian Murphy I know would never ..."

At this point Millicent's voice stopped abruptly. A toddler stood pulling at Gillian's skirt, babbling in a language unknown to both women. Gillian reached down to pick him up, pulling him close to protect him from Millicent's curious glances.

Gillian suddenly felt a burst of courage rise within her. It didn't matter anymore: about the Opera Society, about her standing in society, about anything. Nothing mattered but doing the right thing. And that's exactly what she would continue to do.

"Millicent, what you have heard is in every way true," she said, smiling.

"Why, I simply don't believe it."

"Believe it," Gillian said. "And, truth be told, you and the others should be just as charitable with your own homes. You've plenty of room."

"Well, I never!"

"No, I don't suppose you have," Gillian said with a

smile. "But Millicent, it's time you started. It's a wonderful feeling to help out your fellow man every now and again."

"I do believe this storm has thrown your mind into a tizzy," Millicent said, turning. "But I'm sure the Opera Society will have a few words to say about this."

"Let them talk," Gillian said, suddenly realizing that it didn't matter what anyone thought. "Let them all talk. In the meantime, I'll be here—singing my own song."

And with that, she promptly shut the door.

SUNDAY, SEPTEMBER 9, 1900, 5:00 P.M.
THE COURIER

Everett wrote quickly and furiously, trying to put together the lead story for tomorrow morning's paper. For once, there was no need for yellow journalism. Any headline he could come up with would be inadequate to describe what the island had just been through.

"Some were perched on rooftops. Others were in trees, hanging on for dear life. Some of them were clinging to whatever the water threw their way," he wrote. "The victims remain nameless and faceless in the maddening mess of what has become Galveston Island."

He sat back, noticing for the first time that his hands were trembling. He bore in his own body the depth of the words he was writing, and, try as he may, he could not make it stop.

Nineteen

*B*rent made his way through the maze of people at John Sealy Hospital, hoping to find Sadie, the young woman he had carried into the hospital in the middle of the storm. He had to know; it had been gnawing at him all day. Had she survived? He had risked his own life to get her there, even given her his own blood. She *had* to be alive.

"Have you seen that nurse ... ? He asked an older woman.

"Which one? I've seen half a dozen, at least."

"She's about my age," Brent explained. "I think her name was ..." *Okay, I'm ashamed to admit it, I don't remember her name.* He could only remember her amazing blue eyes, gazing anxiously into his. He had become her hero in the night, and yet he didn't feel much like a hero. He felt the oddest mixture of emotions—pain, agony, relief, joy, sorrow—almost too much to contain.

Emma. The nurse's name was Emma.

"Excuse me," he asked a doctor, "Is there a nurse named Emma here?"

"I think she's up on the second floor."

"Well, what about her sister, the young woman I brought in last night?"

The young doctor turned to look him squarely in the eye. "Oh, it's you. The hero." Brent now recognized the doctor as the one who had been eyeing Emma earlier.

"Yes, it's me," he said curtly. "Brent Murphy. I'm with the *Courier*." He didn't know what made him say the words, except, perhaps, habit. He followed them quickly with, "Where's Sadie?"

"They've moved her to the children's ward right over there." Rupert gestured to his right, and Brent nodded as he headed off in that direction. He made his way through the maze of people in the hallway, some crying, others lying so still that he knew they must have already passed on. Surely, Sadie had not suffered the same fate. Turning into the children's ward, Brent was suddenly overwhelmed with the amount of beds, the number of children. In a room that should have housed fifteen or twenty, there were at least fifty or more. Mosquito netting covered many of the beds, though it did little to protect the injured from their pain.

"Sadie?" He called out her name lightly, hoping not to disturb the others.

No answer. He made his way up and down the row of beds, looking for the familiar angelic face. She would be the one with the freckles and pale skin.

Ah, she was the one directly in front of him. Brent looked down at the young woman, breathing a sigh of relief. She appeared to sleep soundly. A bandage encompassed her head, and her eyes were black and blue, probably as much from blood loss as the beating she had taken out in the storm.

"I'm here, Sadie." He squeezed her hand as he spoke. It didn't matter if she knew. He needed to touch her, to know that she was more than a figment of his imagination. He had been used to save her, but Brent had a sneaking suspicion his job had only begun.

Sunday, September 9, 1900, 6:10 p.m.
John Sealy Hospital

"Where's the chapel?" Henrietta asked anxiously. She had to get away from these people and into a room of solace where she could think, where she could pray.

"Down this hall to the right," an elderly nurse snapped. "But ..."

There was no time for "buts." Henri took off in the direction pointed out, needing to get there quickly, knowing otherwise she would surely explode with emotion in front of this crowd. There had already been enough public displays today. It went against everything she had been taught. She must learn to control her emotions. They were not what needed to be guiding her, especially not now, but she couldn't seem to stop them.

Henri made her way to the chapel, the floor still muddy with water that had washed in during the storm. Candles stood perched atop an altar, unmoved by the storm. That fact brought an eerie sense of comfort. As Henri made her way to the front of the room, groans echoed on every side. For the first time, she realized she was not alone. On the narrow wooden pews, people in abundance slept, cried, grieved. But it didn't matter. She didn't need the solitude. She didn't need the privacy to cry out to God. These people were her equals. They were all one in this room.

"God?" Henri felt the word slip through her lips aloud. That had not been her intent. She would never have prayed out loud. "God, where are you?"

Overcome, she fell to her knees, the mud covering her gown. Frantically, Henri began to pray. She cried out for Sister Elizabeth, who had so bravely gone into town to fetch food for the children. She wept for Sister Grace, who had last been seen defiantly clutching children to her like a mother hen. She agonized over Sister Abigail, whom she had tried so desperately to love. But most of all, Henrietta prayed that Lilly Mae's blessed song would live on, far beyond this weekend of death and devastation, that the song, itself, would bring hope. It would keep Henrietta going.

She began to hum the simple melody, suddenly feeling strength rise within her. Pressing herself to stand, Henri turned to the people. They needed her. She would do what she could to help them.

SUNDAY, SEPTEMBER 9, 1900, 7:00 P.M.
JOHN SEALY HOSPITAL

Brent entered the chapel, startled at what he found there. The room was filled with people, in every sort of distress. He had come there, hoping for a quiet place to write. He had to write. Within him, a story ached to be told, one that would not wait.

"Can I get you to help me over here?" a young woman about his age asked.

"What can I do?" he responded quickly, pressing paper and pen back into his pocket.

"I'm Henrietta," she said.

A beauty, even in muddy gown. But something about this one couldn't be explained. She seemed to be set apart for the task at hand, well suited for the role she now played.

"Henrietta … ?"

"Oh, I'm sorry," she said, clamping her hand over her mouth. "That's Sister Henrietta. I always forget to add that part."

A nun?

"Could you see if there's any food to be found?" she asked. "We've got to get something into these people, even if it's just coffee or warm broth."

Brent nodded lamely, torn between wanting to write and needing to help those in distress. Of course he would help. He sprinted from the room, making his way to someone who looked official.

"Excuse me," Brent spoke to a man mopping the floors at a frantic pace. "I'm wondering where to find food for these people."

"Food?" The elderly man looked up, shaking his head. "I don't rightly know if there is any food left. You need to go up to the kitchen and ask that question. Second floor, on the left."

An agonizing twenty minutes later, Brent emerged with nothing but a pot of coffee, lukewarm, to offer the people below. A small offering, but one they would not turn away at such a dire time.

"Coffee? That's it?" Henrietta asked.

Brent nodded lamely. "There's nothing else. This will have to do until provisions are brought in."

"From where?"

A logical question. If the island is shut off from the mainland, we could all be without food for days. Without food and fresh water, they could all die.

"I'm not sure."

"Well, we'll just have to pray about that," the young nun spoke gently. "Won't we?"

"Yes, I suppose so."

"Not a praying man, Mr ... . ?"

"Murphy. Brent Murphy."

"Not a praying man, Mr. Murphy?"

A rather blunt question, one that would have offended him greatly under different circumstances. Brent knew how to pray. From infancy, the nuns of St. Mary's had ... No, he wouldn't think about that right now.

"I know how to pray."

The young nun smiled in his direction. "Well, get to it then."

"You mean here? Now?" Surely she didn't expect him to stop what he was doing and fall on his knees. That would be a bit absurd, all things considered.

"A little silent prayer never hurt anyone."

Brent looked at her intently. She was a hard one to figure out. There were tears in her eyes, and yet she bore the glow of one who rose above such things. She seemed to carry an immeasurable strength.

For some time, the two worked side by side. Brent labored diligently, yet found himself glued to every word she said. Henrietta told a horrific tale of St. Mary's. A tale of children and nuns roped together. A tale of a little girl who had sung her song against the backdrop of a ravaged sky. A tale of life, and death.

Brent listened closely, taking mental notes. He would write about this child, an orphan of St. Mary's. He would write about the home itself. He owed them that much. This was the story he had been searching for, and yet he hadn't searched for it at all. It had fallen directly into his lap. The article formulated in his mind, even as Henri unveiled the tale—"A Song in the Wind: A Story of Courage and Hope."

He would write about Lilly Mae. He would write about the orphanage. He would write about himself.

"Emma?" She heard Rupert's voice as she re-entered the hospital and tried to steal past him like an invisible ghost. She didn't want to talk. She didn't want to listen. She just wanted to find someplace to collapse. She had to forget all she had seen out on the streets. But how could she forget?

"Emma."

"Not now, Rupert." Her words were curt, but she didn't care.

"Just thought you'd want to know that reporter fellow was back, snooping around your sister."

"What reporter?"

"The one who brought Sadie in last night."

Emma's heart fell. That young man, the one who had played the role of hero, he was nothing but a lousy reporter looking for a story?

"Where is he?"

"Everywhere," Rupert said, frowning. "Every time I turn around, he's under my feet. He's in the ward. He's in the kitchen. He's in the chapel. He's in the lobby."

"Where is he now?"

"Chapel. Playing up to the ladies, I hear."

Emma turned angrily toward the chapel. Her eyes were focused. She was driven. She would find this man and kick him back out into the street where he belonged. She turned the corner, heading into the chapel. There he was, in the corner, the pretty young woman who had come in with the little girl from the orphanage sitting across from him, smiling.

SUNDAY, SEPTEMBER 9, 1900, 7:18 P.M.
JOHN SEALY HOSPITAL

"Just who do you think you are?"

Brent looked up into the cold, blue eyes. They were ablaze with anger. What had he done?

"I'm ... I'm ..." he wasn't quite sure how to answer the question.

"You're a reporter, aren't you?" She asked the question with a clear opinion on the matter.

"Well, yes, but ..." He didn't have time to answer. She wouldn't let him.

"You think you're really something, don't you? You come waltzing in here, under the pretense of helping, and all you want out of it is a story." Here her eyes glanced toward Henrietta. "Among other things."

What's that supposed to mean? I'm here to help. I am. She has some nerve.

"I think you've made a mistake, Miss," Henrietta tried to come to his defense. "He's just ..."

"There's no mistake," Emma said, eyes fixed on his. "And it's pretty clear what he's doing."

"What do you mean?" Brent spoke angrily now, more confused than ever. He had suddenly turned from hero to villain, with no knowledge of how or why the transition had taken place.

"I mean," she said sternly, "the party's over. You're leaving. You can get your story elsewhere." She reached out to grab his arm.

"You've got this all wrong." He spoke with anger surfacing. "I'm just helping *Sister* Henrietta feed and care for these people."

168

SUNDAY, SEPTEMBER 9, 1900, 7:20 P.M.
JOHN SEALY HOSPITAL

"Sister?" Emma spoke the word, feeling her cheeks flush. The pretty young woman was a *nun*?

"That's right," Brent said. "Emma, I'd like you to meet Sister Henrietta Mullins of St. Mary's Asylum. She has taken it upon herself to care for these people, since there's no one else available to do so."

Emma's heart sank to her toes. She looked into the young woman's eyes. They were bloodshot from tears, and yet had a renewed strength in them.

"I thought you were ..." she stammered. To be honest, she hadn't known or cared who the young woman was. She had just been one of hundreds washed in from the storm, near naked and scared to death. A nun? That was the most improbable of all. Nuns were supposed to be older, not as pretty. Weren't they?

"That's all right," Henri said, smiling. "It's understandable, considering my attire. But I would surely hate to lose Mr. Murphy as an assistant."

"But Rupert said ..." Why continue? It all sounded so ridiculous now. Overcome with emotion and exhaustion, Emma began to feel weak. Suddenly nothing mattered anymore. She felt herself slipping away, the room beginning to spin. She was going down ... going down ...

SUNDAY, SEPTEMBER 9, 1900, 7:21 P.M.
THE MURPHY VILLA

"Where is that son of mine?" Gillian asked. "He comes home and then leaves again."

"There's so much work to be done, Miss Gillian," Pearl said. "And you know Brent. He was never one to slack off."

Gillian thought about that comment for a while before answering. Douglas had always accused Brent of being lazy, unmotivated, but their son had always been a hard worker. *Why are you so angry at him, Douglas? Is it the fact that Brent is interested in different things? Your son isn't like you at all, is he, Douglas?*

Your son ...

They *were* father and son, weren't they? It didn't matter that Douglas hadn't actually fathered Brent. They were still father and son.

SUNDAY, SEPTEMBER 9, 1900, 7:26 P.M.
JOHN SEALY HOSPITAL

Brent gazed down at Emma's pale face anxiously. Splashes of freckles covered her pale cheeks. He hadn't noticed them before. Why were they so clear to him now?

"The doctor is coming," Henri said, entering the room, breathless. She had gone off to fetch someone ... anyone.

Enter the young doctor. His foe.

"What happened?" Rupert asked, tossing Brent an undeniable look of distrust.

"One minute she was standing, the next ..."

"She fainted," Henri explained. "She just hit the floor."

"No doubt," Rupert said. "She's been on her feet for days. We all have."

He pulled a bottle of smelling salts from his coat, waving them under her nose. Emma stirred, making faces.

"What ... I ... ?" Her face contorted as she came to. "What ... what happened?"

"You fainted," Brent said.

"I did?" she responded. "I ... I don't remember anything."

"What you need is a good night's sleep," Rupert said, reaching down to pick her up.

"No. Let me." Brent scooped her up into his arms, feeling her heartbeat through the damp clothes.

"I ..." she tried to argue, but fell silent against his argument. In a matter of moments, her eyes were closed again. Brent carried her up to the ward, placing her in the bed with Sadie. She needed sleep, and lots of it. He would make sure she got it.

SUNDAY, SEPTEMBER 9, 1900, 11:46 P.M.
THE COURIER

Everett paced around the pressroom, fighting with machinery. Everywhere he turned he met water, mud, or debris of some sort. *This is maddening.* "Any chance we'll get her up and running?" He pointed nervously to the printing press.

"Should be dried out in a few hours," Nathan said. "I've got Joe and Bill working on it. Don't worry, Everett. You just go home to your family. We'll get a paper out tomorrow, I promise. I just hope we beat the *Daily* to print, that's all."

"Still got that competitive edge," Everett said, shaking his head. "After all that's happened."

"Nothing wrong with that, right?" Nathan looked at him curiously.

Suddenly Everett wasn't so sure anymore. To be honest, he wasn't sure about anything anymore. Another familiar voice startled him. He turned, gazing into Brent Murphy's wide eyes. "Murphy? What, in the name of all that's holy, are you doing here?" *Crazy young man must have risked his life to get here.*

"I've got a story for tomorrow morning's paper."

"We've already laid down the story. We're about to go to print."

"Can we add another?" Brent asked, his eyes looking wild.

"Another?"

"Yes, please." Something in the young reporter's expression caused Everett to hesitate for just a moment. He would listen to Brent's story.

Twenty

Brent gripped the ink pen, writing frantically. *My story is long and complicated. Will one article be enough?* "Perhaps Everett can be talked into a series," he mumbled aloud, then returned to his scribbling:

When I turned eighteen, they gave me the news: "Everything we've ever told you about yourself was a lie." I became a stranger, not only to myself, but to my family as well. The parents I had always called my own turned out to be parents in name only. Good Samaritans. They had taken this homeless waif of a child and given him a home eighteen years earlier. The St. Mary's Orphan Asylum, it turns out, had been my first home. To this day, I have no memory of it, though I have stood at its doors time and time again trying to remember.

But I can stand there no longer.

St. Mary's, along with most of its children, vanished into the night, a victim of the storm. Her departed charges will never know the love of a mother or father, never feel a tender goodnight kiss pressed against their brow. They will never again skip along the shore to pick up shells. Their voices will no longer be heard echoing across this island.

They are no more. But their memory lingers still. They touched our lives, and, as one of them, I feel compelled to share their story ...

Here Brent paused, reaching up to wipe the tears that flowed down his cheeks unashamed. He couldn't seem to stop them. Taking a break from the writing, he lay his head on the desk, letting the tumultuous emotions wash over him like salty ocean waves.

MONDAY, SEPTEMBER 10, 1900, 6:27 A.M.
JOHN SEALY HOSPITAL

"Sadie, can you hear me?" Emma spoke the words gently, almost afraid to move. She had slept soundly with her younger sister at her side. But daylight called. Work summoned.

"Hmmm?" her younger sister mumbled.

"Are you awake, sweet girl?"

"I am now."

Still that amazing sense of humor, Emma thought with a smile.

Sadie grumbled, rolling over. "I want to go back to sleep."

"You've been sleeping a long, long time," Emma said, slipping off the edge of the bed.

"What do you mean?" Sadie tried to sit up, but toppled back over. "Oh, my head."

"You've had a bad time of it," Emma said, reaching over to embrace her. "But you're going to be fine." She spoke the words as firmly and confidently as she could.

"The storm ..." Sadie spoke the word, her face suddenly conveying the memory of what had happened.

"Try not to think about it now, dear," Emma said, holding her close. "You just get better, and everything will be alright."

"Is mother here?" Sadie asked, her eyes filling with tears. "I need mother."

"She's ... she's not here," Emma said, feeling a lump grow in her throat.

"Where is she? Where is Papa?"

"I don't know, Sadie. But I'm going to find out. I promise you that. I'm going to find out."

Monday, September 10, 1900, 8:14 a.m.
John Sealy Hospital

Henrietta glanced up as Emma entered the chapel. "You look much better this morning," she said, satisfied at the improvement in the young nurse's countenance.

"I feel better," Emma said hurriedly. "But I need something, and I was hoping you could help."

"Tell me."

"I need to find out about my family. I made it as far as our street yesterday, but everything is gone, washed away." Emma's eyes filled with tears.

Henrietta instinctively reached to embrace her. "What can I do?"

"I've heard that many from our neighborhood have gone to the Convent Academy for refuge. Maybe my parents are there."

Henri knew the academy well. It occupied four city blocks on the island, Avenues N to O and Rosenberg Avenue to 27th Street. She was relieved to hear it had survived the storm, though that news didn't surprise her. The grounds were surrounded by a massive, ten-foot brick wall.

"I'll be glad to go," Henri said, "But I'll need clothes and a shawl, if you can muster one up."

"I think we can manage that."

Henri asked a lot of questions as she dressed. She would need to know something of Emma's parents: what they looked like, their names, and so on. With those issues addressed, and finding herself clothed in a modest blue dress and shawl, Henrietta set out.

"Where in the world?" She stood still for a moment, trying to figure out which way to go. Nothing seemed to make much sense. *With all this rubble, I can't tell north from south.* Henrietta turned to gaze at the sun, trying to gauge its position in the sky. "Ah, I think I've got it now," she said, turning to the right.

She made her way slowly and carefully, fighting both the debris and the stench of swollen corpses. She fought against her churning stomach, hoping against hope that she could keep from being sick.

About two blocks east of the hospital, Henrietta stumbled across a group of men pulling bodies from the piles of rubble. Dozens of corpses, already discovered, littered the side of the road. She covered her nose, forcing herself to the other side of the street.

Lord, I need you. Show me the way, Father. Help me to know what to do, and how to go about doing it. Help me, Lord.

"Sister, Sister." A familiar voice called out to her. Henrietta pressed her eyes open, afraid of what she might find. A wave of relief swept over her as she spied Big John. He was certainly a sight for sore eyes.

"Big John!" She reached out to embrace him. The rancid smell of stale sweat greeted her, but it presented no barrier. *He's been working so hard.*

"How's that little angel I carried over to the hospital fer ya?" he asked, reaching up to wipe the sweat from his brow.

Henri felt the lump in her throat immediately. A lone tear dribbled down her cheek.

"Oh, Miss Henri, I'm so sorry. I sure am."

"She went to be with Jesus yesterday afternoon," Henrietta said. "But I still want to thank you. If you hadn't come along just when you did, we never would have made it to the hospital."

"Where you headed?" John asked. "You ought not be out on the streets like this."

"I have to get to the academy," Henri said anxiously. "A friend hasn't been able to locate her parents, and she's hoping they're there."

"Oh, Miss Henri, so many folks is missing, all over the island. I sure hopes you can find 'em fer her."

"I'm going to do my best," she said. "But tell me, is there a clearing where I can get through?" The street ahead lay covered in debris on every side.

"We been stackin' timbers and such up and down every side," John said. "And the bodies ..." Here he stopped, an obvious attempt at politeness. "Well, anyways, Miss Henri. You don't want to go around to the right. If'n I's you, I'd take the way to the left through here." He pointed off down the left. "But you best be prepared. I hear tell they got a passel of folks down at the academy. Sure hopes you know who you lookin' fer."

"I think so," Henri said. "And if they're not there, I'll see about staying and helping out a bit."

"Oh, they could sure use it, Miss Henri. They sure could."

Henrietta worked her way through the rubble on her

left, finding a clearing just beyond it. The smell of death hung like a thick cloud in the air above. Her head began to grow light, and suddenly she felt faint.

Be my ever-present help in time of trouble. Be my ever-present help in time of trouble!

Forcing her eyes open once again, Henrietta made herself look. *I owe it to those who have lost their lives here.* Their stories were important, though there would be so little time to hear them all now. Henri's chest began to ache, thinking of Elizabeth, Grace, and Abigail. Were they among the dead? She tried to force such thoughts from her mind. Perhaps there would be news of them at the academy, good news.

Though nothing appeared familiar, Henrietta realized she must be approaching the academy. None of the regular landmarks were in place to guide her. Everything seemed amiss. Even the brick wall, which had surrounded the building, had disappeared. A mob of people stood before her, many weeping and wailing. A large contingent of blacks sang a dirge, wailing in a slow, melancholy manner. Their grief, open and apparent, ripped at her heart.

Children of every ethnic background sat alone, some fully dressed, others nearly naked. Some wandered among the rubble, looking for trinkets, or even bits of food. *Lord, help them. How awful.* Henri forced her way through the crowd and into the academy.

"There's no more room in here." A familiar voice spoke.

"Sister Abigail." Never in her life had Henrietta been so overjoyed to see someone she had so despised. "You're here."

"Sister?"

Henri realized how odd she must look to the older

nun in this contemporary dress and shawl. But what did it matter? They were alive. They were together.

"Tell me about the others," she implored.

Abigail's gaze shot down to the ground, a clear sign the news would not be good. "We've had no sign of Grace," she said softly. "And Elizabeth ..."

What about Elizabeth? Surely she had found safety.

"Elizabeth's body was found early this morning on the west end. She had made it very nearly all the way back to the asylum. Her wagon had been torn to bits."

Henri shook back the tears that tried to tumble so freely out of her eyes. *There is no time for mourning now.* "Tell me about the asylum," she said hoarsely.

"It's gone, child," Abigail said. "Both dormitories washed away. The infirmary stands, but there's little way to care for the patients. As soon as I can get back there, I'm going to do what I can to help."

"You've tried to go back?"

"Yes. This morning," Abigail said sadly. "A hopeless situation, I'm afraid. In some places the wall of debris stood nearly two stories high. There were the cries of those who were dying, buried alive." Tears welled up in the older nun's eyes. Henri reached out to embrace her as the older woman continued to speak. "Inside the wall were animals and children—some dead, others dying." She dissolved into tears again. "And pieces of furniture, pots and pans, walls and windows—too much—too much to bear."

Henrietta's heart wrenched. "Oh, Abigail, at least we have each other." *How odd that the two of us, such formidable foes, survived. Is there now to be a friendship?*

"You blessed girl," Abigail said, suddenly weeping. "I've always been so hard on you."

"Not too hard, Sister," Henri said. "I needed it. I did."

She quickly gathered her wits about her, remembering why she had come. "I'm here to look for the parents of a friend," she explained. "Mr. and Mrs. Weldon Sanders."

"Sanders?" Abigail's face contorted slightly. "There are so many people here. But that name doesn't sound familiar. Would you know them if you saw them?"

"I'm not sure, to be honest," Henri said. "But I'd like to have a look, if you don't mind."

"Of course, child," a very softened Abigail said. "Come on inside."

Monday, September 10, 1900, 9:20 a.m.
The Courier

Brent yawned and took a final look at the newspaper he held in his hand. He clutched it tightly, feeling the need to embrace it as a friend. The office door swung open, startling him. Everett stood before him, dressed in fresh clothes and looking like a man who had finally slept.

He gazed at Brent curiously. "Did you stay here all night?"

"Yep. Got it out."

"Well, let me have a look at it."

Brent reluctantly handed the newspaper over to the editor, knowing he had given up a piece of himself in writing it. It had not been an easy story, tracing his roots back to the asylum, but now the story was out. And Lilly Mae's life would now serve its purpose. Everyone would have a chance to get to know this amazing little girl, to share in her song.

Everett read it intently, looking up on only one occasion at Brent. "I had no idea," he said quietly.

"No. I don't suppose you did. Not many people knew."

"They will now." Everett said, looking at him closely. "Are you alright with that?"

"I'm alright with that."

MONDAY, SEPTEMBER 10, 1900, 11:15 A.M.
THE MURPHY VILLA

"Pearl, could you come in here and help me?" Gillian called out from the dining room where a third round of people sat for breakfast.

"Coming, Miss Gillian." The older woman rounded the corner with a plateful of potato pancakes.

"How's the food holding out?" Gillian asked, lowering her voice.

"Well, we got enough for a meal or two tomorrow— thanks to your party goods."

Her party. Gillian hadn't thought about it since Millicent's visit last night.

"We got a kitchen full of chocolates and taffies," Pearl said with a grin. "That oughta keep the young'uns happy, for awhile anyhow."

"That's all they need right now," Gillian said, glancing about. Already, the children were under her feet at every turn. "Can we send some of them out back to play?"

"In your garden, Miss Gillian?"

Yes, in her garden. She didn't care about that. Not anymore. Not when these children had lost so much. *If my garden can't be used as a playground, then why bother having it at all?*

MONDAY, SEPTEMBER 10,1900, NOON
THE MURPHY VILLA

"Brent, you're here. I've been so worried."

Brent stifled a yawn as he looked into his mother's worried eyes. He fought off the sleep that almost overwhelmed him as she wrapped her arms around him. "I'm sorry, Mother," he said sleepily. "I've been at the *Courier* all night putting together a story about the storm."

"Why doesn't that surprise me?" she asked. "Can I read it?"

Brent hesitated, but only slightly. Surely his mother would understand why he had written the article. She, of all people, would understand. "Sure you can," he said with a smile. "I brought home four or five copies just for posterity's sake."

"You look like you haven't slept in days, son," Gillian said. "Why don't you head on up to your room and get some rest?"

"Great idea." Brent was completely and totally exhausted. And yet ..."What about all of these people?" The house remained full, brimming with children playing, mothers talking and weeping, men working to mend the pieces of the house that had been touched by the storm. A noisy place, it didn't look like things would be quieting down anytime soon.

"Oh, posh," his mother said. "You can sleep through this. Why, when you were a boy, you could sleep through anything."

"True." Brent yawned again, reaching out to hug his mother tightly. He would sleep. He might never wake up again.

MONDAY, SEPTEMBER 10, 1900, 4:13 P.M.
THE GALVESTON COURIER

Everett entered his office after a detailed visit with Isaac Cline, the island's chief meteorologist. Cline had suffered terribly during the storm, losing several of his own family members. Everett felt a deep sorrow for the man.

Information floated about everywhere, like debris and bodies. One thing was for sure: The loss of life on Galveston Island now surpassed both the Chicago fire of 1871 and the Johnstown flood of 1889. In every way, the storm had been catastrophic.

The arduous task of collecting bodies and transporting them to sea had already begun, but not before the looting. People stole anything and everything they could get their hands on as they made their way through the remains of shops and houses. Already word had reached Everett that more than three thousand buildings had been destroyed by the storm, and the official tally wasn't in yet. Whole neighborhoods had been obliterated, wiped off the face of the map. Shipping facilities were damaged beyond repair. This whole island sat separated from the rest of the world.

Worse still, some human vultures stole from the corpses themselves. Scavengers plundered everything from jewelry to bits of clothing, some going so far as to chop off fingers of the deceased in order to obtain their rings.

Gruesome, thought Everett. *Will history remember Galvestonians this way? Is this our story?*

Everett began to look over his notes from Cline, amazed at all he read. The barometric pressure recorded thirty miles from the eye of the storm read an amazing 27.49 inches. At its highest point, Galveston stood eight feet, seven inches above sea level. The storm surge, by all estimates, had reached nearly sixteen feet. A seawall could have, probably would have, saved the city, but the argument against building it had won out. The island never stood a chance.

The death tally rose steadily, and the cost of repairs would soon reach staggering proportions. Everett dropped into his chair in disbelief as he considered the inevitable. *This could very well turn out to be the most awesome storm ever to strike the United States of America.*

Twenty-One

*B*rent tossed and turned, the victim of a terrible dream ...

Restless waves pitched him to and fro as he fought with every ounce of strength to stay afloat. *Won't someone please help me? Someone? Anyone?* Off in the distance, the beach sparkled white, like crystal. He stared, longing for its security. With outstretched arms, he reached, but found himself fighting the undercurrent once again. *I need to get out of here. I need to get home.* He began to paddle madly, working his way toward shore, only to find himself pulled out to sea once again.

Suddenly, he recognized someone off in the distance. His father stood along the shore, nibbling a sandwich and visiting with friends. *Doesn't he see me? Doesn't he know I'm about to ...* Brent felt himself being pulled under again and gasped for breath. Rising to the surface, he let out a shrill cry. "Help me!" He raged against the current.

His father never even looked his way.

A curious song suddenly filled the air, wrapping him like a blanket and giving him the courage to continue fighting for his life. It rose and fell like the waves themselves. Brent began to hum the melody, realizing it might very well be his only lifeline.

TUESDAY, SEPTEMBER 11, 1900, 6:33 A.M.
JOHN SEALY HOSPITAL

Emma took one look at the *Courier* and let out a groan. "I don't believe it." The paper's headline read, "A Song in the Wind: A Story of Courage and Hope." She could not mistake Brent Murphy's byline below the title.

He did it. That awful reporter took Lilly Mae's story and publicized it for the whole world to see. How insensitive can he be? Disgust almost forced Emma to toss the paper altogether. *On second thought, maybe I'd better read it. That way I'll know how to confront him if he dares to show his face around here again.* Her eyes settled on a particular paragraph that described Lilly Mae with depth and beauty. It conveyed real meaning, real hope. She read on, pricked by Brent's description of the orphanage and his journey through its doors into a home of his own.

Maybe there's more to this story than meets the eye. Maybe Brent Murphy isn't such a bad guy after all. Emma read on, mesmerized by the carefully woven tale. *No. Maybe Mr. Murphy isn't quite what I made him out to be.*

TUESDAY, SEPTEMBER 11, 1900, 7:53 A.M.
THE ACADEMY

Henri made her way through the Convent Academy, offering cups of water and small pieces of soda crackers as they became available. People of every color sat huddled together, cold and hungry, some still in a dismayed state of shock, others overcome with despair. Those with any energy at all mourned openly. Others sang their dirges, weeping and wailing until the whole crowd began to moan in unison.

> *"Dere's no rain to wet you,*
> *O, yes, I want to go home.*
> *Dere's no sun to burn you,*
> *O, yes, I want to go home;*
> *O, push along, believers,*
> *O, yes, I want to go home;*
> *O, yes, I want to go home;*

An eerie sound, she had to admit, and yet oddly soothing. There seemed to be a depth to these people she had not seen before. *Is it because I never took the time to know them?* They knew this "home" of which they sang. Intimately, they knew.

> *Dere's no hard trials,*
> *O, yes, I want to go home;*
> *Dere's no whips a-crackin',*
> *O, yes, I want to go home;*
> *My brudder on de wayside,*
> *O, yes, I want to go home;*
> *O, push along, my brudder,*
> *O, yes, I want to go home;*
> *Where dere's no stormy weather,*
> *O, yes, I want to go home;*
> *Dere's no tribulation,*
> *O, yes, I want to go home*

Sometimes Henri found herself caught up in the haunting melody of their song. It reminded her of Lilly Mae, the youngster who had claimed to hear angels singing over her. Perhaps she had. Perhaps she sang with them now. Just as quickly, she would push memories of Lilly Mae away. They weren't fair, her memories. They were too fresh, too crisp. In them, the child was always healthy, perfect, so very alive.

Lilly Mae. Grace. The asylum. They're all gone. I have to accept that. I must. Henrietta's eyes filled with tears at the thought of her beautiful and loving friend, who had given her very life to save those of the children. *If only I could manage one-tenth of Grace's goodness, what a wonderful person I would be.*

As she reflected, Henri prayed, questioning herself and the Lord. *Why should I remain here on the island? What's left for me here?* Certainly, there were those to be tended to, but couldn't someone else fill that need? *Lord, I want to go home. I long for Virginia now, more than ever. I ache for my mother and father. I need them, Father. I need them.*

The frustrated young nun continued to work, calculating how she might go about achieving the task of leaving the island once the bridge to the mainland was rebuilt. "Unless God speaks," she whispered aloud, "I will leave Galveston Island soon and never look back."

TUESDAY, SEPTEMBER 11, 1900, 8:02 A.M.
THE MURPHY VILLA

Brent awoke to the stark smell of mold all around him, puzzled by the sound of a child crying. He sneezed three times consecutively, unable to control himself. The sun streamed in brightly through the window, blinding him, but he felt sure, at least almost sure, that a child sat next to him in the bed, a little boy.

"Mister, mister."

He squinted, trying to see past the streams of sunlight that wreaked havoc with his vision.

"Mister, where's my mama?" He looked into the inquisitive eyes of a little boy probably no more than four or five, who sat on top of his feet.

"I, uh …" Brent tried to collect his senses. *Where am I again?* He looked around the room, settling the question. *Home. I'm home.*

A young woman appeared in the doorway, her face aflame with embarrassment. "I'm so sorry, sir," she said, scurrying into the room. "I don't know how he got away from me. I really don't."

She pulled the youngster into her arms, his little face lighting up with the joy of his recognition. "Mama!"

Brent nodded in their direction, pulling the covers up around himself. They turned and went on their own way, and he found himself free to slip into some clothes. *What clothes? Everything I owned is still at The Tremont.* He thumbed through the remains of a wardrobe several years old, trying to decide on an appropriate outfit. *Does it matter? Who am I dressing for anyway?*

His thoughts immediately shifted to Emma—that nurse—the one with the beautiful brown curls. For some reason, he just couldn't seem to shake the memory of their last conversation or the glare in her eyes as she tore into him.

TUESDAY, SEPTEMBER 11, 1900, 11:16 A.M.
ALONG THE STRAND

Everett paced up and down The Strand, fighting the unbelievable stench and taking in all the damage he could. The smell certainly wasn't the worst of it. He had forced himself not to look too closely at the bodies that littered the streets. For every corpse carried off, another seemed to appear in its place, washed up on shore with the morning's tide. They were stacked upon each other like pieces of meat at the butcher shop, awaiting a final resting place.

Within hours, the burning would begin. The whole island would become an inferno of funeral pyres. *It's the only way*—or so the majority of masterminds had concluded. *We've already been tried by flood. Are we now to be tried by fire also?*

Everett pondered the question as he gazed at the workers. They wore rags across their faces in a vain attempt to avoid the odor, and they worked long and hard. Would this nightmare ever end? People were leaving in droves, paying outrageous amounts to be boated to the mainland, and who could blame them? Even Maggie, bless her soul, had wished for an escape. She had pleaded with him just this morning to get them to Houston. "Somehow," she had said. It didn't matter how.

I can't leave. Not now, anyway, while the story's still unfolding. Like it or not, I'm still a newspaperman, and this is my bread and butter. Tragedy abounded, to be sure, but in the midst of it all Everett had managed to find a few humorous stories as well. One Galveston matron had stumbled across a live cow in her parlor just after the storm. With no food or water handy, her unexpected houseguest had provided nourishment for her four little ones during those first dark days. *Now that's a story folks would love to hear. It will give them hope, and hope is a precious commodity these days.*

Hmmm. What about this one? He looked over his notes. *Local pastor clings to wooden cross.* This cross, once perched atop his church's steeple, had come dislodged during the storm, floating about like a piece of driftwood. Somehow it had managed to stay afloat, in spite of everything, a testament to the wonders of the pastor's faith.

Faith: a word Everett rarely considered anymore. And now, in the aftermath of the storm, he wondered if he would ever understand such a word.

TUESDAY, SEPTEMBER 11, 1900, 11:57 A.M.
THE MURPHY VILLA

"Miss Gillian, are you alright?"

Gillian leaned against the wall for support, completely overcome with exhaustion. Her hair, now matted to her head, had grown thick with perspiration. Her dress, torn in at least a half-dozen places, did little to enhance her appearance.

"I'm exhausted, Pearl," she said, feeling the tears begin to sting her eyes. "I just need to lie down awhile."

"Well, take the sofa, Miss Gillian," Pearl said, shooing several children out of the way. "You been workin' too hard, and you need yer rest."

Gillian made it to the sofa, where she stretched out for a much-needed nap. *How can I relax when there's so much work to be done, so many people to be cared for?* Suddenly, all of the tea parties and social events in the world seemed so pointless, so trite, so frivolous. *If only Douglas were here. He would know what to do. He would ...*

No telling what he would do. Surely, his heart had not been as changed as hers had. That would be asking too much, far too much. *Please, Lord, let him be alive.* She hated to even think otherwise, but already news had come in of those who were in railroad cars when the bridge had gone down. *If Douglas was among them, I don't know what I'll do. How will I go on?*

No. She wouldn't let herself think that way. *He's*

alive, and he's coming home. And he would welcome their son with open arms.

Brent scribbled frantically, trying to remember every detail, every event.

They are burning the bodies. The smoke, thick and horrible, covers the island. The smell is ghastly, unlike anything I have ever imagined. We close our windows and doors, but we cannot escape its torment. We are live corpses, wandering blindly in a fog of smoke. The ashes of our friends and loved ones float through the air like storm clouds, rising and falling like the tide itself. We are afraid to breathe. We are afraid not to.

Emma sat at the small table in the nurses' lounge, sipping a glass of weak tea, trying to relieve the piercing headache that had consumed her for the past few hours. Try as she may, the pain would not lessen. The overwhelming smell coming from the fires nauseated her, making her continually dizzy. She tried to drive it away with thoughts of happier things, but no thoughts would come. The headache, aggravated by lack of sleep and tension, prevented them. For days, she had worried and fretted over the condition of her parents. And there was still no news. *This is unbearable,* she thought. *How long can I go on like this?*

Emma turned her thoughts to her sister, Sadie, who was recovering nicely upstairs. *At least, thank the Lord, she'll be fine.* There seemed to be no serious aftereffects to her injuries. Thanks to a kindhearted stranger, she had escaped death.

Kindhearted stranger. Emma thought of the young journalist again. She had come to see him in a different light after reading his article in the *Courier*. His own story of loss and gain had touched something in her heart. But would she ever see him again?

Twenty-Two

Brent stood at the shore, looking out onto peaceful waters in the gulf. How strange to think all the devastation surrounding him had come at the insistence of the once angry waves. They were angry no more. His eyes brimmed with tears as the cool saltwater eagerly lapped the shore, dancing against the tepid morning sun. Reaching to pick up his tablet, he began to write.

So you have won at last. You have captured the soul of this island and buried it beneath your current. What you have taken, we give back to you ... the bodies of those who have no breath left in them will be yours once more. We carry them out on boats and weight them down, as if, in doing so, we could offer them as sacrifices. And yet, you give again. Their bodies wash up on shore, a grim reminder that you are, indeed, more powerful than we. It has always been this way, and it will forever continue.

He stopped writing to think: about the father he still

had not seen, about the reasons his life had been spared. *Am I still here for a reason?* Perhaps someone, somewhere, knew his life meant something, that he could make a difference. Brent could not help but think of Sister Henrietta. She had lost much, but her countenance was golden, at least most of the time. She seemed to rise above it all. Clearly something greater than ordinary courage or tenacity drove the young nun. Could he obtain such courage? Where did it come from?

For the first time in years, Brent Murphy bowed his head to pray.

WEDNESDAY, SEPTEMBER 12, 1900, 11:47 A.M.
THE COURIER

"Three days in a row, sir."

Everett looked at Nathan curiously. "What do you mean?"

"Three days in a row we've beat those suckers at the *Daily* to print. That's the best we've ever done. People are fighting each other to get their hands on the *Courier*. They want the news."

"And we're giving it to them," Everett mumbled.

"What was that, sir?"

"Oh, nothing," Everett said, biting his lip. He turned away from the young reporter, unable to share his joy. In the past, it would be been excellent news. Now, it just seemed futile. What difference did it make if the story made it to print in one paper before another? It was still the same story, regardless of who printed it first.

WEDNESDAY, SEPTEMBER 12, 1900, 2:52 P.M.
JOHN SEALY HOSPITAL

Brent couldn't help but stare as he made his way through the front door of the hospital. *This place is a wreck.* Outside, men of every color worked alongside one another to shore up the building, which had been knocked off its frame a few inches. Inside, workers scrubbed frantically at the walls, trying to wash away any trace of mold they might find there. They worked diligently at the near-impossible task, seemingly unaware. They wore crude masks over their faces, but still struggled against the smell of the mildew that now seemed to almost overwhelm the building.

Brent wound his way through the halls, looking for Emma. *I need to be here for her.* He couldn't explain what suddenly drove him, but his mind wouldn't rest until he found her.

Wednesday, September 12, 1900, 3:01 p.m.
John Sealy Hospital

"Are you Emma Sanders?"

Emma turned to face the stranger, knowing in her heart he brought bad news. "Yes," she half-whispered, half-spoke.

"I'm afraid I have some bad news for you, Miss," he said, removing his hat.

Her heart at once began to twist within her. "No!" she cried out, not even waiting for his words.

"Your parents ..."

She heard the rest through the numbness consuming her. Her father's body had been found the afternoon before, washed up onto the beach. Her mother's body, the man informed her, had been located by neighbors, just this morning. Both of her parents had been carried out to sea for burial. There would be no opportunity for goodbyes.

"I'm so sorry." He seemed to be speaking in slow motion. "Is there anything I can do? Anyone else I can help you locate?"

She shook her head back and forth, drawing in a deep breath. "There is no one else," she whispered, suddenly realizing that she, alone, was left—to care for herself, and to care for Sadie.

"The neighbors thought you might like to have this," he said, pressing something into her hand. The room spun madly.

"Thank you, sir," Another voice, a familiar voice, spoke. Through the haze, Emma saw Brent Murphy speaking to the man who had brought the news. Emma never heard or saw anything else. With her back pressed against the wall, she felt her knees give way. She slid all the way down until she sat in a curled ball on the floor, weeping openly.

WEDNESDAY, SEPTEMBER 12, 1900, 3:13 P.M.
THE ACADEMY

"I need to get off of the island." Henrietta spoke the words forcefully, hoping to somehow convince herself. She felt the pangs of home calling out to her louder than they ever had before. It was no longer an issue of whether she would stay or leave. The minute she could go, she would go. No looking back.

"Miss Henri, I just don't rightly know ..." Big John tried his best to reason with her, but Henrietta's mind was made up. She would go home.

"Just tell me right out, John," she said stubbornly. "Can you take me to the station?"

"I can gets you there, Miss Henri," he said hesitantly, "but you gonna be waitin' a long time before you gets off the island, an' that's a fact."

"They're ferrying people across the bay, John," she said firmly. "And I'm going to be one of them. Now, can you get me to the station or not?"

Just as he opened his mouth to answer, Abigail interrupted, "Sister?"

"Yes?" she answered abruptly, turning to face the older woman. "What do you need?"

Abigail's face fell, and immediately Henri was sorry she had spoken so abruptly. "I, uh ... I was hoping you could help me dispense some medications," she said, her eyes shifting downward. "But I can see you're in the middle of something."

"No," Henri said impatiently. "I'm not. Really. It can wait."

"Are you sure?" Abigail asked. "Because I could ask one of the others. You've been on your feet nonstop for days."

"I guess it goes with the job," Henri said, turning away from Big John and moving toward the older nun.

"Does that mean you'll be stayin' on, Miss Henri?" Big John asked, looking at her curiously.

She shrugged. "At least for the moment," she said. "But don't go very far. I'll be sending for you shortly."

Wednesday, September 12, 1900, 3:15 p.m.
John Sealy Hospital

Brent sat down on the floor, reaching to put his arm around Emma. She wept loudly, openly. As his arm slipped over her shoulder, she buried her head in his embrace. Unashamed, he pulled her closer to himself.

"You go ahead and cry," he whispered. "If anyone ever deserved it, you do."

She had been through so much over the past few days, and now this. This news. It was devastating. Brent held Emma's tear-stained face against his chest for several minutes, feeling her heart beat against his.

"I ... I'm so sorry." Emma looked up at him with eyes full of unshed tears.

"Please don't be," he said, offering her a handkerchief. "I'm just glad I got here when I did." She would never know how glad.

She brushed a lock of hair out of her face. "Why are you here?" she asked, looking up at him curiously.

"I came to check on Sadie, of course," he said, mustering up a smile. Truth was, he had come to see Emma too. But he couldn't bring himself to tell her that.

"Sadie ..." Emma mumbled, looking down. The tears began to fall like torrents rushing toward the floor. "She doesn't know yet—about Mama and Papa." She spoke of her parents in such an endearing way that it shook him to the core of his being. Did some families actually care for each other in such a way?

"I ... I have no one now," Emma said, looking up at him, completely defeated.

"You have Sadie. God has spared her, Emma. And she needs you."

"But I have nothing to give her. I don't even have a home to take her to. What am I going to do?"

What, indeed? For days, she had been shut up at this hospital with little but the uniform she was wearing and a grueling schedule to keep her company. He had to do something, but what?

Suddenly the answer came. *How perfect. How completely logical.* He would take her home. He would take them both home. His mother would welcome them with open arms, just as she had already welcomed those who had come before her.

"Emma," he said, squeezing her hand tightly. "I think I have an idea."

WEDNESDAY, SEPTEMBER 12, 1900, 3:17 P.M.
JOHN SEALY HOSPITAL

Emma sat quietly listening to Brent's strong, reassuring words. They offered hope when she really had none of her own to spare. He was offering so much: a place to stay, food, a family. How could she possible say yes to such an offer?

Then again, how could she possibly say no? She looked up into his eyes. They were kind, compassionate. This was a man she could trust.

"You dropped something," Brent said, pointing to the floor.

Emma looked down curiously. "What?"

"I don't know," he said, reaching to pick up something shiny and silver. "That man gave it to you."

"He did?" Emma barely remembered taking anything from him.

"Looks like—"

"A ring," she said, grabbing it out of his hand. A tiny diamond sat perched atop a shining silver band. She had looked at it hundreds, if not thousands, of times before. "It's my mother's wedding ring." Emma clutched it tightly, barely able to breathe.

WEDNESDAY, SEPTEMBER 12, 1900, 5:00 P.M.
THE COURIER

Everett threw open the window to his office, seeking air. The overwhelming smell from outside nauseated him immediately. No breeze in the world was worth that. He slammed the window shut with a vengeance, turning back to face Nathan. This was not a conversation he wanted to participate in.

"So, what are you saying, Everett?" Nathan asked the question pointedly.

"I'm just saying too many lives have been lost already," he said sadly. "That's all. I don't want to risk any more."

"So you don't want me to get over to Bolivar for a few photos? Is that what you're saying?"

Everett shrugged. He knew the story. At Bolivar Point, forty-six people had drowned. That wasn't the real story. The real story hadn't been written yet. More than a hundred others were saved in the lighthouse there. That would make a killer story.

If he were interested in stories.

"So I shouldn't go?" Nathan asked, shaking his head in amazement.

"Not this time," Everett said, sitting down and staring placidly out of the window. "Not this time."

Nathan left the office in a huff, not even trying to hide his anger. Everett didn't blame him. This was the news business. They were supposed to be tracking down stories.

Everett Maxwell didn't feel like doing that anymore.

WEDNESDAY, SEPTEMBER 12, 1900, 5:18 P.M.
THE MURPHY VILLA

"Mother." Gillian heard her son's strong voice, and her face lit up. Brent was home. She needed him, today of all days. It seemed like an eternity since the storm. She had done little but care for strangers and pray her husband would return safely. For days, she had slept little and worked much. But Brent was home now. Just having him here would make everything all right.

Gillian rounded the corner into the entryway, prepared to throw her arms around him. She stopped just short when she found that he was not alone. A young woman, probably near twenty, stood beside him. Her long, brown hair was matted, and her white nurse's uniform appeared badly stained. *Still, she's a pretty young thing.* Next to her stood a rather weak-looking young woman, barely a teen, if that.

"Mother," Brent said with a smile. "This is Emma." He gestured to the young woman in the uniform. "And this is her sister, Sadie."

"Emma. Sadie." She repeated the words, extending her hand toward the older of the two. "How do you do?" It hardly seemed a fair question, since they both looked so weary and worn.

"I'm ... fine," came Emma's forced response, though Gillian noticed her eyes shifting toward the floor.

"Mother," Brent said firmly, "Emma and her sister are needing a place to stay."

Gillian's eyes lifted and looked into his. *So that's what this is all about. More wayfaring strangers to be cared for.* "But ..." she tried to interject. Her mind began to calculate how they might accomplish the feat. *The guest bedroom is already taken, and every square inch of space in the parlor is being used too. That only leaves my room and Brent's.*

"Do you remember me telling you about the girl I carried all the way to the hospital the night of the storm?" he continued.

She nodded. "Of course."

"Well, this is the young woman and her sister," he said.

"Yes, of course," Gillian said, her heart softening immediately.

"Have you had any word about your parents?" she asked carefully, wishing at once she could take the words back by the look on the young woman's face.

"Yes, Mother," Brent said, looking at her with concern. "And, um ... I'm, uh ... I'm afraid the news wasn't very good."

"Oh, my dear," Gillian said, wrapping her arms around Emma first, and then Sadie. "I'm so sorry." Tears began to flow as she looked Emma in the eye. "You'll stay here with us, of course. You will take my room. You and your sister are welcome to it for as long as you need."

"Oh, we couldn't do that," Emma said nervously.

"Pooh. Of course you can," Gillian said stubbornly. "I won't take no for an answer."

Emma smiled in gratitude. "Thank you so much, Mrs. Murphy," Emma said, her tear-stained eyes looking up momentarily. "I don't know where else we could have gone. There's no one left ... no one."

"Well, we're here," Gillian said matter-of-factly, reaching for the young woman's hand and squeezing it tightly. "And life is going to go on. Just you wait and see. Now, are you hungry?"

Wednesday, September 12, 1900, 5:20 p.m.
The Murphy Villa

"Am I hungry?" Emma's stomach rumbled at the very thought of food. For days, she had eaten little but tea and crackers. "I'm starving."

"What can I get for you then?" Mrs. Murphy asked, looking her squarely in the eye. "I've got a bit of ham left over, but not much in the way of bread. I do have yeast for rolls, but that would take some time. Oh, and I have a large kettle of beans cooking for the others. Pintos. Does that sound at all tempting? And I believe Pearl could rustle up some cornbread, if you're interested."

"Oh, yes ma'am," she said, trying not to sound too

excited. Just the thought of hot food made her feel better already.

"Now," Mrs. Murphy said, scrutinizing her. "Let's see about getting you into some decent clothes."

Emma looked down at her nurse's uniform in shame. Once crisp and white, it was now a dingy gray with splatterings of dried blood everywhere. "I'm so sorry," she mumbled, shrugging.

"Don't give it another thought," the older woman said with a smile. "Just follow me upstairs. I daresay I've got something that will fit you; that is, if you don't mind this old woman's taste in clothing."

Nothing was further from Emma's mind at the moment. Just getting into clean clothes would be great.

"And what about a bath?"

"A bath? That would be heavenly." She couldn't help but notice Brent's grin as she squealed her response. She was suddenly embarrassed, though she didn't know why. He had been very kind to her, to be sure, but beyond that, there was nothing in their relationship to warrant embarrassment.

"Pearl," Mrs. Murphy called out.

A large black woman entered from the kitchen, her hands loaded with a mixing bowl and spoon. She stirred frantically as she spoke. "Yes, Miss Gillian?"

"Pearl, this is Miss Emma, and this little one is her sister, Sadie." Pearl's eyes shot back and forth between Brent and Emma, as if trying to figure out the relationship between them. "She'll be needing a bath drawn with fresh towels. Oh, and be sure to pull out some of my honeysuckle soap. I'm sure that would make it nice for her."

"Yes'm." Pearl turned back toward the kitchen, returning moments later empty-handed. She made her way up the stairs, shooing children right and left as she went. Her voice sounded firm but kind as she scolded the youngsters. Emma's eyes followed her, curiously.

"Pearl's been here since I was a young boy," Brent explained. "She practically raised me."

"Well, where was I, I'd like to know?" his mother asked incredulously.

"To be honest, usually off at some tea party or something," he said with a laugh.

For a moment, Emma thought the older woman might become angry, but was relieved to hear her chuckle the awaited response, "You're so right. Well, I'm making up for it now."

"Yes, you are," he said, slipping his arm around her waist. "And we're all grateful. Aren't we, Emma?"

"Oh yes, very," she said, embarrassed at how childish she suddenly sounded.

"Well, come with me then, child," Mrs. Murphy said, taking her by the hand and heading up the stairs. "Let's get you into a warm bath. I've got some wonderful bath salts, imported from Italy. I'm sure they will help relax you."

They made their way down the long, dark hallway with birch paneling and stenciled plaster.

Moments later, with Sadie sleeping soundly in the large four-poster bed, Emma practically melted into the yellow-tiled tub. She did all she could to put the events of the last few days behind her. Her eyes drifted shut as the memories ran over her like a flood. They were mixed with the scent of burning flesh and honeysuckle, an eerie combination. She drifted down into the warm water, letting it wash over her. The honeysuckle scent grew stronger, and the fires from outside all but washed away as she began to fade into the mist of a wonderful dream.

"I'm so proud of you, Emma."

"Mama!" Her eyes flew open instinctively. "Mama?" She looked around anxiously. Nothing.

"Honey, are you okay?" Mrs. Murphy's voice over the gentle tapping on the door convinced Emma she had only been dreaming.

"I ... I'm fine," she whispered, then dissolved into an ocean of tears.

Twenty-Three

*B*rent awoke to the inviting smell of food cooking downstairs. He turned over in his bed, amazed to find that the sun was up. "What time is it?" he mumbled to himself, reaching for his pocket watch on the bedside table. He squinted, finding it hard to see past the streams of sunlight pouring in through the large bay window.

Nine-fifteen. I've been sleeping for nearly eleven hours. That's unheard of. It's ...

It was completely wonderful. He rolled back over in the bed, stretching. His mother had been kind enough to let him get some much-needed rest. Not that he had anything pressing to get out of bed for.

Emma.

Brent sat up suddenly, remembering. *Emma is here.* She had slept in the room just across the hall. *How could I have forgotten?*

He staggered out of the bed, stopping to look at himself in the mirror. His hair stood up all over his head. He did his best to comb it down, but it was hopeless.

Slipping into a pair of slacks, he headed downstairs. Familiar voices rose and fell from the breakfast table.

Glancing into the kitchen, he could hardly believe his eyes. Emma stood at the kitchen sink next to his mother, peeling potatoes.

"How long have you lived on the island, Mrs. Murphy?" she was asking.

"Oh, honey. I've lived here all my life," his mother responded with a laugh. "I've got sand in my blood, I daresay. And my husband has the railroad in his. We had this house built when Brent was just a boy, not much older than Sadie."

"It's a lovely home," Emma said, looking about. "Very stately. And so beautiful. I just love homes fashioned with that lovely new gingerbread trim. The large gallery out front is my favorite part. Our home has ... had ... no porch at all. It was just a simple wood-framed home built by my father's parents years ago."

Brent listened from a distance, drinking in her words. She liked it here.

"What about you?" Gillian asked. "How long have you lived here?"

"Oh ..." Emma responded, reaching up to wipe her brow with the back of her hand. "My father brought us here when I was just about three or so."

"Really? What sort of work does your father do?" Mrs. Murphy asked. Just as quickly as the words were spoken, she clamped her hand over her mouth, ashamed. "Oh, I'm so sorry, honey. Really, I am. I meant to say, 'What sort of work did he do?'"

Brent cleared his throat loudly, deliberately interrupting their conversation. He couldn't help but notice the tears in Emma's eyes as she glanced his way.

"Good morning, sleepyhead," his mother said with a grin. "I was beginning to think you were going to sleep all day."

"Oh you did, did you?" he asked, reaching across her to pick up a piece of raw potato and popping it into his mouth.

"Don't do that," she said, swatting his hand away.

"Why not?"

"It's not good for you. They're not cooked."

"I thought it tasted a little funny," he joked, swallowing it. "But something sure smells good. What's cooking down here?"

"I've got biscuits and gravy left over from this morning," his mother said, reaching to open the oven door. "They've been sitting awhile waiting on you. Might be a bit stiff."

"That won't be a problem, I assure you," he said, barely taking his eyes off of Emma to look at the food. "I'm famished."

"What about coffee?" Emma asked. "Would you like a cup?"

"Oh, Brent's not much of a coffee drinker," his mother began.

"I'd love a cup," he interrupted, looking intently at Emma. *There's something different about her this morning. What is it?*

"You drink it black or with a little sugar?" she asked, filling the cup. Their eyes met in an extended gaze, so extended that the cup overflowed. "Oh, I'm so sorry," she said, reaching to wipe the table.

"That's okay." He smiled in her direction, unsure of the emotions now gripping him. He barely knew this woman, and yet ...

There was undeniably something there. Suddenly, everything began to make perfect sense to him. He hadn't just come back to Galveston Island to face his father.

He had come to meet Emma.

THURSDAY, SEPTEMBER 13, 1900, 11:46 A.M.
THE COURIER

"So, they're coming, are they?" Everett said, pacing around his office. He had just received the news. Press members from all over the country were descending on Galveston Island. Many had already arrived, but there was one team in particular that drew his interest.

It would draw Brent Murphy's too.

Journalists from Joseph Pulitzer's paper, *The New York World*, were set to arrive in the next few days. They would be sharing headquarters with the Red Cross just up The Strand at 25th Street. Everett couldn't help but feel a twinge of jealousy as he thought about those big-city reporters and their take on Galveston's disaster. They were sure to take advantage of the situation, sure to ...

They were sure to do exactly what he had done—reach for the best, the most tantalizing headline possible. That was their business, after all.

They would certainly have their hands full, sharing space with the American Red Cross. Clara Barton was due to arrive on the island at any moment. From what Everett had heard, she would arrive with plans to start a new orphanage. Now *that* would be newsworthy. Many of the island's surviving children were still at the infirmary, waiting for food and necessary supplies, but most, sadly, had perished in the floodwaters, their tiny bodies unable to fight off the sting of death.

Traffic from the mainland had been steady and strong as boats made their way across the bay. Supplies were coming in, though not in abundance. Local merchants, moved by the situation, had already begun to offer goods at manufacturer's costs, but their lack was overwhelming. Would Galveston Island ever crawl back up out of the mire and stand to her feet again?

Everett gazed out of his window one last time before heading down to the pressroom. *There's only so much one editor can do about that.* Right now, it was just a matter of piecing things back together—one life at a time.

THURSDAY, SEPTEMBER 13, 1900, 3:38 P.M.
THE ACADEMY

"Miss Henri, what you gonna do?" Big John asked, looking at her intently. "You cain't leave the island. No ma'am."

"What do you mean?"

"There's little 'uns ever'where who's lookin' fer a place to stay now," he argued. "They done lost everything, most of 'em. They ain't got no ma or pa, and no place to go. They cain't stay here forever." He waved his arm toward the academy, still nearly full to bursting with refugees. "The sooner they get out of here, the better."

"What am I supposed to do about that?" Henrietta asked nervously. "I'm just one person. Besides, my family needs me back in Virginia." Her heart began to pound. It wasn't that they needed her, she suddenly realized. She needed them.

"But these little 'uns need ya more," John argued. "And you know it. You got to listen to the Lord, Miss Henri! He's tellin' you what to do now."

"John, I really don't think we need to be talking about this right now."

No sooner were the words spoken than a youngster attached herself to Henrietta's skirttails. "Miss Henri," the little one spoke up excitedly. "We get food today, real food!"

"Yes, Amelia," she spoke in response. "They're bringing in food from the mainland today. But it will still be awhile, so why don't you go and play with the other children?"

"I don't want to, Miss Henri," Amelia said, tugging tighter at her skirt. "I want to stay with you."

Henrietta sighed deeply, finally reaching down to scoop the six-year-old waif into her arms. The storm had been cruel to this little one. It had taken every family member from her: mother, father, and older sisters. She was all that was left of what had once been a well-to-do family on the island's east end.

"Do you believe in heaven, Miss Henri?" The youngster's blue eyes gazed into hers.

"Of course I do," she said as she instinctively wrapped her arms around the child.

"My mommy's there now," Amelia said with a sigh. "And Poppy. He's looking down at me right now." She began to wave her arms frantically toward the sky.

"Stop it, Amelia," Henrietta scolded. "Don't do that."

"Why not?" The youngster said, a tear now running down her freckled cheek.

"Yes," John echoed. "Why not, Miss Henri?"

"It's just so foolish to wave to the sky like that," Henri whispered, feeling the inevitable lump in her throat. Somewhere up there, Lilly Mae was probably waving back, just as frantically. *No, I won't let myself think about it.* "We must try to be brave," she said firmly, looking at Amelia. "And not worry. Everything will work out. I know it will."

The little girl ran off with a newfound smile on her face.

"See there, Miss Henri," John said with a grin. "You has a way with the chilluns. They need ya."

"Tell me, then," she said with a huff. "Tell me what I'm supposed to do."

"Only the Lord can tell ya that." He broke into a long resounding laugh. "But I got a sneakin' suspicion it's got somethin' to do with that orphanage you came from."

"St. Mary's? St. Mary's is gone. Washed out to sea."

"So she is," he said, suddenly looking serious. "Which is 'zactly why somebody has got to stick around to rebuild her."

THURSDAY, SEPTEMBER 13, 1900, 6:59 P.M.
THE MURPHY VILLA

Emma made her way through the maze of people out onto the front porch of the Murphy's large Victorian home. She leaned against the railing, deep in thought.

What do I do now, Lord?

It was more than a simple prayer. If she didn't receive an answer quickly, no telling where she and Sadie might end up. And yet, God had already provided a place, at least for the time being. Not just a place, but a home on Broadway. Emma had envied the people in the large Victorian homes since childhood. Now she stood along-side people of every race and social status in one of the island's finest homes. It was ironic, tragic.

Emma's eyes traveled up and down Broadway, trying to absorb what she saw. Many of the homes in this area had taken in water, but most were still standing strong and firm.

"... having done all, to stand."

The scripture raced through her mind, startling her,

but where had it come from? Ah yes. Her mother had shared it with her just a few short days ago, when she was struggling with her decision to work at the hospital.

"When you've done all you can do," her mother had said with a smile, "then you have to stand firm. It's really all you can do."

Emma looked at the houses once again. They were battered and bruised by the storm, as she was, and yet they stood as a testament to the wonder of good construction. They were strong.

She would be too.

Twenty-Four

Brent made his way out onto the front gallery, a cup of coffee firmly clutched in his right hand. Off in the distance, the smoke from the fires rose above the city, but even that couldn't hold his attention now. A lovely young nurse by the name of Emma stood at the far end of the porch, completely unaware of his presence.

"I thought I might find you out here," he said, walking to her. She turned to face him, her eyes puffy and red, a sure sign she had spent the night in tears. Not that he blamed her; she had lost so much. Brent's heart skipped a beat as their eyes locked. "This is for you." He handed her the cup, almost dropping it in the process.

"Oh, thank you." She took it willingly. "I need this."

"I had a feeling. Are you sure you should be out here? The smoke is awful."

"I know, but I feel like I'm suffocating inside. I have to get out." She began to cough, using a handkerchief to cover her mouth and nose from the smell. "I won't stay out long, I promise."

He gave her a deliberate smile. "I'm just looking out for you."

"Thanks again. I don't know what I would have done without you these past few days. I really don't."

He smiled again.

A silence stood between them for a moment before Emma spoke quietly. "I was just standing here trying to decide whether or not I should go back in to the hospital this morning." She glanced off in the distance.

"Are you sure you're ready for that?" Brent asked softly. *She needs to stay here. She's not ready to face the madness of the hospital. Not yet, anyway.*

"They need me." Her voice quivered. "That's why I went into nursing in the first place. I need to be needed."

He gazed at her tenderly. *Have I ever met anyone this marvelous before?* "A wonderful motive," he assured her. "No one can fault you there."

"I've always wanted to help people," she said with a shrug. "But I never thought it would be like this. Sometimes I'm not sure I've done the right thing."

"How can you say that?" he asked, amazed. "If anything, this whole thing should have convinced you that you made the right decision."

"How do you know what I'm thinking or feeling? How do you know anything about me?" Her words were suddenly curt.

He responded softly. "I'm sorry," he said. "I'm the last person on the planet to give anyone else advice on what they ought to do with their life."

"Why is that?"

He shrugged impatiently. "Never mind. We can talk about something else."

"No, come on," she said, her face suddenly lighting

up. "I'm sorry. Really. I'll talk if you will." She coughed again, covering her mouth and nose with the handker-chief. "But not out here. Could we go back inside?"

"I hoped you might say that." He gestured toward the door, following behind her as she made her way inside. *I'd follow you anywhere.*

"What would you like to talk about?" he asked, as they made their way into the kitchen to sit at the table.

Emma smiled. "I'd like to know what you were doing off in New York, for one thing, when you have such a wonderful family right here."

"Ouch." Brent's heart twisted inside of him as he looked up and saw his mother standing just a few feet away peel-ing potatoes. *That's a little personal, don't you think?*

"I'm sorry," Emma said, obviously sensing his frus-tration. "It's none of my business." Her cheeks turned crimson.

"No, it's okay."

"It's just that my family has always meant every-thing to me," Emma said, tears welling up in her eyes. "I couldn't imagine ever being away from them. I ... I still can't."

"I love my family," Brent argued. "I do."

"Well then, how could you leave them? I don't think I could ever ... I mean, I don't think I could have ever ..." The tears began to tumble down her cheeks. "None of this matters now. There is no family for me anymore. No one but Sadie, I mean."

"Don't you have grandparents? Aunts and uncles?" Brent asked, taking her hand and pressing it into his own. His heart felt like it would break for her. Had he really only known this incredible woman a few days? It seemed more like a lifetime.

"My dad's parents are somewhere in Chicago. My mother's parents were too—until the fire."

"I'm so sorry, Emma." He paused, gripping her hand tightly, not wanting to let go.

"I just don't know if I'm strong enough to get through all of this by myself," she whispered, leaning her head down until her forehead rested on their clutched hands.

"Maybe you won't have to," he said, lifting her chin.

"What do you mean?"

"I mean," he said, "you and Sadie can stay here as long as you like. Even after the others have gone. My mother loves having you here. Don't you, Mom?" He turned to gaze at his mother, anxiously awaiting her response.

"Of course," she said, reaching to hand Emma a clean handkerchief.

Brent tried to sound reassuring as he spoke. "Just relax and stay put for a while. Don't worry about the future. Each day has enough grief of its own."

"That's a scripture," Emma said, dabbing at her eyes.

"Is it?" he said, his forehead wrinkling as he thought about it. "Maybe I learned something in Sunday school, after all."

"You were a Sunday school kid?"

"Of course. But I was a little monster—at least that's what I've been told."

"That's hard to imagine."

"A holy terror," he said with a laugh. "Or so they tell me. A lot like some of these kids my mom has taken in." A couple of youngsters chose that very moment to race across the room, chasing one another. They bumped into Emma, nearly spilling the cup of coffee.

"Sorry, miss." Off they ran, their laughter and chatter almost contagious.

"If I ever get married, I'm going to have daughters," Brent said, looking at them. He couldn't help but notice his mother clear her throat loudly.

"Oh, you're so sure, are you?" Emma argued with a smile.

For the first time in days, Brent saw a smile cross her lips. "Well, pretty sure. I figure girls are easier than boys. What about you?" His mother cleared her throat again, but Emma forged ahead with her answer.

"Me? I'm probably never going to get married, at least not now. I've got Sadie to think about. She needs me."

"Of course she does, but don't give up completely on the idea of finding the right person," Brent said, grinning at her. "I'm sure some dashingly handsome fellow is going to come along and snatch you up."

"Well then," she said playfully. "I'll have boys. Four boys."

"That's funny," Brent said softly.

"What?"

"Oh nothing," he said, feeling his hand begin to tremble a little. "It's just that I've always wanted four kids too."

"But girls. You want girls," Emma said, pulling her hand away. "So that settles it."

"Settles what?"

"You're not the dashingly handsome fellow who's going to sweep me off my feet," she said with a laugh. "Couldn't be."

"I wouldn't be so sure," Brent said, reaching for her hand once again. This time, for some reason, he couldn't seem to let go.

FRIDAY, SEPTEMBER 14, 1900, 7:51 A.M.
THE MURPHY VILLA

Gillian's eyes shifted back and forth from Brent to Emma. They were lost in conversation, completely unaware of the fact that she had entered the gallery. They seemed so completely unlike each other, and yet ...

In so many ways they complemented each other. The last couple of days had convinced her that Emma's visit here was far more than coincidental. In some unique way, the storm had brought Brent and Emma together.

Her heart began to break within her, as she thought about Douglas. *Where are you? Will you come back to us?* Their marriage had already weathered so many storms. Brent's article in the *Courier* had pretty much captured the story: the tale of how she had longed for a child but couldn't have one, the reality of adopting a little boy who turned out to be such a difficulty.

Had he really been that difficult, that rebellious? Looking across the room at him now, all Gillian saw was a well-mannered young man who seemed to always look out for the interest of others. *He's so wonderful, even if he's not our own flesh and blood. Some things run deeper than that.* But would Douglas ever forgive her for not being able to bear him the son he had longed for, someone to carry on the Murphy name? Someone to pick up where he left off when he retired from the railroad? Someone who loved the things he loved and hated the things he hated? Would he always hold her responsible?

"Come home to us, Douglas," she whispered, "and see your son. See what an amazing man he is. See what others see in him. See what I see in him." Turning her head away from Brent and Emma, Gillian immediately dissolved into a haze of silent tears, tears for a son who needed a father and tears for her own broken heart. An unbearable ache gripped her. *Lord, bring my husband home to me. I'm not too proud to beg, Father. I need him. I love him. In spite of everything, I will always love him.*

FRIDAY, SEPTEMBER 14, 1900, 9:52 A.M.
THE COURIER

"Miss Barton, it's so wonderful to meet you." Everett extended his hand in the direction of the elderly woman. She gripped it firmly. Even for a woman in her late seventies, she had quite a grip.

"How was your trip down from Washington?"

"Long and extremely tiring," she responded, taking a seat across from his desk. "Getting across from the mainland was quite a chore. Folks all the way up to Houston are fighting to get here—but I guess I'm not telling you anything you don't already know."

"It's going to take some time to get everything in place," he responded. "But I'm so glad you're here now. How are you, Miss Barton?"

"I'm fine," she said, her face never losing its serious edge. "We've settled in and are preparing to set up a temporary office to work out of. We're sharing headquarters with *The New York World.*"

"So I hear," Everett said. "Right here on The Strand."

"The folks at that newspaper have been so kind," she said.

Sure. Since when have big-city reporters been kind?

"They've agreed that all contributions the paper receives will go toward our efforts at the Red Cross."

Everett shook his head in disbelief. "Really?"

"Really. And I plan to take advantage of this opportunity for the children of Galveston."

"That's very kind of you," Everett said with a nod. "So,

223

with all those newspapermen over at your place, what brings you here, to the *Courier*?"

"Those gentlemen aren't Galvestonians," she replied. "You are. You know this island inside and out, at least from what I've read in your paper."

"You've read our little paper?" he asked, feeling his lips turn up in a smile.

"Absolutely. And I particularly loved that story about the little orphan girl. What was her name again?"

"Lilly Mae."

"Yes," Clara said, looking him in the eye. "She's the reason I'm here. I, and I'm speaking for the Red Cross here, want to establish an orphanage for the storm's smallest victims."

Everett nodded. "Much needed."

"We'll also need lumber to help people rebuild homes," she said, jotting down notes. "But that will take money, which is one of the reasons I've come to you."

Everett swallowed hard. *Money? She thinks I have access to money?*

"I had an idea about raising funds," she continued. "We'll take dozens of photographs of the devastation and sell them."

"Sell them?" *A novel idea.*

"Naturally. I'll be speaking at a conference on the East Coast in a few weeks. I'll take photographs with me. We'll sell them anywhere and everywhere. Once people see the destruction with their own eyes, I have no doubt they will be filled with compassion for you Galvestonians. What has happened here is simply unbelievable."

Everett nodded in agreement. "Let's pray it never happens again."

"Mr. Maxwell, that is the prayer of the entire country. Now, tell me more about that young whippersnapper, the one who did the write-up on the little girl. One of these days, I'd like to meet him in person."

"Brent Murphy?"

"Yes, I believe that was his name."

"Mr. Murphy is on a bit of a sabbatical for a few days, but should be back in the office before you leave town."

"Wonderful." She gave him an impish grin. "I'll wait till he's back at work to come in for a visit, then. Trust me, Brent Murphy is one young man I'd like to meet while his hands are still wet with ink."

FRIDAY, SEPTEMBER 14, 1900, 11:45 A.M.
GALVESTON ISLAND

Henri paced back and forth across the beach, sand between her toes, and the now-familiar smell of putrid smoke rising to her nostrils. She choked back the wave of nausea that suddenly swept over her.

"This doesn't make sense," she said to herself, stopping to review the situation in her mind once again. "I need to go home. The very last thing I need to be doing is staying here and ..."

Helping.

There are children everywhere who need help. And, according to Big John, I have a mission here. Maybe I'm not alone. Clara Barton is here now. With both of us on the same team, who knows what might happen?

"But Lord," she argued aloud in prayer, "this is ridiculous. I'm so young."

Immediately she was reminded of the biblical story of Timothy, a young man who was used mightily of God. His age hadn't been a hindrance.

"But I'm not good at leading, and they're going to need leaders," she argued aloud.

I have called you. I will equip you.

For the first time in ages, Henrietta Mullins heard the Lord's voice—and she wept with sheer relief.

FRIDAY, SEPTEMBER 14, 1900, 10:22 P.M.
THE MURPHY VILLA

Emma entered the Victorian home, completely exhausted. It had been a long walk from the hospital, one she did not care to repeat anytime soon.

"Just couldn't stay away, could you?" She looked up into Brent's eyes. They were kind, compassionate.

"No," she said wearily, feeling every muscle in her body ache. "I had to go back and see what could be done. Your mother said she didn't mind keeping an eye on Sadie."

"Sadie's fast asleep," Brent said. "Has been ever since I got home from the paper. I think she's enjoying her stay here."

"There's much to enjoy here," Emma said. No sooner were the words out than she realized what she had said. "I mean," she stammered, "it's such a lovely home, and your mother is so kind."

"Is that all?" he asked, taking hold of her hand gently. She couldn't help but notice the ink under his nails, even in the warm, soft glow of the lamplight. Emma felt her heart begin to flutter. Their eyes met for a brief moment.

"No. That's not all," she said, her eyes shifting to the ground. "I, uh ... I have enjoyed getting to know you too, Mr. Murphy."

"Mr. Murphy?" He let go of her hand abruptly. Emma looked at him curiously.

"What did I say?"

"I'm not Mr. Murphy, that's all," Brent said with a shrug. "I'll never live up to that name. Trust me."

"There's more to a man than his name," she said, reaching for his hand once again. "And, at least as far as I'm concerned, you are a remarkable man. You risked your life to save my sister. You've given of yourself several times over to help others in need. If that's not a man, I don't know what is."

FRIDAY, SEPTEMBER 14, 1900, 10:53 P.M.
THE MURPHY VILLA

She called me a man. For the first time in years, someone has referred to me as something other than a child. In my heart, I know that I have become a man my father could be proud of. All that separated us seems so nonsensical now, in light of all that has happened. When he comes back ...

Brent looked up from his tablet, scratching his head. "If you will come home," he whispered, "I will make you proud."

Twenty-Five

Brent tossed and turned, the victim of another night of terrifying dreams:

Standing alone at the station, a fog began to roll in. Brent gazed to the right and then the left, searching for his father's train. It should come in anytime now, just as it had done so many times in the past. At that moment, it pulled into the station, emptying its cars of all passengers. They waved excitedly as they greeted their loved ones. Brent waited alone, hoping, praying. His father was nowhere to be seen.

"Do you know a Mr. Douglas Murphy?" He posed the question to a lady in a rather large, awkward-looking hat. "He's tall with black hair." She shook her head and marched off in the opposite direction.

Brent's heart raced against his chest. He ran up and down the tracks, his face pressed against the window of each car. His father had to be on board. Surely he's coming home to us.

Waking with a start, Brent realized he was soaked in

sweat. *It's hot in here, but not that hot.* He shot out of bed, making his way to the window. There he gazed out into the darkness. Utter darkness. For some reason, Brent couldn't seem to get the lump out of his throat. Tears began to course down his cheeks.

Lord, are you there? I don't even know if you can hear me anymore, Lord, but I need you. My mother needs you. My father ...

The lump grew so large he could barely swallow.

My father needs you, Lord. Watch over him. Bring him home again. Help us to be the family that you want us to be. I forgive him, Father. I forgive him for all of the times he hurt me, for all of the times he ignored me. Bring him back to us, Lord.

The tears flowed like rain. Brent stood in the window until the sun crept up and swallowed the darkness. He prayed as never before and wept for the father he had never even realized he loved—until now.

SATURDAY, SEPTEMBER 15, 1900, 5:20 A.M.
THE MURPHY VILLA

Emma awoke in a pool of tears after a heartbreaking dream. "Mama, I need you," she cried out, still half-asleep. "Sadie needs you."

Her sister stirred in the bed next to her. "Emma?"

Now fully awake, she responded with trembling voice. "Yes, baby?"

"I miss them too," Sadie whispered softly. "So very much." Emma reached to take hold of her. Together, they cried openly, unashamed.

"We're going to wake the others," Sadie said finally.

A gentle rap on the door confirmed her words. "Everything okay in there?" Brent's voice immediately consoled her, though Emma couldn't begin to explain why her heart suddenly leaped within her.

"Yes," she answered.

"I'm not sure I believe you," he said firmly. "Can I open the door?"

Emma scurried for a robe, wrapping the sash tightly around her middle. "Just a minute."

The door opened just a crack. "I just want to make sure you're really all right."

"I am." She stepped out into the hall.

"I thought I heard crying in there," Brent said, holding up a kerosene lamp. He moved in her direction until the light shone on her face. "I was afraid of that. Are you alright?"

Emma stared into his eyes. *Red. Just like mine probably are.* "Looks like I'm not the only one," she whispered. "You've been crying too."

"Who, me?" he asked, feigning innocence. "Nah. I just, uh ... got something in my eye."

"Yeah. Mine too." Her tears began to fall again. Emma hung her head in shame. It wasn't right to grieve openly like this, especially not in front of someone like Brent, who had already been so kind, and who was going through so much himself. "I'm so sorry," she whispered.

He set the lamp down and wrapped his arms around her. "You go ahead and cry, Emma. Don't let me stop you. Don't let anyone stop you."

His arms were exactly what she needed. Emma's head fell to his chest, and his fingers stroked her hair gently as he spoke words of comfort and reassurance. *I needed arms to hold me, Lord. Thank you so much for sending him when you did. He's here at exactly the right moment.* Emma wept until she could weep no more. From out of the room Sadie came, pressing herself into the middle of their locked embrace. When Emma finally felt courageous enough to look up into Brent's eyes, she was amazed to find them full of tears. Even in the soft glow of the lamplight, she saw herself in their reflection.

SATURDAY, SEPTEMBER 15, 1900, 9:10 A.M.
GALVESTON ISLAND

Henrietta paced up and down the patch of land that had been St. Mary's Orphanage. To her right, the infirmary still stood, though it had certainly suffered its share of damage during the storm. The dormitories were gone, the chapel had completely disappeared—everything she had known and loved had been swept out to sea. All that remained was a huge heap of rubble to her left. Most of the debris appeared unfamiliar, probably from houses and buildings miles away. Sofas, mattresses, chimney stones, and windowpanes were all wedged together with a wall of sand holding them in place. It might be days, even weeks, before anyone could get to this mess. But what could she do?

Henrietta's heart ached to start right away, to begin the building process again. There were children everywhere who would need a place to stay. The familiar dirge of the island's victims filled her ears again:

> *"Dere's no rain to wet you,*
> *O, yes, I want to go home.*
> *Dere's no sun to burn you,*
> *O, yes, I want to go home;*
> *O, push along, believers,*
> *O, yes, I want to go home;*
> *O, yes, I want to go home."*

The words cut to her heart, and for the very first time since arriving on Galveston island, Henrietta Mullins realized she did not want to go home. She whispered a prayer of thanks as she headed to find others who could assist her with the momentous task ahead.

If you're asking me to stay, Lord, I'll need help. Lots of it.

SATURDAY, SEPTEMBER 15, 2:02 P.M.
THE TRAIN STATION

Gillian stood in the crowded lobby of the train station, straining to see. *They must have some word for me today, Lord. If he doesn't come back soon, I don't know what I'll do.* She held her lace handkerchief over her nose, trying to distract herself from the stench that hung like a mist in the air as she made her way to the familiar counter.

"Can I help you, Miz Murphy?"

She turned to face Daniel, a small black man who worked as a porter for the GH&H. He had served as mediator for the past few days as she quizzed anyone and everyone about her husband's whereabouts. "Is there any word yet?" she asked breathlessly.

"We received a telegraph just this morning," he said with a smile. "From the conductor on your husband's run. Said they ran into trouble trying to get back on the island the night of the storm, so they backed up all the way to Texas City. They've been put up at the station on that end for a week, from what I hear, but there's word they're sending them over by boat, now that the bodies ..." Here he paused, looking down. "Um, now that the debris has been cleared from the bay, and the piers have been rebuilt."

"So they're ... they're ..." Gillian could hardly speak, for fear the words would curse the outcome.

"Now, we don't have any specifics, ma'am," Daniel said hesitantly.

"But I have every reason to hope ... ?"

"Oh, yes ma'am." He smiled broadly, showing off large white teeth. "Praise God. We all have reason to hope—even in the middle of this mess." Daniel turned to respond to another person, a nervous-looking young woman clutching a child at her side.

Gillian muttered a quick "Thank you" before heading out of the station. As she walked in the direction of the villa, her heart soared. *Is it possible, Lord? Have you already answered my prayer?* Her spirit sang as she made her way through the mud-caked filth toward home. For the first time in ages, she actually felt some sense of relief. The past few days had been unbelievably difficult, but Gillian had borne them well.

Most of her houseguests had left this morning, many opting to head to the mainland, now that the journey could be made without fear of peril. Still others had decided to return to the remains of their homes, hoping to rebuild. A handful remained at the Murphy villa, but they planned to move on within a few days. Gillian's life would soon return to normal.

Oh, but I dread that. I'll simply die if things go back to the way they were. I'm not the person I was—or the person I thought I was, at any rate. Over the past several days, Gillian had come to know herself—not as the haughty woman others in society perceived her to be, but as the compassionate woman she had become. *I like who I really am. Now, if only Douglas would return. I would be completely whole again.*

Everett made his way up The Strand, taking inventory. *The confectionery window is out. Tables and chairs have all but disappeared. That one will take a lot of work.* He made his way to the emporium, relieved to see that it was back up and running. Most of the businesses in this district had managed to pull themselves up by their bootstraps and get back to work.

"That's what this island needs," he said aloud, trying to convince himself. "To get back to work. It takes courage. Tenacity. We've got plenty of that in us."

Though he spoke of courage, he felt little as he made his way toward Market Street and Frankie Dolan's Barbershop. His heart twisted with anxiety. *Will it still be there? I haven't heard from Frankie since the day of the storm.*

He rounded the corner onto Market, shaking his head with disbelief as his gaze rested on the shop in question. A new sign adorned a shattered front window, but through it he could clearly see the answer to his question, and it caused his heart to jump for joy.

Brent returned home from a long day of helping with the seemingly never-ending disposal of bodies. His gut had wrenched at the sights and smells the day had offered him, but a long bath had served to wash most of it away. Now he stood clean and refreshed on the front porch, pacing anxiously. His eyes were fixed on the spot where Emma should arrive shortly. For some reason, his heart would not calm itself until she had returned.

"Brent, what are you doing out here?" Sadie's gentle voice brought him back to his senses.

"I, uh ... I was just ..."

"Enjoying the view?" she said, forcing a smile.

"Obviously not."

"Well, what then?" she asked. "You've been out here for nearly half an hour looking up and down the street for something, or should I say someone."

"Sadie."

"Admit it," she said with a laugh. "You're sweet on my sister."

"That's crazy," he responded. "We hardly know each other." Had it really only been a week? It seemed more like a lifetime. Every moment with Emma had been precious, and he found himself looking forward to seeing her more with each passing day.

Sadie spoke knowingly, a glimmer in her youthful eyes. "She's sweet on you."

"How do you know?" *Did I respond too quickly? Give myself away?*

"Girls talk." She erupted into a fit of laughter. "But I've said too much already."

"No, tell me more," he urged her.

Sadie shook her head, pointing off in the distance. "Not right now," she said, turning back toward the house. "Looks like you're about to have company."

Brent turned, his gaze falling on Emma. His spirits immediately lifted. "She's here," he whispered, and then headed down the stairs to greet her.

SATURDAY, SEPTEMBER 15, 1900, 9:15 P.M.
THE MURPHY VILLA

Emma walked out onto the front porch of the Murphy home for a few moments of quiet reflection before heading off to bed. Secretly, she had hoped Brent would join her, but he had fallen asleep on the sofa a few minutes earlier.

"Just as well," she said aloud. *Spending time with a young man, any young man, is the absolute last thing on earth I need to be doing right now. What I need is a plan—a plan that will provide enough money to rent a small house on the island. The Murphys have been wonderful so far, but surely they didn't mean that we should stay on here forever.* Most of the others had parted, headed for relatives or the mainland. Emma's heart raced as she contemplated the reality set before her. *It's just a matter of time before Sadie and I will be expected to move on as well.*

Twenty-Six

Brent awoke, thinking of Emma. The touch of his hand against her cheek, the scent of her hair as he comforted her. He rolled over in the bed, hoping not to lose the last of his dream. It had been amazing—amazing because it centered on her.

Emma awoke, thinking of her dream. It had been an odd mixture of sadness and joy. The faces of her parents still haunted her, and the ache remained in her heart. But there was something wonderful about the dream too, though she couldn't quite put her finger on it.

Brent.

Brent had been in the dream. He had been the one who had rescued her from darkness, from death. He had been the one to comfort and console her.

No. That isn't a dream.

That's reality.

SUNDAY, SEPTEMBER 16, 1900, 9:21 A.M.
THE MURPHY VILLA

Gillian moved through the house, doing what she could to clean up. Days of entertaining houseguests had left her beautiful home in less than perfect shape, but she really didn't mind. *It's been worth every bit of work.* And now, with Pearl gone off to church, she could finally set her sights on getting things in order once again. She made her way through the large parlor, picking up blankets and pillows. A loud knock at the door distracted her. The knocking was forceful, almost demanding.

"I'm coming, I'm coming," she called, brushing her loose, mussed hair behind her ears and wiping the flour off of her hands using the torn dishcloth which draped her waist. "Be patient."

Gillian pulled the door open, prepared to face another potential houseguest, another wayfaring stranger. What she found on the other side was nearly enough to knock the very breath out of her.

SUNDAY, SEPTEMBER 16, 1900, 9:58 A.M.
THE COURIER

"Here's how this is going to work," Everett said, addressing a room full of young reporters. "We're going to try a whole new approach to journalism."

"What do you mean?" Brent asked curiously. Everett couldn't help but notice the look of concern on his face and the faces of the others in the room.

"I mean, we're going to help each other out," Everett said firmly. "We're going to work for the good of the people. No more, no less."

"Are you kidding, Everett?" Nathan asked nervously.

"I mean, remind me if I'm wrong, but isn't journalism about beating the other guy to the punch?"

"Maybe that's the way it has worked in the past," Everett said, shaking his head. "And maybe that's the way to sell papers. I don't know. I just know that it doesn't work for me anymore."

"What are you saying, Everett?" Nathan asked. "Are you saying we shouldn't find stories?"

"Of course not. We're still all about stories," Everett responded. "But we've got to be careful not to cross any lines, not to step on anyone to get those stories." That was the part he couldn't stand, reporters rushing here and there, trampling over anyone and everyone to get the latest tidbit. It sickened him.

"I also want the *Courier* to be the first paper on the island to adequately cover the building of the new orphanage."

"New orphanage?" Brent suddenly sat up straight in his chair.

"Yep. That's the plan." Everett smiled in Brent's direction. "As most of you know, Clara Barton is here, along with a team from *The New York World*. We're going to link arms with them to get the necessary provisions for this orphanage. In other words, we're going to use this paper for the good of the island, and especially the island's children."

"How, exactly?" Nathan asked, still looking worried.

"The Red Cross has come up with a plan," Everett answered. "They're going to raise money by selling photographs of the storm's devastation."

Nathan lifted his Kodak in the air proudly. "I've got plenty of those," he practically shouted.

"Yes, but are you willing to part with them?" Everett asked. "I mean, are you willing to give them away?"

"I, uh ... I suppose," Nathan said, somewhat less enthusiastically.

"We've got to be bold here, because the need is so great," Everett continued. "And that's Pulitzer's plan too, I might add." He looked in Brent's direction.

"You mean to tell me the *World* is going to become a benefactor to the island?" he asked incredulously.

"That's right," Everett responded. "They've made an agreement with the Red Cross to donate any contributions they receive to that organization."

"Wow." Brent's one word said it all.

"Are you sure this isn't some sort of publicity stunt?" Nathan's question was an honest one.

"I don't think so," Everett said. "I really don't. Mrs. Barton is seventy-eight years old. But she's come here to help, in spite of her age. She's never been one to shirk her responsibilities, especially when people are hurting."

"That's true." Brent said. "I did a piece on Clara Barton when I was at the *World*."

"So I've been told," Everett said with a smile, "which is exactly why I'm going to be looking to you for some great stories. In fact, she's asked for you, personally."

"She has?"

"Yes. Now, I want you to travel with her: go where she goes, talk to her, get to know her."

"Are you sure?" Brent asked, looking around. "I've only been back a few days, and you've got a room full of other guys here waiting for a chance to—"

"I'm sure," Everett said in the firmest voice he could muster. "You're just the man for this job, Brent. Now get out there and get to work."

SUNDAY, SEPTEMBER 16, 1900, 10:30 A.M.
THE ACADEMY

"This may be a bit awkward," Henrietta said, "but I believe we should hold a service this morning."

"With all of these people?" Abigail asked. "How in the world ... ?"

"Let's gather them all together in the courtyard, and go from there."

"But who will speak?" Abigail looked shocked. "We haven't got a priest, or a pastor of any sort, for that matter."

"I think I've got just the man for the job," Henri said with a smile. "If he's willing, that is."

Yes. Big John would be just the right one for the job.

SUNDAY, SEPTEMBER 16, 1900, NOON
THE MURPHY VILLA

Gillian listened carefully as Douglas spoke. "We tried to cross over on Saturday night, but the winds were too strong. On Monday after the storm passed over, we tried again. The train hadn't quite reached the Bay Shore—about six miles out—when we got the answer to our question. The prairie was littered with debris and dead bodies. Hundreds of bodies. They lay there—so still and quiet—most stripped of all clothing, all dignity. What we saw horrified us. We had no way of knowing if our own loved ones might be among the deceased."

Here Douglas broke, his voice quivering with an undeniable passion. "I have to tell you, my heart just broke. I didn't know if you were dead or alive." He reached over and pulled Gillian to himself. "I've never been so scared in my life. I just kept praying, 'Lord, protect my family. Keep them safe.'"

"We were praying the same thing for you," Gillian said, pressing against her beloved husband as tightly as she could.

"My life is nothing," he said stubbornly, "but you and Brent ..." Here, he dissolved into a puddle of tears. "If anything had happened to either one of you, I don't know what I would have done."

"You ... you knew Brent was back on the island?"

"I knew. I'm so sorry I didn't tell you. I found out the day I left. Remember old man Spencer down at the station? He's been with the GH&H for years. He used to let Brent help clean the station as a child."

Gillian nodded. Of course she remembered him.

"Well," Douglas continued, "he told me he had seen Brent on the morning run from Houston to the island. He was there in the station when Brent stepped off the train. Our son was actually on the island when I left, Gillian. On the island when I left. And I never said a word. I didn't even try to find him."

Gillian gazed at her husband curiously. His eyes were misty with tears. Douglas had never shown this type of tenderness before. If the storm had brought this out in him, then there was truly something to be thankful for.

Sunday, September 16, 1900, 5:42 p.m.
The Murphy Villa

Brent entered the house, finding it amazingly quiet. Now that most of the houseguests had moved on, an eerie tranquility hung in the air. Regardless, it was still far better to be inside than out. With the odor that now seemed to permeate the island, Brent was more than happy to remain inside for hours at a time.

What a day it had been. His mind began to race back

to all that Everett had said. The renowned Clara Barton was on the island, a new orphanage was going up, and Joseph Pulitzer himself was coming for a visit. If that didn't beat all.

"Brent?" He looked up to see his mother standing in the stairwell. There was something rather mysterious about the look on her face, but he couldn't quite place it.

"Mother. I was beginning to think no one was home. Is Emma here?"

"Yes. She had a long morning at the hospital, but she's up in her room with Sadie, having a little nap now."

"That's nice." Somehow just thinking about Emma made him feel better. He looked at his mother once again, trying to read the expression on her face. "Is everything alright?"

"Yes, as a matter of fact it is," she said with a smile. "But I don't want to talk too loudly." She put her finger over her lips and gestured toward the rooms upstairs. "I don't want to disturb anyone."

"Oh, I don't think there's any fear of that," he reassured her. "From what I've been able to gather, Emma could sleep through just about anything. And Sadie's still on enough medication to keep her from being bothered for awhile."

"No, not the girls," his mother whispered.

"Then who? Please don't tell me you've taken in more people, Mother. We've already had more than we can handle."

"Just one more," she said with a smile. "But I really don't think you're going to mind this one."

They made their way into the parlor, where Brent sat next to his mother on the sofa. At that very moment, a voice rang out, shattering the silence in the house.

"Gillian? Gillian, have you seen my spectacles? I'm having a devil of a time trying to find them!"

Brent's heart immediately went to his throat. *Father. My father is home.*

SUNDAY, SEPTEMBER 16, 1900, 6:00 P.M.
THE MURPHY VILLA

Emma stood silently in the stairwell trying not to move. A stair creaked underneath her as she shifted her position slightly. She wasn't trying to be nosy, exactly. However, she couldn't help but overhear. Mr. Murphy had arrived. He was in the parlor with Brent and Mrs. Murphy. His words to Brent were soft, kind. This was not the man Brent had described. He was no tyrant. He was a saint.

"Brent, there are so many things I want to say to you." Mr. Murphy's voice was gentle, loving. "I'm afraid I've waited too many years to say them."

"Say them, Father." Brent's voice sounded nervous, almost skeptical.

Emma wished she could see his face, judge his expression. "This is none of my business," she whispered, then leaned a little closer so that she could hear every word.

SUNDAY, SEPTEMBER 16, 1900, 9:59 P.M.
THE MURPHY VILLA

Brent scribbled frantically, tears flowing:

Who is this man in my home? He resembles my father, and yet he is nothing like him. His once stern face appears far more relaxed, even soft at times. His voice is laced with a tenderness I have never before known. His entire countenance is changed, altered. It seems too wonderful to be true.

This stranger of a man embraced me. For the first time in twenty-six years, he actually put his arms around me and held me like a father holds a son. My silence must have been deafening in his ear, but there seemed to be no words to convey what I felt in that moment. Joy? Relief? Confusion? All of those things and so much more.

I want to understand him. He is a new man, transformed, and yet I have not discovered the secret behind this transformation. Do I dare trust my feelings? I am still at arm's length, but the arm grows shorter as the minutes tick by. It is just a matter of time before we are truly father and son. I feel it in the evening breeze. We are almost family.

Twenty-Seven

Brent looked across the backyard at his mother. She seemed like a carefree schoolgirl, humming as she pulled sheets from the line. He made his way across the stretch of yard to meet her.

"Could you hand me that sheet, son?" She pointed to the clothesline. Brent reached over to pull the bedsheet down, handing it to her carefully. His mother began to fold it rapidly, talking almost as fast. "God has truly blessed us, hasn't he, son? I can't remember ever feeling this blessed. Your father is home. And he's so different, so completely different. It's just so amazing."

"You've known him for nearly thirty years, Mother," Brent said hesitantly. "Has he ever been like this before?"

"Oh my, yes. The first few years, he was gentle, loving. It wasn't until after, well, after we discovered that we couldn't have children, that he changed."

"I see." That made sense, at least to some extent.

"You see, he always wanted a son," Gillian continued,

"but it was starting to look like we would never have one. Your father is the last one in his line of Murphys. He needed a son to carry on the family name."

"I'm not quite what he was looking for," Brent mumbled. He never had been. That had always been made obvious.

"Let me see if I can make you understand, honey," his mother said carefully. "Your father is a very proud man. It was humiliating to think that he hadn't been capable of producing a child of his own. And then, once we made the decision to choose a little boy from the orphanage, I thought he had resigned himself to the inevitable. But apparently he still struggled with the decision. He kept it hidden for years. In fact, when you were really little, he would have done anything for you. Anything."

Brent vaguely remembered his years as a young boy. There had been a tender side to his father once, at least his somewhat confused memory now told him so. "What happened?"

"When you were about five or six, your father became very ill. Do you remember that?"

Brent shook his head. "Not really. What happened to him?"

"Scarlet fever," his mother said with a sigh. "It was a really bad case."

"I had it too," Brent said, remembering. "When I was five."

"That's right."

Suddenly Brent understood. "Are you saying I made him sick?"

"Well, you did develop symptoms first," she answered quietly. "Though, of course, no one could blame a sick child for infecting someone else. But your father became very ill—deathly ill. For several weeks we thought we might lose him."

Lord, I remember. I remember walking into his room as a young child and finding him in bed in the middle of the day. He was sick, Lord. I made him sick.

"His illness progressed," Gillian continued, "developing into rheumatic fever. The doctor said it weakened his heart, and the scarring would remain for the rest of his life. He was never the same after that."

"He has a weak heart?" Brent could hardly believe it. His father seemed so strong.

"He had always worked for the GH&H as a lineman," she said, "but he had to resign himself to office work after that. Every move he made had to be carefully monitored by the doctor."

"I can't believe you kept this from me all these years," Brent said softly.

"I'm not sure why we never talked about his illness in front of you, son," she said gently. "Perhaps I was just afraid you might feel the weight of it too strongly."

"I tried so hard to show him how much I loved him."

"I know."

"Mother," Brent argued, "this still doesn't explain why he has always accused me of being lazy. That's the one thing that still doesn't make sense. I'm not lazy."

"I know you're not. But don't you see, Brent? You recovered. You were young, strong. You could have done anything with your life."

"I did exactly what I wanted to do, exactly what I felt I was supposed to do," he argued.

"He always thought you would follow in his footsteps and work on the line. It was a pride issue."

"Ugh. I would have been awful at that," Brent said,

looking down at his hands. "These fingers were meant to write."

"I know that now, honey, and I think your father does too. Speaking of which, I showed him your piece in the *Courier*."

Brent's heart began to beat wildly. "You're joking."

"No I'm not. He thought it was very good," she explained. "There were some parts of the story that were difficult for him to read, but he made it through. He even told me that he was proud of you."

"Why didn't he tell me himself?" Brent asked, feeling a lump begin to grow in his throat.

"Perhaps he will," Gillian responded. "Perhaps he will."

MONDAY, SEPTEMBER 17, 1900, 9:59 A.M.
THE COURIER

Henrietta paced back and forth in front of the *Courier* building, afraid to go in.

"Be my ever-present help, Lord," she whispered, then she bravely knocked on the door.

MONDAY, SEPTEMBER 17, 1900, 10:00 A.M.
THE COURIER

"Could I speak with you, sir?" Everett looked up to a see a young woman standing in the doorway. Her faded yellow dress was tattered and torn, her wispy hair pulled back loosely at her neck. Perspiration beads shone across her face, a rather young face.

"Sure. Come on in." Everett gestured to a chair nearby. She entered, rather hesitantly it seemed. Nerves seemed to have the better of her.

"I've been wanting to speak with you ever since I heard the news," she said, a smile suddenly lighting up her face.

And what a pretty face. She had delicate features, which complemented her petite frame.

"What news would that be?"

"About the orphanage," she answered breathlessly. "Oh, I'm so sorry, I forgot to introduce myself. My name is Henrietta Mullins. I mean Sister Henrietta Mullins." She stuck out her hand. He reached to take it, shaking it gently.

Everett couldn't seem to hold back a chuckle. So this was the rugged nun he had heard so much about. "Well, we meet at last, Sister. Brent Murphy has told me much of your story. I was so impressed that you took such pains to care for that precious little girl."

"Lilly Mae." She spoke the name with a solemn reverence. "I was just doing my duty."

"I daresay you went beyond the call of duty on the night of the storm," Everett said. "As did so many. Now, what was it you were saying about the orphanage?"

She squirmed a little in the chair, clearly anxious about something. "I know I'm young," she said finally. "And I'm not the most spiritual person I know."

Everett bit his lip and tried to control the grin threatening to escape. He didn't wish to poke fun at her, after all, but she was charming.

"But I know I have a call on my life to work with the orphans on Galveston Island," Henrietta said, looking him in the eye. "I've known it for some time now. I'm sad to say it took this storm to convince me that I really belong here. Until then, all I wanted to do was catch a train back to Virginia."

"Your home?"

She nodded. "It was my home. But this is my home now. And even though we've lost so many children, there are so many more needing a place to stay. The Ursuline Academy is nearly full to bursting. I'm convinced the orphanage must be rebuilt, and I want to be a part of that."

"And you've come here because ... ?" Everett gazed at her curiously. She had a lot of spunk, this young nun.

"There's a rumor you can help me. I've been told Clara Barton is here, along with a host of reporters from around the country."

"Yes, that's right."

"Mr. Maxwell, I want to meet them, to tell them about the children I've been caring for these past few days." She spoke firmly, with conviction. "I'm convinced that I could be a help in some way, and I feel compelled to try to do something."

"Do you now?" He smiled at her warmly. She returned the smile, hope etched on every curve of her young face. *She's quite the crusader.* Somehow, just looking at her encouraged him. Everett had the feeling this was just the beginning of a new and very exciting friendship.

MONDAY, SEPTEMBER 17, 1900, 12:45 P.M.
THE MURPHY VILLA

Gillian looked across the room at her husband, who paced up and down in front of the bay window. "Anxious about something, dear?"

"I'm just worried about Brent. He's been gone quite some time."

Gillian smiled. It was the first time Douglas had ever expressed concern over their son's whereabouts, and she wanted to savor the moment. "I'm sure he'll be here soon," she said. "He was up at the newspaper earlier, but I believe he's gone over to the hospital to pay Emma a visit."

"Ah, Emma," Douglas said, nodding. "I see."

"I believe I'm beginning to see something there too," Gillian responded with a wink. "I think she's a lovely girl."

"I agree," he said, turning toward her, "though not half as pretty as you."

Tears instinctively sprang to Gillian's eyes. She rose, crossing the room to stand next to her husband. "I've thanked the Lord a hundred times at least," she said. "He's brought you back—really brought you back." Her words held a deeper meaning, and she hoped Douglas would understand their depth.

"I'm here to stay," he said, pulling her close. "That's a promise."

"Here to stay, eh?" she teased. "Does that mean you're not going back to work this afternoon? I can have you all to myself?"

"I'm afraid I have no control over that," Douglas said with a sigh. "There's so much to be done, and they need every man they can get."

"But you've hardly touched your lunch," she said with a pout. "Egg salad is your favorite."

He smiled, reaching to take another bite of the sandwich. "There. Happy?"

"I suppose," she answered, rising to her feet. "But I'd be happier if you stayed put today. You need your rest."

"There will be plenty of time for rest later. I need to do my part, Gillian. There's so much left to do, but if we all work together, Galveston can be restored to her former self. I know it."

With her husband's loving arms wrapped tightly

around her, Gillian Murphy felt more hopeful than she had in many years. "I believe our little island will be better than ever," she whispered.

MONDAY, SEPTEMBER 17, 1900, 4:00 P.M.
JOHN SEALY HOSPITAL

"Where are you going in such a hurry?" Emma turned as she heard Nurse Phillips's stern voice.

"I'm ... My shift is over. I even put in an extra hour. I'm going home."

"Hmmm. So it is." The older woman looked up at the clock as she spoke. "Well, just be sure you're here on time tomorrow. You were three minutes late today."

"Yes ma'am." Emma shook her head in disbelief. In spite of everything, Nurse Phillips still hadn't lost her touch.

"Three minutes late? Heaven forbid." Emma looked behind her to see Brent with a broad grin on his face. "What do you get for three minutes' tardiness?" he asked.

"Knowing Nurse Phillips, I'll be docked half an hour's pay," she said with a shrug. "But I don't care. And besides, I wasn't even late. She's just looking for a reason to dislike me."

"Why, do you suppose?"

"I don't know," Emma said. "I haven't been able to figure it out. Most people find me very likable."

"Oh they do, do they?" he said, reaching to take her hand. "Well then, as one of your many admirers, I was wondering if you would do me the honor of dining with me tonight."

"I dine with you every night," she said with a laugh. "At your mother's table. Remember?"

"No, I had something a little different in mind tonight, if you're up for it."

"Up for it? Sounds intriguing. What do you have in mind?"

"Just leave it to me," he said with a grin. "I have a wonderful idea."

MONDAY, SEPTEMBER 17, 1900, 5:45 P.M.
GALVESTON ISLAND

Brent placed the picnic basket in the boat and stepped inside. His fear of the water was momentarily pushed aside as he gazed into Emma's beautiful blue eyes. She could make him forget anything, even the pain of the past week and a half. "Are you ready?" he asked.

She shrugged. "I suppose, though I still don't know where we're headed."

"I'm just going to row out into the bay a ways. The waters are pretty calm, and I thought we could sit and talk while we're eating."

"Sounds nice. My father used to take Sadie and me out on the water at sunset when we were younger." Her voice cracked, and she couldn't continue.

"To be honest," Brent said, "I just feel like I need to get off of the island for a while." He knew his voice sounded tense, but didn't care.

"I can certainly understand that," she responded softly, reaching to take his hand.

He loved the feel of her hand in his, though it did present a rather interesting problem. "I, uh ... I'm going to need that hand for rowing."

"Ah." She pulled her hand away.

He reached to take it once again, squeezing it reassuringly. "Not for long, I promise."

Brent rowed until they were about three hundred yards out. The sun continued to put itself to sleep off to his left, its reds and oranges dancing across the shimmering water. Emma's soft brown hair seemed to come alive. Brent's heart was so full that he could barely contain himself.

Thank you, Father, he prayed silently. *You've brought me back home, and given me back the father I never knew existed. Now, about this girl, Lord ...*

There he stopped, not knowing what to pray next. He reached to take hold of Emma's hand, gripping it until he thought his heart would explode.

Twenty-Eight

Son, can I talk to you?" Brent looked up from his breakfast as his father entered the room.

"Of course."

"I've been trying to work up the courage to do this for days," the older man said, sitting next to him. "But I'm such a coward."

"You? A coward?" That made no sense at all to Brent.

"I have done so many things that I'm ashamed of, son. But there is one thing above all that is unforgivable."

Brent began to tremble, anticipating his words. "What do you mean?"

His father looked down at the table, and then raised his head abruptly, with a determined look. Brent was almost sure he saw tears forming in his eyes. "I've been a hard worker all my life. I've done everything I could to make sure you and your mother were well taken care of, that you lived a good life."

"We have. A very good life."

"I guess what I'm trying to say is, I stayed so busy

trying to give you things that I didn't bother to give you the one thing you needed most of all."

Brent's heart raced. "What is that, Father? You gave me everything."

"No, son. No, I didn't." His father wept in earnest now. He fought to gain control of his emotions as he spoke. "You see, Brent, the one thing I held back, the one thing I didn't give you ..."

Brent felt a lump begin to grow in his own throat as his father reached out and grabbed his hand.

"The one thing I didn't give you," his father said again, "was me."

TUESDAY, SEPTEMBER 18, 1900, 9:39 A.M.
THE COURIER

"Bishop Gallagher, thank you so much for seeing me on such short notice." Everett extended his hand toward the elderly man, who took it willingly.

"I'm just happy to be included in your plans," he said with a smile. "Now, tell me what you're thinking."

"Well, you know the piece of property on the corner of 40th and Q streets?"

"Of course." The bishop nodded, reaching to hand Everett a cup of tea.

"I happen to know it's available for purchase. I was thinking perhaps it might be an appropriate place to rebuild the orphanage."

"You were, were you?" The bishop smiled broadly.

"Correct me if I'm wrong, but you've been wanting to move the orphanage into the city for some time now. Am I right?"

"That's right. We've put it off far too long. Sadly, the storm has taken most all of our children from us."

"But there are so many more who need a place now,"

Everett said excitedly, "and I'm convinced we can work together to give them one."

"We?"

"Yes," Everett said with a smile. "We. We owe it to the children."

TUESDAY, SEPTEMBER 18, 1900, 11:23 A.M.
THE MURPHY VILLA

Henrietta knocked on the door of the large Victorian home on Broadway. Mr. Maxwell had willingly given her the address. She only hoped it was correct. Nothing would embarrass her more than soliciting the wrong family for help. The door swung open wide. A beautiful woman dressed in a fashionable housedress greeted her with a smile. "Hello?"

"I'm Henrietta Mullins," she said, extending her hand. "I mean, Sister Henrietta Mullins."

"Sister?"

"Yes," she said, looking down at her own feminine attire. "I know I don't look like a nun—at the moment, anyway. But I assure you I am."

"You're lovely," the woman said. "I'm Gillian Murphy. Can I help you with something?"

Henri was so distracted looking at Mrs. Murphy that she almost forgot why she had come. "Oh, please forgive me," she said finally. "I'm looking for Brent."

"My son? I believe he's gone up to the station with his father to help with the cleanup on that end of town."

"Oh dear."

"Could I help you with something, Sister? Would you like a glass of lemonade?"

"Lemonade?" It sounded absolutely divine. "To be honest, I haven't had lemonade since I arrived on the island."

"Well then, why don't we remedy that?" Gillian ushered her through the door into the beautiful entryway of the home. It was exquisite. A mammoth portrait of the Murphy family hung on the wall. For a brief moment, Henrietta's heart leaped within her. A similar portrait hung in the entry of her Virginia home. She felt the tears begin to work their way out, but she forced them to stop before they had a chance to start.

Mrs. Murphy chattered on and on about the storm, the weather, totally oblivious. "Let's go in the kitchen," she said, leading the way. Henrietta followed her past the grand stairway and into the spacious kitchen with its tall ceiling and large open window.

"Have a seat, dear." Mrs. Murphy gestured toward a massive oak table in the center of the room. Henrietta sat willingly. Her eyes grew wide as she watched the older woman pour long, cool glasses of yellow lemonade.

"You know, our kitchen at home is very much like this one," Henri said, looking about.

"Really?"

"Yes, but not as long. Perhaps a little wider. But there is a window just above the counter like that one."

"I do apologize for leaving it open," Mrs. Murphy said, "but it's so hot in here when it's closed. Do you mind?"

"Of course not." After countless days, she had grown used to the smell by now. It was bound to linger long past the cleanup process.

"Now, what was it you said you needed my son for?" Brent's mother looked curious, even a little nervous.

"He was so kind to me after the storm," Henri said. "The little girl I had cared for during the night ..." She couldn't go on. The knot in her throat wouldn't let her.

"Oh, my dear," Gillian said, taking a seat. "You're the

one, the one he wrote the article about. And that precious little girl, what was her name again?"

"Lilly Mae." Henrietta could barely whisper her name.

"Lilly Mae. I have the article right here." Mrs. Murphy reached across the table, picking up a copy of the newspaper. "My Brent says you were quite the hero."

"I'm no hero," Henrietta said softly. "But I want to be."

"What do you mean?"

"I want to be a hero to the children of this island," she said, regaining strength in her voice. "That's what I wanted to talk to Brent about. He's such a good writer. I hoped he could help me. Mr. Maxwell has already agreed to print anything Brent writes."

"But, agreed to what, dear? I'm afraid this still isn't making much sense."

"Oh, I'm so sorry," Henri said, wrapping her fingers around the cool glass of lemonade. "We want to begin work on a new orphanage. Though we lost most of our own children from St. Mary's, there are so many more now that need a home, need a place to stay. It only makes sense that we should give them a place. Don't you agree?"

"I do."

"The infirmary is still standing, and will remain on the current property, but it's not large enough to house the children, especially now with so many sick and injured."

"Of course. But tell me, what are your plans? How will you begin?"

Henrietta took a sip of the heavenly lemonade before answering. "I've already gone to Mr. Maxwell, as I said." She seemed to gain strength with each word. "And he's spoken with the bishop just this morning. The new orphanage will be here, in town. It just makes so much more sense that the children should be here, don't you agree?"

"Yes, of course," Gillian responded.

"We'll be looking for people to lend their support, both financial and emotional. That's where Brent comes in. He's got such a way with words. I just know he could stir the people's hearts."

"That he could."

"I didn't mean to take up so much of your time with this," Henri said, sipping her lemonade. "But I'm just so excited at the prospect of doing something for the children."

"It's a marvelous idea, Sister. I'm so very pleased that you've taken it upon yourself to do this."

"How could I do any less?" Henrietta spoke passionately. She took a long drink, relishing every delicious drop. "Mrs. Murphy, it was so wonderful of you to invite me in like this. I can't tell you how wonderful. I miss my home in Virginia so much. It makes me feel very much at home to be here."

"Well, you come back any time and sit here," Gillian said with a smile. "In fact, I insist. You will always be welcome in the Murphy home."

Henri leaned back in her chair, content to sit and visit a while longer.

TUESDAY, SEPTEMBER 18, 1900, 1:25 P.M.
GALVESTON ISLAND

Gillian put on her best bonnet and headed out of the door. She made her way up Broadway, pausing in front of the familiar green Victorian home with the exquisite gingerbread trim. For nearly an hour she had contemplated the young nun's words, and she knew that she must do something to help.

Now she knew exactly what that something was. Her years in society had not been in vain. She could return something to the people of Galveston. And she knew just the person to help.

Gillian traced the cobblestones up to the front door of the impressive home. One knock. Two. The door opened suddenly, startling her. There was no turning back now. She took a deep breath and dove in.

"Millicent, there's something I need to talk to you about."

Tuesday, September 18, 1900, 7:00 p.m.
The Murphy Villa

Emma looked across the dinner table at Brent. His hair hung over one eye in a lopsided way. It drew her to him as never before. She wanted to run her fingers through that hair, to straighten it out. She wanted to let her fingers rest against his as they had on the boat just last night.

"Would you like some more potatoes?" Mrs. Murphy asked, peering at Emma curiously.

"Oh, no ma'am." She wasn't the slightest bit hungry.

"How about some of these rolls?" Mr. Murphy suggested, lifting the platter. She took one without even looking at it. Her eyes were fixed on Brent's. His were equally fixed on hers.

"You two are about to drive me mad," Sadie said suddenly, startling them all.

"Sadie!"

"No, I mean it," she argued. "You're both so moonstruck you can hardly see straight. And I'm not going to get a decent night's sleep until you two just come out and tell each other how you feel."

"Sadie, I can't believe you—"

"No, she's right," Brent said with a smile. "She's right." His eyes twinkled merrily.

"Well, it's about time, that's all I've got to say," Mrs. Murphy said with a broad grin.

"Sadie, I haven't a clue what you mean," Emma tried to argue. They shouldn't be talking about this here, in front of everyone, but now with every curious eye on her, Emma had no choice but to plow ahead.

"I mean," Sadie said emphatically, "you hardly sleep a wink at night. And you must be dreaming about him—unless there's some other Brent that I don't know about."

"What?"

"You call his name out most every night," Sadie said with a shrug.

"I do not."

"Do too."

"Do not!" Emma said, standing. She felt the color begin to rise in her cheeks, but couldn't control it. Mrs. Murphy had started to giggle, and reached out to clutch her husband's hand. His lips were tightly pressed together, as if trying to keep himself from saying something.

"Sadie, you're just being dramatic," Emma said, shaking her napkin in her sister's face. "And I want you to stop it at once."

"I'm being dramatic?" Sadie rolled her eyes.

"It would appear that you have a flare for drama as well," Brent said, standing. "But, then again, I've always had an interest in the theatrical." He moved toward her slowly, reaching to take the napkin from her hand and laying it on the table. Her heart began to race as their fingers locked. His eyes riveted into hers. They were kind, loving eyes.

"I, uh ..." she stammered.

"Now, if you will all excuse us, I believe Emma and I have some business to take care of out on the porch."

Brent led Emma out of the house and onto the large front porch. His heart guided him toward the swing, where they sat together. She looked frightened, like a young child.

"Are you still angry?" he asked, gripping her hand.

"Yes. No. I don't know." She dropped her head into her hands. "I'm just so humiliated. I can't believe Sadie said that in front of your parents."

"She was right, you know," Brent said, reaching to lift her chin.

"She was?"

"Well, I don't know about the dream part, but I can assure you she was right on the money when she said that we are both moonstruck. At least I know I am." *I am, and I love the feeling.*

"You are?" Emma looked up at him for confirmation. Her eyes pooled with tears.

Brent nodded, suddenly unable to speak. He slipped his arm around her shoulder, and her head instantly found its spot next to his heart. He could feel her tears through the linen shirt he wore. He would be content to stay like this forever, except ...

"Emma, there's something I must say to you."

"What is it?"

"Could you look at me?" he asked.

She gazed up into his eyes.

"All of my life I've been a coward," Brent explained. "I've run from my father, run from my faith, run from my home. I couldn't look anyone in the eye—until now. Suddenly, I feel invincible. It's because of you, Emma. With you, I'm strong. With you, I can do anything."

She began to weep openly. "I'm not strong," she whispered finally. "I'm so weak right now, I can barely stand."

"Then let me stand for the both of us," he said, lifting her face to his.

"Oh, Brent."

"Let me hold your hand, hold your heart, and walk you through this valley. The storm is over, Emma, and the winds are dying down. It's time to start over. Do you understand what I'm trying to say?"

"I think so."

"I'm usually pretty good with words, but everything is coming out backwards right now. What I'm trying to say is ..." His heart began to pound in his ears. "What I'm trying to say is ... I love you, Emma. I love you. I think I loved you the moment I laid eyes on you the night of the storm. My heart has almost turned itself inside out over these past ten days. I can't imagine living one minute without you. I hope I never have to."

He looked into her eyes for the answer he prayed would come. His lips softly brushed against her hair as she buried her head in his chest and wept. When the tears gave way to joy, she lifted her head once again, and their lips met in a kiss that sent his heart soaring heavenward.

He didn't care if it never touched earth again.

EPILOGUE

*Galveston Island has returned in all of her glori-
ous brilliance. She remains a garden of oleanders, wispy
as they dance along evening breezes. The gulf, teeming
with life, continues to roll in and out, completely undisturbed. The people are much the same, though some
have moved on to Houston, where they seek a life with
less risk. The competition between the two cities grows
daily, though I fear our sister city may soon have the
upper hand.*

*I don't mind, really. Whatever happens in other
places is fine and good. I am truly home. Galveston, the
island of my youth, has drawn me back, and I will forever remain her friend and inhabitant. My whole future
lies before me. I remain a dreamer, though reality has
certainly reared its head more than a few times in my
life. I have little trouble reconciling the two.*

Brent laid down his pen as he gazed out at the gulf
waters, calm and tranquil. They seemed to symbolize his

life. All of his memories rose and fell with the tide, but only the good remained.

SATURDAY, SEPTEMBER 7, 1901, 11:30 A.M.
THE NEW ORPHANAGE

Everett stood in front of the new orphanage, a smile working its way across his face.

"It's lovely, Everett," his wife, Maggie, said. "I'm so very proud of you."

"Don't be proud of me, honey," he said, wrapping his arms around her. "It's just proof of what we can accomplish when we all work together. If Clara hadn't come, I'm not sure we would have made it this far." He pointed across the lawn to Sister Henrietta, who had a child wrapped around each leg. Bishop Gallagher stood nearby, sipping from a glass of lemonade and talking to her. Off in the distance, the Murphy family stood, arm in arm. Everett smiled in Brent's direction.

"You know, honey," he said, turning his attention back to his wife, "I've been giving a lot of thought to retiring."

"Really?" Her voice had a hopeful edge that could not be ignored.

"Really. In fact, I think I have just the man in mind to take my position at the *Courier*." He tipped his head in Brent's direction.

"Everett, I think that's a wonderful idea," she said, embracing him tightly. "When are you going to tell him?"

"There will be plenty of time for that later. Right now I just want to make sure you won't mind having me around the house. I can be a real pain in the neck when I'm bored. You know that."

"Well, you won't have the opportunity to be bored for long," she said, smiling up at him.

"What do you mean?"

"I mean," she said with a gentle kiss to the tip of his nose, "I've been thinking it's time the two of us took a trip."

"A trip? Where?"

"Oh, someplace completely different," she said. "Someplace where there's lots of excitement. Maybe Europe, or Africa, or someplace like that. Heaven knows nothing exciting ever happens on this island."

"Are you teasing?" he asked.

"Perhaps," she said with a smile. "But I would love to take the train up to Houston for a few days of adventure. How does that sound?"

"Anywhere with you sounds wonderful," Everett said, sweeping her into his arms. "You are my life."

SATURDAY, SEPTEMBER 7, 1901, 11:45 A.M.
THE NEW ORPHANAGE

Henrietta looked up at the beautiful orphanage and whispered a prayer of thanks. No longer St. Mary's, this new facility would be known as the Wharton Davenport Estates. Her precious orphans, all ninety of them, would soon be permanently moved from the infirmary, where they had stayed for the past year, into their new home. This large frame house had proven to be the perfect choice, and she was happy to join the eight other Sisters of Charity as they took their new place here.

"Henri?" She looked up into Abigail's merry face. "We made it. We really made it. Can you believe it?"

"We weathered the storm," Henrietta agreed, reflecting. "I hope we never have to go through anything like that again, but even if we do, I'm ready for it. I'm a completely different person today, Abigail. I really am."

"I think I am too," her friend said, taking her hand and squeezing it tightly. "But I never would have made it through this without you, Henri. I mean that."

"You would have," Henrietta scolded. "The Lord would have seen you through."

Lord, you are my refuge and strength, my very present help in time of trouble! Why the words came back to her now, she was not sure. Suddenly the picture of Lilly Mae's face was in front of her: a bright, shiny face, full of hope and excitement. Her song, as clear as the day it was first sung, seemed to fill the air, riding the winds. Henrietta looked up to the skies, her heart swelling with joy.

"This is for you, little one," she said, looking back to the orphanage where the children played happily on the lawn. "This is for you."

Out of the corner of her eye, Henrietta saw Brent Murphy approaching with his new bride, Emma. They were such a lovely couple. God, in his great goodness and wisdom, had brought them together under the worst of circumstance. Now here they stood, under the best of circumstance, as husband and wife.

"Would you mind if I asked you a couple of questions?"

Henrietta turned as she heard Brent's voice. "Of course not."

"I'm going to be doing an article on the orphanage, and I wanted to get your opinion of how it turned out. Are you happy with the new building?"

Happy? "Oh my, yes," she exclaimed. "In fact, I don't know when I've ever been happier."

"So you'll be staying here on the island then?" Brent asked, looking at her carefully. "I seem to recall a young nun who couldn't wait to leave Galveston. Have you changed your mind?"

Henrietta smiled, knowing in her heart that the decision had not been her own. "I'm content to be exactly who I am," she said, reaching down to scoop a precocious youngster into her arms, "and to minister right here—where God has planted me."

SATURDAY, SEPTEMBER 7, 1901, 11:55 A.M.
THE NEW ORPHANAGE

Gillian walked through the dorm rooms of the new orphanage, relishing every moment. "It's just perfect," she said, clutching Douglas's hand tightly in hers. "Thank you so much for letting me participate in all of this."

"For letting you?" he teased. "Wild horses couldn't have stopped you."

He spoke the truth, but she knew his words were spoken in love. So much had transpired over the last year. So very much. The homes along Broadway had returned to their original splendor, though attitudes within the homes had changed immensely.

"I want to tell you something, Gillian," her husband said, reaching to gently touch her face.

She looked at him curiously. "Douglas?"

"I want to tell you how proud I am of you," he said, tears forming in his eyes.

"Proud? Of me? Whatever for?" Douglas drew her so close that she could feel his heart beating.

"I'm proud to call you my wife, Gillian Murphy," he whispered in her ear. "You are a loving, giving woman. You would give your last dime to someone who needed it."

"But—"

"No, let me finish," he said, putting his finger over her lips. "I wasted so many years not telling you how much I loved you, how much I appreciated you. I want to make up for it. I'll do anything it takes to make up for it."

Gillian wept silently, her face buried in her husband's chest.

Thank you, Lord. You've brought my husband back from the dead. You've resurrected our marriage. Are you really so good that you would bless me with even more?

Gillian turned her face up toward her husband, the man she loved with every fiber of her being. He reached down with a fingertip to brush a tear from her cheek. "You've just given me all I could ever want," she whispered. "How could I ever ask for more?"

SATURDAY, SEPTEMBER 7, 1901, NOON
THE NEW ORPHANAGE

"Mrs. Murphy?" Emma looked up as Everett Maxwell approached.

Just two short months into married life, she still hadn't quite gotten used to being called Mrs. Murphy. "Yes?"

"I hate to intrude, but I have a bit of news for your husband."

"Should I ... should I go?" she asked, pulling her arm from Brent's.

"No, please." The older man reached to take her hand, placing it back in her husband's. "This news is for both of you."

Emma began to tremble, fearing the worst. Would Everett want Brent to leave the island in search of a story? She had dreaded this possibility for some time now.

"What is it, Everett?" Brent asked curiously.

"I've been thinking about retiring," the older man said with a sly grin.

"Retiring?" Emma and Brent spoke in unison.

"That's right," Maggie said, coming up behind him. "I'm getting him all to myself."

"How wonderful." Emma smiled in Maggie's direction.

"Anyway, I was thinking perhaps you might like the job," Everett said, looking at Brent.

"Me? An editor?" Brent sounded stunned.

Emma's heart began to swell with pride. She looked up at her husband to gauge his response. He grinned madly. "Oh, honey," she said breathlessly. "You'd do such a wonderful job. And best of all, it would keep you close to home."

"It would, at that," he said, pulling her close. "And there's no place I'd rather be."

"Say yes," Emma whispered in his ear. "Please."

Brent extended his hand in Everett's direction. "You've got yourself a deal, Mr. Maxwell," he said. "And I couldn't be happier."

Everett and Maggie turned back toward the orphanage, and Emma threw her arms around her husband's neck, squeezing tightly. "I'm so happy, Brent."

"I can tell. You're about to choke me."

She put on her best pouting face, loosening her grip only slightly. "There's just one thing that might make me happier," she said with a pout.

"What's that?"

Emma's eyes raced to and fro across the lawn, seeking out the one thing that had held her attention all morning. There, near the porch, Sadie was playing with a little girl, a toddler. The youngster had thick black curls and rich brown eyes. Sadie had placed a pink ribbon in her hair to keep the unruly curls from tumbling into the child's eyes as she played.

"There," Emma said, pointing. "That would make me happy."

"What?" Brent's eyes searched the place over until they fell on the child. "Are you saying what I think you're saying?" he asked.

"There are so many who need a home, Brent. We can't take them all. But we could start with this child. Her name is Teresa. She'll be three in a couple of months, and she's simply precious. Sadie is just mad about her, and I am too. I want to adopt her, honey."

"Are you sure?" he asked, cupping her chin in his hand. "Because if you're teasing me, it's a very cruel thing to do."

"I'm not teasing," she said, her eyes traveling to the youngster once again. "We'll have children of our own soon enough. I know that. But she needs parents right now—a mother and a father who will love her and take care of her."

"Yes, she does."

"The storm took my parents from me," Emma said, struggling to control her emotions. "It was cruel and heartless. But honey, don't you see? I know just how she feels. I know what she's been through. I can give her something back. *We* can give her something back. We can give her a wonderful life—and love. Lots of love."

"Emma, you're the most wonderful woman I've ever known," Brent said, kissing her forehead, then her cheeks, then the tip of her nose.

"She needs us, Brent. And, to be honest, I can't think of a better father on all of Galveston Island." Emma wasn't just saying the words to flatter him. They came from the depth of her soul.

"Do you mean that?" her husband asked, tears forming in his eyes.

"I do," she whispered, and melted into his arms.

SATURDAY, SEPTEMBER 7, 1901, 12:07 P.M.
THE NEW ORPHANAGE

Brent held his wife close, listening to her words of wisdom. She was a rare jewel, by far the most amazing thing that had ever happened to him in his twenty-seven years on this earth. His eyes fell on the youngster across the lawn. *Pretty little thing.* Emma was right. She deserved a chance at life, at happiness.

He would give it to her.

"Would you like to tell her now?" he asked, looking at his wife tenderly. Emma nodded, squeezing him harder than ever. Together, they crossed the lawn until they stood at the porch's edge. His beautiful bride reached down and swept the child up into her arms. Sadie joined the circle, tears tumbling down her rosy cheeks. Brent wrapped his arms around them all, holding them close. Through an upstairs window he caught a glimpse of his mother and father as they stood in a tight embrace. Brent's eyes met his father's, and unspoken words of love traveled between them.

After years of wandering, Brent Murphy was home at last.

READERS' GUIDE

FOR PERSONAL REFLECTION
OR GROUP DISCUSSION

Hurricane

FINDING THE EYE IN THE MIDDLE OF THE STORM

*T*he storms of life wear many faces. Many would appear to be small gusts of wind that merely shake us and test our faith, but don't really threaten our lives. Still others, like serious relational issues or the death of a loved one, can appear catastrophic. How we learn to deal with the storms of life says a lot about our faith—or lack thereof.

The Bible teaches us that we are to expect stormy times to come. How we deal with them is the real test. In Isaiah 43, we read: "Do not be afraid, for I have ransomed you. I have called you by name; you are mine. When you go through deep waters and great trouble, I will be with you. When you go through rivers of difficulty, you will not drown!" There will be troubles, no doubt; but God has not left us adrift on the waters. Just as Peter stood to walk on the sea toward Christ, we can rise above the circumstances that the storms in our lives present.

The characters in *Hurricane* are faced with several

different types of storms—both inner and outer. They learn to face the challenges of the natural and the emotional alongside one another. Together, they learn that obstacles can be overcome. Prodigals can return home. Fear can be replaced with hope. Seemingly impossible struggles can bring victories. The key to all of these successes, however, lies in strategically locating the eye in the middle of the storm.

Jesus is that eye, not just in this fictional setting, but in the midst of our very real storms. He offers us peace when violent winds are raging. He is the stillness, when everything around us seems to be whirling out of control. He is the key to our survival. If we turn to Him, we will do more than make it through the storms in our lives—we will overcome them.

1. In the opening chapter of the book, Brent Murphy is struggling with his decision to return home after years of living on his own. In what way does he remind you of the prodigal son (story found in Luke 15)? In what ways is he different?

2. What seems to be the motivating force in Gillian Murphy's life as this story begins? What do you suppose has driven her to this point? Does she appear to care for anyone but herself?

3. Henrietta Mullins is struggling with the call on her life. Why doesn't she simply leave and return to her home, where everything is safe and comfortable? Why stay, when everything within her is telling her to go?

4. How are the lives of Henrietta Mullins and Emma alike? How are they different? Who seems to be the happiest with her "calling"?

5. What role did newspapers play in the early twentieth century? Likewise, what role does the media play in today's society? How have things changed? How are they the same?

6. How do Brent's journal entries provide a glimpse into his struggles? Why is it often easier to write things down on paper than to voice them openly?

7. In chapter five, we read: "Henri wiped away warm tears with the back of her hand and tried to comfort herself with a familiar scripture: 'Lo, I am with you always...' God would always be with her, wherever she went, whatever obstacles

befell her." Why does Henri rely so heavily on this scripture? Why should we, as well?

8. Everett Maxwell is looking for a story that will put his newspaper a position of prominence in society. He can't imagine such a story actually exists on Galveston Island. What is Everett really dealing with?

9. In what ways does the pending storm approaching the island parallel the storms Brent Murphy is facing in his own life?

10. Different people prepare for approaching storms differently. Explain how some of the people on the island prepared (or refused to prepare) for the incoming storm. How do we, as Christians, brace ourselves for approaching storms? Do we take shelter under the wings of the Almighty or do we pretend that all is well?

11. "Do not be afraid, for I have ransomed you. I have called you by name; you are mine. When you go through deep waters and great trouble, I will be with you. When you go through rivers of difficulty, you will not drown!" (Isaiah 43: 1–2). Discuss this scripture in depth. What promise does the Lord make in this passage?

12. "Greater love has no man than this—that he lay down his life for a friend" (John 15:13). Which characters best exemplify this scripture? Who was most willing to lay down his or her life to help others during the storm? Who was least willing?

13. Henri faces the challenge of her life when she and Lilly Mae ride out the storm together. What decision would you expect her to make after discovering the child has lost her life?

14. Facing the death of a loved one is one of the most difficult struggles any believer can face. When Emma learns that she has lost her parents, how does she react?

15. When the storm hit, Everett Maxwell finally gets his "story of a lifetime." How do you think he feels once the headlines begin to roll?

16. In the middle of the storm, the reader begins to see a very different side of Gillian Murphy. What is her greatest desire at this point?

17. In what way does "Big John" appear as a hero in this story? Why is he an unexpected hero?

18. The stench of death is everywhere on the Island after the storm. Is it possible for "the stench of death" to be on those who fall victim to life's storms? Explain.

19. What might have become of Galveston Island had the storm moved in a different direction? How might history have been changed? Have you ever "barely missed" a major storm (real or symbolic)?

20. At one point, Galveston Island is completely cut off from the mainland. She is all alone. Is it possible for Christians to let the storms of life separate them from the safety of the mainland? Explain.

21. Is it possible to rebuild your life after a major tragedy like the one the characters in this story faced? Explain.

22. How does Gillian ultimately become a hero in this story? How does she have to change along the way? What does she have to lay down?

23. Some very real people (like Clara Barton) came to Galveston Island and helped bring restoration to the people. Are you a Clara Barton to those around you who are going through storms? Do you do all you can to bring a message of hope and healing to those in need?

24. Brent is ultimately restored to his father at the end of this story. Have you ever reconciled with someone you had been estranged from? What does the Bible have to say about such reconciliation?

25. In the final chapter of this book, Brent and Emma decide to adopt a child. In what way does that child symbolize a fresh start for the two of them?

The Word at Work Around the World

A vital part of Cook Communications Ministries is our international outreach, Cook Communications Ministries International (CCMI). Your purchase of this book, and of other books and Christian-growth products from Cook, enables CCMI to provide Bibles and Christian literature to people in more than 150 languages in 65 countries.

Cook Communications Ministries is a not-for-profit, self-supporting organization. Revenues from sales of our books, Bible curricula, and other church and home products not only fund our U.S. ministry, but also fund our CCMI ministry around the world. One hundred percent of donations to CCMI go to our international literature programs.

CCMI reaches out internationally in three ways:

• Our premier International Christian Publishing Institute (ICPI) trains leaders from nationally led publishing houses around the world.

• We provide literature for pastors, evangelists, and Christian workers in their national language.

• We reach people at risk—refugees, AIDS victims, street children, and famine victims—with God's Word.

Word Power, God's Power

Faith Kidz, RiverOak, Honor, Life Journey, Victor, NexGen — every time you purchase a book produced by Cook Communications Ministries, you not only meet a vital personal need in your life or in the life of someone you love, but you're also a part of ministering to José in Colombia, Humberto in Chile, Gousa in India, or Lidiane in Brazil. You help make it possible for a pastor in China, a child in Peru, or a mother in West Africa to enjoy a life-changing book. And because you helped, children and adults around the world are learning God's Word and walking in his ways.

Thank you for your partnership in helping to disciple the world. May God bless you with the power of his Word in your life.

For more information about our international ministries, visit www.ccmi.org.

CA+

Additional copies of *Hurricane*
and other RiverOak titles are available
from your local bookseller.

If you have enjoyed this book,
or if it has had an impact on your life,
we would like to hear from you.

Please contact us at:

RIVEROAK BOOKS
Cook Communications Ministries, Dept. 201
4050 Lee Vance View
Colorado Springs, CO 80918
Or visit our Web site: www.cookministries.com

RIVEROAK®
Good News in Fiction